Praise for the

Wind Dragons Motorcycle Club

series

Dragon's Lair

"*Dragon's Lair* proves a badass chick can tame even the wildest of men. . . . Not to be missed. A biker book unlike any other . . . [with] a heroine for strong-willed women and an MC of hot bikers. Chantal Fernando knows how to draw you in and keep you hooked."

—Angela Graham, *New York Times*– and
USA Today–bestselling author

"*Dragon's Lair* was witty and fast-paced. A delicious combination of badass biker men and laugh out-loud humor."

—*Bookgossip*

Arrow's Hell

"Redemption and forgiveness form the basis of the story, while laughter, tears, and some erotic sex scenes keep the reader engaged. Low-key violence blends well with the multiple plotlines and drama-drenched characters."

—*RT Book Reviews*

"Cheek-heating, gut-wrenching, and beautifully delivered! *Arrow's Hell* took me on the ride of my life!"

—Bella Jewel, *USA Today*–bestselling author

"*Arrow's Hell* is a fast-paced, entertaining, and intoxicating story line with some fun and humor to offset the intensity of guilt and grief."

—*The Reading Cafe*

Tracker's End

"Fernando's vivid characters burst onto the page, . . . pulling readers into their world immediately and completely. This tightly told tale will leave readers eagerly waiting for the next installment."

—*Publishers Weekly*

"The physical chemistry between Lana and Tracker burns up the pages."

—*RT Book Reviews*

"The charismatic characters have captured my heart. . . . *Tracker's End* is my favorite book in this series."

—*Smut Book Junkie*

"Don't miss out on the Wind Dragons MC series. . . . Chantal can really pull off the sexy times and give you some new BBFs to add to your list!"

—*The Literary Gossip*

Rake's Redemption

"You'll find yourself sitting on the edge of your seat in anticipation of how [*Rake's Redemption*] will unfold."

—*RT Book Reviews* (4½ stars, top pick)

"*Rake's Redemption* is a story about betrayal and loss, revenge and retribution, second chances and falling in love. The premise is emotional and entertaining; the characters are passionate and energetic; the romance is fated and hot."

—*The Reading Cafe*

"If you haven't read this series, pick it up now. . . . *Rake's Redemption* is a definite must-read for lovers of the series or for anyone wanting a hot MC read!"

—*Reading Past My Bedtime*

The Wind Dragons Motorcycle Club Series

Dragon's Lair

Arrow's Hell

Tracker's End

Dirty Ride*

Rake's Redemption

Wolf's Mate

Wild Ride*

Last Ride*

*ebook only

Crossroads

CHANTAL FERNANDO

G

Gallery Books

New York   London   Toronto   Sydney   New Delhi

G

Gallery Books
An Imprint of Simon & Schuster, Inc.
1230 Avenue of the Americas
New York, NY 10020

First Gallery Books trade paperback edition March 2017

GALLERY BOOKS and colophon are registered trademarks of Simon & Schuster, Inc.

For information about special discounts for bulk purchases, please contact Simon & Schuster Special Sales at 1-866-506-1949 or business@simonandschuster.com.

The Simon & Schuster Speakers Bureau can bring authors to your live event. For more information or to book an event contact the Simon & Schuster Speakers Bureau at 1-866-248-3049 or visit our website at www.simonspeakers.com.

Manufactured in the United States of America

10 9 8 7 6 5 4 3 2 1

Library of Congress Cataloging-in-Publication Data

Names: Fernando, Chantal, author.
Title: Crossroads / Chantal Fernando.
Description: First Gallery Books trade paperback edition. | New York :
    Gallery Books, 2017. | Series: Wind Dragons Motorcycle Club ; book 6
Identifiers: LCCN 2016037611| ISBN 9781501139628 (paperback) |
    ISBN 9781501139635 (ebook)
Subjects: LCSH: Motorcycle clubsFiction. | Motorcycle gangsFiction. |
BISAC: FICTION / Romance / Contemporary. | FICTION / Romance / General. |
FICTION / Action & Adventure. | GSAFD: Love stories.
Classification: LCC PR9619.4.F465 C76 2017 | DDC 823/.92dc23 LC record
    available at https://lccn.loc.gov/2016037611

ISBN 978-1-5011-3962-8
ISBN 978-1-5011-3963-5 (ebook)

To my sons,

for showing me what love truly is

Acknowledgments

First of all, I'd like to thank all my readers for wanting more from the WDMC world, and for Gallery Books and Abby Zidle for making it a reality.

To my agent, Kimberly Brower, I'm so lucky to have you! Thank you for everything you do. As always, I know I can always count on you, and I'm so grateful.

Arijana Karcic, thank you for all you do for me. You're seriously the best and deserve the world.

Natalie Ram, thank you for being the most versatile best friend ever, from helping me proofread to making me swag, I appreciate everything that is you. I know I can always count on you to have my back, or help me when I need you. I kind of adore you, and I don't know how I survived before I had you by my side. You're my one-woman army, and I love you heaps.

Thank you to my parents and sisters for helping out whenever I need more writing time, and to my three sons for being patient when they know their mama has to work. I love you all so much.

FMR Book Grind, thank you for everything; I appreciate all the hard work you all do for me!

Rose Tawil, I really don't know what I'd do without you. I can't say thank you enough for all the work you put in to support my dreams, and you never ask for anything in return. You truly are one of the best people I've ever met. Love you infinity.

The way to make people trust-worthy
is to trust them.

—Ernest Hemingway

ONE

Ranger

"**N**o," I tell her, for what must be the millionth time, even though the word doesn't fall easily from my lips. I can see why no one says no to this woman. Not only is she unbelievably sexy, although I'd never admit that out loud because Sin will fuckin' kill me, but she also has this charm and charisma about her that just makes you want to do whatever she asks.

No doubt, her team is always the winning team, so why wouldn't I want to get on board? It just happens that what she's asking—to help her with some fuckin' case she's working on—doesn't appeal to me at all. Working with the cops and the feds? No fuckin' thank you. I don't think I've ever been around a cop without the words "you have the right to remain silent" being said shortly thereafter, and I have no intention of voluntarily being around them now.

Do I feel bad about what's happened? Sure. A woman is missing, after all, but I'm not a hero and I'm not going to pretend to be. If I had any type of hero complex, I'd have joined the military or some shit like that—hell, maybe I'd even have become a cop.

But nope, I'm just a biker. Don't expect shit from me.

"Ranger, why the fuck not?" Faye continues, pursing her lips. I can see the determination in her hazel eyes. She wants me to help her, although I have no idea why. "I could really use your brain on this case. Don't you want to be challenged? To do something good, to give back to the community? To help this poor woman, because who knows where she is right now or what's happening to her!"

All valid points. I just don't see why out of all the men she knows, she's so adamant about having me be the one to help her.

"Come on, Ranger, you can at least look at the case before you say no again. You might pick up on something we've all missed, who knows. Anything you can think of will help. I'm at a dead end right now. You're a fuckin' genius, Ranger!" When I raise a brow, she adds, "I know exactly how high your IQ is. Talon told me."

I groan and shut my eyes. Only Talon knows about that, and as far as I know he hasn't told anyone, until now. Fuckin' Faye. Looks like she got to him—he's already spilling secrets to her.

"No one ever tells you no, do they?"

"Not without changing their mind," she replies, not sounding smug, just stating a fact. "Especially after I was kidnapped."

I open my eyes and look at her. I mean really look at her. "I didn't join this MC to help you on your missions to save the world, Faye. I don't want to work for the feds, or the cops, or for anyone for that matter. Yes, I'm smart. So are lots of people. I don't really see how I can help though. It's a missing-persons case. I don't even know why they put you on it—how is a lawyer supposed to help?"

She slams the file down on the table, obviously losing her temper, the contents spilling out.

It's the picture that gets my attention.

"Elizabeth Chase is a good woman, Ranger," she says, softening her tone. "She volunteers to feed the homeless, she babysits her neighbors' kids for free because they can't afford a babysitter, and she sends all the money she can to help her younger sister pay for college."

In the picture, Elizabeth is smiling, her long blond hair tumbling down her slender shoulders. Her blue eyes are looking right at me.

Judging me.

I pick up the photo, then glance at Faye, my expression giving away nothing. The thing is, I already know that Elizabeth Chase is a good woman. I know this firsthand. "Tell me everything."

Her eyes dance with satisfaction.

She won. Like she usually does.

This time though, it's not about Faye. The only reason I'm helping her is the woman in the photo.

Faye can be as smug as she likes.

All I care about right now is saving a woman I once used to know.

Six Years Ago

"Hello," the girl says to me, tucking her hair back behind her ear. "You're Cameron, right?"

I nod, smiling at her. I've seen her around the last few days but have never spoken to her. I came on this tour alone, a cruise around Scotland and Ireland, before all of us in the tour group head off to continental Europe, and it's been one huge party from the second I got here. Everyone on board is young and looking for my kind of good time—no strings attached, just enjoying the right now and not worrying about tomorrow.

"Yeah," I say, lighting up my cigarette and inhaling.

"I'm Elizabeth," she says, smiling and then ducking her head, like she's shy all of a sudden. I'm not a person who ever feels shy, so for some reason it amuses me. It's an emotion I don't really understand. I'm usually confident at best, comfortable at worst. I don't generally give a shit what people around me think. If I did, there's no way in hell I would have survived high school.

Wait a second, is this her trying to flirt with me? Yesterday, a pretty dark-haired girl walked up, pressed herself against me, and asked if I wanted to fuck. This is definitely a different approach, from a different type of girl. No judgment from me—after all, I did fuck that girl yesterday, and we both got what we wanted out of the night—but I have no idea what a shy, nice girl would be wanting from me. I have nothing to offer but my dick and a good time.

Maybe I'm wrong though; maybe she's not as innocent as she comes off. Or maybe she wants to be a rebel for the night—to see what it's like to be with a bad boy. I'm completely aware of how women see me. I'm six foot five, built, with a dark scruffy beard and longish hair that women seem unable to get enough of. I have tattoos, and I'm rough around the edges. No one would guess that I'm on break from my double major at college. No one really bothers to look beyond the exterior.

"Nice to meet you, Elizabeth. Did you have a good time last night?" I ask, attempting to make small talk with her. I'm not very good at it, but I think it will put her at ease a little. She's a pretty enough girl, and I wouldn't mind spending the night with her at some point during the trip if that's what she's after. My gaze drops to her chest, where her small breasts are pressing against her white top. Yeah, I wouldn't mind having a taste of her one bit.

She clears her throat, so I raise my eyes back up to hers, grinning. "You were saying?"

She shakes her head, eyes looking a little sad before answering me. "It was good, yes. The club was pretty packed though. You don't remember me at all, do you?"

I squint my eyes, wondering where the fuck I'm meant to be remembering her from. Have I fucked her before? This could get awkward if that's the case, because I don't remember doing so. Then again, I've kind of lost count of how many women I've been with. I cringe as that fact is brought to light. She watches me squirm for a few moments, before laughing, shaking her head at me. "No, we haven't slept together, if that's what you're racking your brain over. We both went to Miles together."

I instantly still, my expression going blank. My years at Miles High School aren't the fondest. I moved away from that place for a reason, for a fresh start, and never did I think I would run into someone from there, especially on vacation, in a completely different country.

"Small world," I mutter under my breath. Then louder, "Can't say I remember you, Elizabeth."

"I'm two years younger than you." She nods, grinning, her blond hair bouncing. Even her hair is perky. "Probably not on your radar, but I remember you."

If she remembers me, she would definitely remember my reputation, which has me wondering why she's standing here, talking to me like we're good friends. Or like she wants to be. Maybe she wants to fulfill a high school fantasy of fucking the bad boy, the man from the wrong side of the tracks. I didn't grow up with money; in fact, I grew up living in a trailer park, and everyone knew it. I got into a lot of fights, hung out with the wrong crowd, and was generally a waste of fuckin' space. I graduated only because I was able to ace all my exams without any kind of studying, or even attending most of the classes. The teachers were suspicious as fuck—they thought that I cheated but couldn't prove it.

I didn't cheat.

I decide to change the topic away from a subject I'd rather not talk about, a part of me that I had buried. "You want to grab a drink?"

She nods, beaming. "I'd love to, Cam."

TWO

"So she's been missing for two weeks now?" I ask, running my hand through my hair. Two fuckin' weeks. She's either dead and I'll be bringing back her body, or she's alive and being kept somewhere and will return in who knows what condition. If it's the former, at least she can be laid to rest, and her family can have some closure.

"Yeah, two weeks," Faye says, her tone strictly business, as she scans the papers in front of her. I have to wonder why, out of all the cases, she chose to work on this one. Faye is a lawyer who assists the feds on cases when she chooses to. I don't know how she got into this position, or whatever deal she has going with them, or why they need a lawyer like her, but even I know she's a good woman to have on your side.

I decide to ask, to just put it out there. If she's honest with me, I'll be honest with her.

"What interests you about this case?" I ask her boldly, testing her.

She lifts her hazel eyes to me, giving me all her attention.

"They suspect that a biker had something to do with her disappearance, but only because she was last seen at a biker bar."

I can't imagine Elizabeth hanging out in a biker bar, but it's not like I've seen her in years. I don't know the person she became after we parted ways.

Faye continues, "That's not exactly solid evidence, but it's something to go by. Someone in the bar must have seen something, and if I go in there asking questions, it's going to be received a lot better than if the cops do."

That makes a hell of a lot of sense. Faye commands a lot of respect, and she definitely has the power to push herself into situations that others don't. Over the years, while I was with the Wild Men MC, even I heard stories about her. She's known for pretty much being a warrior, a woman with skills to take on even the best of men, and with Sin and the Wind Dragons by her side, she's an unstoppable force.

"I'll admit to having another reason," Faye adds, shrugging. "But that reason is my own. The bottom line is this woman needs help, and I'm going to do my best to figure out what happened to her. If she's alive, I want to save her. Her cousin happens to be a police officer and is pushing for all resources to be used in the search for Elizabeth."

"I know her," I admit quietly, then clear my throat. "At least I did. We were friends."

"I know," Faye admits, cringing. "I mean, I didn't know at the start, but I saw a picture of the two of you on her social media."

She has a picture of us? I'm not on any social media, so I wouldn't know, but for some reason this surprises me. Sure, she took a picture or two of us on the tour, but I haven't thought about those photos since. I think we spoke on the phone once before I joined the Wild Men, and never again after that.

"And you didn't say anything?"

"I was waiting for you to," she says, resting her hand on my arm. "I'm just happy you agreed to help. We can do this, Ranger, I know we can." She removes her arm and sighs. "Although we have to work side by side with her cousin, so I hope you're going to be okay with that."

I don't like cops, not even a little bit, but we all have the same end game, and for Elizabeth I can suck it up and work with her cousin. If he's an asshole . . . well, I'll just have to handle it. Not many men are stupid enough to fuck with me, but a cop, well, they think they rule the fuckin' world, so who knows. Cops like to talk big, but if you try to say or do anything back to them, they get you locked up. How the fuck is that fair? I heard all about the situation with Irish's woman, Tina, and her dirty-cop ex-boyfriend.

I don't understand cops. I'm sure not all of them are bad, but let's just say the ones I've met haven't exactly shown me any redeeming qualities. There are so many stories out there about cops who think they're above the law that it's hard to respect such hypocrites. Then again, I'm a biker, the enemy to them, so I guess they'd have no reason to be fair to me. I've been arrested a few times for doing absolutely nothing. It almost seems like they're looking for something that can put me behind bars, anything. I've been lucky each time that I didn't have any weapons on me.

"I'll deal," I tell her. "I assume you went to the bar already? What did you find out?"

"Nothing," she groans, frustration flashing on her face. "She went there alone, and she left alone. The bartender who was working says that she had two drinks, and that a few men came and spoke to her, but he can't remember what they looked like."

"Camera footage?"

"Apparently their cameras weren't working that day," she says, rolling her eyes. "They also only have one on the main bar, not one outside, so either way we wouldn't be able to see what direction she left in, or in whose car."

"How convenient," I add, lips tightening. "I think we should go back there."

Faye nods, straightening her shoulders. "I'm ready when you are."

It's not very often that a woman catches my eye. Yes, many women are beautiful, and I will check them out, but they never make me feel anything. Countless numbers of beautiful women have walked through the clubhouse doors, and more often than not, I decided to sleep alone anyway. After my college years, when I'd fuck anything in a skirt, it became unappealing. The fact that women are so easily accessible to me kind of makes me resent them. Maybe I'm dead inside, I don't know, but it's been a very long time since a woman piqued my interest. The one at the bar right now, however, has me doing more than a double take. Not that this is the time or place, considering I just finished grilling the bartender for information on Elizabeth, but I can't help it.

I look again.

She's on the curvy side—I can see the curve of her ass and the shape of her hips and thighs in the tight pair of worn jeans she's wearing. Her waist is tiny, and her tits are the perfect handful. The black halter top she's wearing shows off her toned arms; she definitely works out. She glances at me from the corner of her blue eyes, narrowing them slightly before returning them to her drink.

"Get what you need?" Faye asks quietly from my other side, sipping on her own drink, her alert gaze touching on everything and anything.

"Yeah," I reply, looking back at the woman. The bartender kept saying that he knew nothing, which is a lie. I can tell when someone lies—it's all in the body language, and this asshole is lying. So yeah, I got what I need—the rest will be carried out tonight.

"Shall we leave, then?" Faye asks, downing her drink and slamming the glass on the table.

I nod and reluctantly follow her out, even though what I really want to do is ask that girl to have a drink with me. I find myself curious, wanting to know everything. Does she have a boyfriend? What does she do for work? Does she enjoy it? Why is she drinking in a place like this? Not all women can pull off having short hair, but on her the style just emphasizes the beauty in her face. I glance back at the blonde once more before walking out the door, then return my attention to Faye, who is giving me a weird look. It's probably for the best anyway—my focus needs to be on Elizabeth right now. I don't have the luxury of distractions until I find out exactly what happened to her. I get back into the passenger seat of Faye's car, even though I'm not a fan of her driving, or her music.

"What is this shit?" I ask as she starts singing along the instant the music turns on.

"It's 'One Dance' by Drake," she says, grinning. "Good, right?"
I shake my head. "Terrible."

She rolls her eyes and puts it even louder.

I look out the window, my mind starting to wander. I haven't been having the best time as of late, but I can't exactly put my finger on why. The move to a new MC maybe? The Wind Dragons are amazing, and they've welcomed me with open arms, but why don't I feel like I belong here? My old club, the Wild Men MC, turned out to be fucked-up. Between our bad history, Slice's betrayal, and the pathetic men who are left over, I really don't know why I stayed there so long. Probably because of Talon. He's a good man, a good friend, and I trusted him and his belief in the club. I still trust him, of course, joining the Wind Dragons with him to be by his side. Is that the only reason I joined? I don't even know anymore. I shake myself out of those thoughts. I need to focus on Elizabeth now, and everything else later.

"I'm going to break into the bar tonight and find the missing camera footage," I tell her, watching in amusement as her head snaps to me, eyes wide.

"That's your diabolical plan?" she asks, sounding incredulous.

"Well, the bartender is lying. So it's either that or I go to his house and give him a different kind of interrogation." An idea forms. "Can't the cop do that for us? Take him in and demand answers? As a matter of fact, why haven't they stormed in with a search warrant to find the footage?"

"They already did, apparently," she says, tone dry. "He's sticking to his story. He didn't see anything unusual. As for the camera footage, they didn't find anything. It might really have been turned off, which makes me wonder why. Either they knew something was going down, or their camera really was busted."

"I'm thinking they knew something was happening."

"Same," Faye agrees, slamming her brakes at the light, making the car jerk.

I brace myself against the dashboard. This is definitely the last time I'll be a passenger in the car with her, not to mention my long legs are cramped as hell.

"If they searched the bar and didn't find anything, maybe the break-in isn't necessary," I think out loud. "But maybe we need to put our own cameras in and have the place under surveillance. They're up to something, and I want to know exactly what it is."

"We can get that done tonight," Faye agrees, nodding. "Arrow and Tracker can handle it. They're both good with that kind of stuff."

"Why don't you just ask the feds to sort it out?" I ask, wondering why she'd ask the MC for help instead of them.

She shrugs and simply says, "I like to use my own resources if need be. I like to show them that I don't need them, they need me."

"Of course you do," I murmur, shaking my head and looking out the window.

Who knows why Faye does what she does? She seems to always have a plan though.

My mind wanders from Faye and her diabolical mind to someone else.

That woman.

I wonder if she'll return to the bar again.

THREE

AFTER speaking to Elizabeth's sister, neighbors, and friends, I head back to the clubhouse, wondering why terrible things happen to good people. She really was a saint, just a good soul, and it hurts my chest to think of what she could be suffering through right now, if she's even still alive. I really hope she is.

When I walk into the kitchen, smelling something delicious, I open the oven to investigate. I have to hand it to the women here: there's always food in the kitchen, something I'm not used to, and something I won't be taking for granted any time soon. We didn't have any women who cooked for us at the Wild Men clubhouse. We had women who came and partied, stayed the night, then left in the morning. We had nothing like the family vibe here. I don't even know which of the women can cook, but the fuckin' lasagna in the oven looks amazing. I close the oven and go to the fridge for a beer, then head outside where I can hear the others laughing. Talon, Sin, and Tracker are sitting there watching the sunset, so I pull up a chair and join them. Ever since Sin stepped down as president, I've noticed that he's more relaxed. It's Arrow we turn to now if anything goes wrong, and I guess that must be a weight off his shoulders.

"How did it go?" Sin asks me, playing with the label on his beer bottle. "Any leads?"

"Not yet," I say, nodding to Tracker. "Apparently you and Arrow have some cameras to plant tonight, so maybe you should stop after that beer."

Tracker smirks, not fazed. "Or perhaps I should drink more. Faye wants me to install cameras where, exactly? Since when did we start working for the feds too?"

I laugh that he already knows it's Faye handing out commands.

"Since Faye decided so. A biker bar about thirty minutes from here," I tell him, giving him a quick rundown of everything that happened today.

"How exactly did you get dragged into this again?" Tracker asks, amusement dancing in his eyes.

"Faye wanted me to help," is all I say, because it really is an answer in itself.

They all nod like they understand.

"You need any help, let me know," Talon says, the look in his eyes telling me that he means *anything*, no matter what. He has my back. I nod, because I already know that he does.

"I just hope we can find her," I say, looking down at my feet. "Two weeks is a long time, you know?"

Silence takes over the group as we contemplate that.

"Let me know if you think Faye is getting in over her head," Sin says, looking at the sunset. "I'm sure you've already figured out that she thinks she can save the world all on her own."

"I'll look after her, don't worry," I reply.

To the other men, he probably wouldn't have even said anything, but I'm new to the MC, so I understand why he mentioned it. Still—it does annoy me a little. I get that trust is earned, but I'm a loyal man, and I will be loyal to this club, just like I was to my last. No one here besides Talon really knows that about me though. I finish my beer, listening to their easy conversations, but not participating. I feel like I'm an outsider looking in sometimes, yet I'm not exactly making any moves to fix it. I'm at a crossroads in my life, and I have no fuckin' idea what I want or what will make me happy.

I'm just wandering, without direction or aim.

I really need to sort my shit out.

It's a few days later when I see something on the previous night's camera footage that has me on alert. I pause the recording, then rewind it. Grabbing my phone off the table, I hit Faye's name and wait for her to answer.

"I feel like we need code names," is how she answers the phone. "Can we call each other Mulder and Scully?"

"No," I reply instantly. This chick is so random sometimes. "I found something I want to show you. Can you come to the clubhouse?"

"Give me an hour," she says, hanging up without saying 'bye.

I take a quick shower and dress in jeans, a black T-shirt, my black boots, and my cut—my standard attire—then grab some coffee from the kitchen, thinking about everything I just saw on the video. When Faye arrives, loud and full of life, I show her the footage and sit back, waiting to see if she picks up on the same thing I did. She watches until the very end, then pauses it and turns to look at me.

"What makes you think there's anything suspicious about the girl getting into the car?" she asks me, eyes locked on mine.

"The car had no license plates."

Her eyes widen. "I didn't notice that. How did I miss it? Shit. How can we track it down if there's no plate?"

She sounds annoyed with herself, which makes me smirk. Looks like I'm not the only one who doesn't like to lose.

"Maybe we should find out if there's another girl missing," I suggest, running my hand down the stubble on my cheeks. "Put the cop on it. If there is, at least we now know where the pickup point is. We're going to have to have someone there, making sure it doesn't happen again, and twenty-four-hour surveillance."

"You think that they think they got away with it when they took Elizabeth, so they tried it again two weeks later?"

I nod. "Must be. Pretty bold move, don't you think? Just how big is the operation? If this girl has also been kidnapped, Elizabeth's disappearance obviously isn't a random act."

Faye picks up her phone and starts typing out a message. "I'll get Jo on it. Maybe this is even bigger than we thought." She sighs heavily, presses SEND, and then turns those eyes on me. "Just what are we getting into here, Ranger?"

Her phone beeps almost instantly. She reads it, then says, "You're going to have to meet the cop. I have to be at Clover's school in thirty minutes. I'm going to text you the address."

My jaw tightens at the thought of meeting and working with a fuckin' cop without having Faye there as a buffer. "Can't we go after your school thing?"

"No," Faye says, amusement flashing in her gaze. "You don't have to sit there and have a deep and meaningful conversation or anything. Just hand over the video footage. And we don't want to bring a cop to the clubhouse, hence a random meeting place."

"Probably a police station," I grumble, crossing my arms over my chest. "Where they proceed to arrest me afterward."

"You're not going to get arrested," she says, rolling her eyes. "There's only room in this clubhouse for one drama queen, Ranger."

With that parting line, she grins, waves, and exits the room.

My phone beeps with the address to meet this cop.

Better get this shit over with.

I don't know why this dude wants to meet at a café. Not very inconspicuous if you ask me. I'd have chosen a parking lot, or a dark alley. Fuck, maybe Faye is right—am I overdramatic?

I arrive ten minutes late, because I had to find the fuckin' place, then glance around the café. I don't even know what this Joe looks like, probably something I should have asked Faye but forgot to. I can usually sense a cop a mile away—I just look for someone who gives off an air of entitlement. I'm not wearing my cut, because that would just be stupid, and I have no idea if he knows what I look like either.

I'm scanning the café when something catches my eye, or should I say some*one*. When our eyes catch and hold, and she continues to stare at me expectantly, I walk over and sit down opposite her, hoping I'm wrong.

I have to be wrong.

"I thought you were just going to stand there all day staring at me dumbly, because that's not obvious, right?" she says dryly, pressing her plump pink lips together. Even her voice is appealing, husky, and sensual.

I open my mouth, then close it.

Why does she have to be the one working on this? And she's Elizabeth's cousin?

Her short blond hair is slicked back today, but it suits her. Fuck, she's beautiful. What a shame. A waste of beauty. There's no way in hell I'd date a cop. Hell fuckin' no.

"I had no idea who I was meeting today," I say, finding my voice. "So you have me at a disadvantage."

"You didn't know that was me next to you at the biker bar?" she asks, raising her brows. "Why exactly do I need your help again?"

Of course she's rude.

A rude cop. Are the two mutually exclusive?

I grit my teeth and reply with, "Probably because you still haven't found her."

Her eyes narrow, and she looks down into her coffee. "Tell me what you have."

That must have been hard for her to ask, after her previous comment, or maybe she has no pride at all, who knows. I pull the disk out of my pocket and slide it over to her side of the table. Just as I pull my hand back, she reaches for it, causing our fingers to briefly touch. I retract my hand as quickly as I can without knocking over the salt and pepper shakers in the middle of the table.

Fuck.

I rub my fingers together, feeling as if I've been zapped. What the fuck was that? I want to be near her yet as far away as possible at the same time. What is it about this woman? She's a cop, for fuck's sake. And she can't stand me either. I can see the contempt in her pretty blue eyes. She doesn't look anything like Elizabeth, but they do have the same coloring with the blond hair and blue eyes.

Right, Elizabeth.

I need to fuckin' concentrate, because she is the real reason I'm here. Not anything to do with the woman sitting opposite me. She is nothing to me.

She clears her throat, also looking uncomfortable, but then her expression goes blank. "Now tell me everything you found out. I need to know. We don't have time to waste, I want my cousin back."

I realize that I don't even know her name.

"What's your name?" I ask, leaning back in my seat.

She licks her lips, then says, "Johanna."

Johanna, I repeat in my head, then lean forward and tell her everything she needs to know.

FOUR

Johanna

EVER since my cousin went missing, I've been a wreck. I wonder if people can tell. I'm barely holding on, but I know that I need to stay strong, that everyone is looking to me with hope in their eyes, like I'm their last chance of finding her.

I have to find her.

I don't know why we need a biker working with us, but at this point I'll take any help I can get. Is he here because of the supposed biker connection to her disappearance? And if so, wouldn't he side with the bikers? I'm curious about the man sitting across from me. Not only have I never seen a biker so good-looking, I've never seen any man so striking. He's tall, extremely so. I wonder if he ever played basketball. Dark, thick hair tied at his nape, bright hazel eyes framed in thick dark lashes. Lashes wasted on a boy. He runs his hand across the stubble on his cheeks as I realize I haven't paid any attention to the last thing he said.

I clear my throat and respond to the last thing I remember. "I'll see if anyone reported another girl missing. We might have to wait another twenty-four hours though. I'll alert the police that the bar might be being used to lure women into whatever they are doing with them. I really hope we can stop this before it happens again."

The thought of my cousin missing makes it hard for me to breathe. What was she doing at that stupid biker bar? It seems so out of character for her. Elizabeth hardly even drank.

While we don't see each other that often, Elizabeth and I are still pretty close, our whole family is, and her disappearance has been hard on everyone. Whenever we have a problem, we call each other to vent. When I'm down, she cheers me up, and vice versa. She's more like a sister to me than anything, since I'm an only child, and we've shared a lot of memories together.

I remember when I visited her over the holidays one year, I think I was about seven. We were playing on the playground with a few other kids, and one of the little boys pushed Elizabeth down because she wouldn't get off the swing. Without thinking, I rushed over to the boy and punched him in the face. Blood started gushing from his nose. I helped Elizabeth up and pulled her into me, protecting her, always protecting her. For as long as I can remember.

Where is she?

I've been a cop for the last four years, just like my mother before me, and I've seen things that will haunt me in my dreams forever. However, when something like this happens to you personally, you get to feel firsthand how the people you usually try to help feel, and it's unlike any pain I've ever known. The helplessness, the worry. I can't sleep; I can't eat; I keep playing out different scenarios in my head. I keep dreaming about her, calling out for help, and I'm trying but I can't save her. I need to save her. I keep telling myself that I'm not doing enough, that I need to push more, try harder. How can I be okay knowing that she's out there, going through god knows what?

"Excellent," Ranger says, looking like he wants to escape. He never told me his name, but when Faye texted me, she said I'd be meeting with Ranger. What kind of name is that anyway? How'd he get it?

"I'll call you and let you know how it goes," I say when he stays silent. "Will you let me know if you find anything else?"

He nods once, throws some money on the table . . . for my coffee? Then stands and leaves before I can protest, my mouth open, about to tell him that I can pay for myself. He didn't even have anything to drink, and he left a twenty-dollar bill.

Who exactly is this man?

The next day, I decide to call Faye instead of Ranger with the bad news. Another girl has gone missing—the same one from the video footage. I let the police know what we found out, and place some undercover cops in the area. Why didn't we think to stake out the bar? Sure, I went there a few times, but I didn't set up cameras. How did the club even set up the video surveillance? Never mind—I don't want to know. These bikers think that the law doesn't apply to them, that they have their own set of rules, but this time it benefited the case, and possibly will save lives, so how can I complain? I just want my cousin back, and the truth is that I'd lie, cheat, and steal to make that a reality.

With the bar now under surveillance, hopefully we catch one of the men involved and can bring him in for questioning. Until then, I'm pushing the media to share Elizabeth's face. I want everyone to be looking for her, and maybe, hopefully, someone has seen her, so we'll know in which direction to look. I tap my fingers on my desk impatiently, wondering where my time will be best spent today. Lucky the sheriff is a friend of the family. Because of that, she's giving me more leeway with this case than she would any other officer.

"Jo," Travis, my partner, calls out as he approaches my desk. He's dressed in his uniform, his brown hair spiked up like it usually is. He wipes his brow with his hand. "Fuck, it's hot outside."

"I know," I say, forcing a small smile. "Sorry I couldn't go with you today. Was everything okay?"

"Yeah," he says, blue eyes softening. "Any leads on Elizabeth?"

"Not yet," I say, shoulders hunching. "Time is running out, you know? I just feel like if we don't find someone ASAP, we never will."

"Don't give up just yet," he says, moving behind me and gently massaging my shoulders. "Her face is all over the news. Someone has to have spotted her at some point."

I nod, but I don't feel so confident.

What if I never find her?

Travis has met Elizabeth a few times—he's basically like family to me. I remember her asking how come I never dated him, because he *is* a good-looking man. He has a perfect build, a handsome face, and charisma that attracts women by the thousands, but to me he's just my good friend and partner, someone who I trust inexplicably to have my back and vice versa. I've seen how women throw themselves at him, and it amuses me. He's a good man though, and an even better cop. Yes, he asked me out once, when we first became partners, but I turned him down and now we pretend it never happened.

"That's what I'm banking on," I say, standing up and turning to face him. "All right, I need to get shit done. You coming?"

He nods. "Whatever you need, especially if you're going to meet that hot lawyer chick."

I laugh at his description of Faye. "You want to die, don't you?"

"I'm not scared of those fucking bikers," he mutters, lips tightening to a thin line.

"They're not scared of you either," I point out, feeling amused.

"I laugh in the face of danger."

I stop, eyes widening. "Did you just quote *The Lion King*?"

He wraps his arm around me and leads me outside. "I'm just playing. I'd never go for a biker chick. Could you imagine? A biker and a cop?"

I have to agree with him on this one. The biker lifestyle is a criminal one; it really is like they live in a world of their own creation. I follow the law, and it's my job to uphold it. The only cops who associate themselves with bikers are dirty. I've never heard of an innocent friendship between the two. Faye seems to be the exception, but even then, I'm wary. Bikers are rebellious and don't like authority.

We are the authority.

"Sounds like a recipe for disaster," he adds, shaking his head.

Ranger's too-handsome-for-his-own-good face flashes before my eyes.

I couldn't agree more.

Two days later, we hit a lucky break. We get one of the men from the surveillance video in custody, and someone phones in with a sighting of my cousin. It's everything I hoped for, giving me something to work with. She was spotted about one thousand miles from here, so I'm taking the next flight out. The con? Ranger is coming with me. I don't know why Faye isn't; all I was told is that she's unable to leave at this time.

I don't really understand why Faye is involved at all, to be honest, but for whatever reason, the feds put her on the case. I have to admit, I'm curious about this woman. Essentially she's a criminal with a law degree, but the feds think she's useful to them. Maybe they need her biker contacts and influence. The worst part is now I'm going to be stuck with Ranger, on the flight, in a car . . . we're pretty much going to be living out of each other's pockets. I don't know why I need him anyway. The local police will help, and without his club at his back, just how useful is he? Why is he working on this case? Or any case?

I don't have time to argue about it though. I need to get over there as soon as possible before we lose one of the only leads we have. As I throw some clothes in a duffel bag, my phone beeps with a text from an unknown number:

Meet you at the airport in an hour.

Ranger?

Must be.

I reply with a simple Okay, then continue to throw things into my case like a madwoman. I can't deal with Ranger right now.

Elizabeth, hold on.

FIVE

Ranger

"I DON'T see why you can't come," I grumble, slamming my suitcase closed. "You're the one who dragged me into this."

"Please. You got involved in this because you know Elizabeth, not because of me," Faye replies, lifting her chin. "You're one of the only men here who has no problem saying no to me." She pauses and grins. "Don't worry, I'll grow on you."

When I continue to stare at her silently, unimpressed, she says, "I can't just up and leave, Ranger. I have two children, and we don't know how long you'll have to stay out there. I can come up for a few days or even a week if you want, but there's no way I'll be able to last longer than that without seeing my kids. Besides, you don't need me there to hold your hand. Is this about Jo? She's cute, right?"

I narrow my gaze on her. "I haven't noticed anything besides the badge she wears."

A lie.

Faye smirks, stepping to my suitcase and locking it. "Even I noticed that she's a babe. Great ass, right?"

"Faye," I snap, not having the time to deal with her shit right now. "I better leave or I'll miss my flight."

"Who's driving you?" she asks, leaning against my bedroom wall.

Not you, I think to myself.

"I don't know. Where's Talon? He can take me," I say, lifting up the suitcase. Faye hands me the little key for the lock and I put it in my pocket. "Thanks."

"Why do you want Talon to take you? Don't you think you should get to know the other men too? I'm sure Rake or Tracker can take you. They're sitting outside doing nothing right now."

"It's just a ride to the airport, Faye," I grumble. "Where's Shayla?"

I feel comfortable around Vinnie's woman, because she's Talon's cousin and I've been around her multiple times before.

"Exactly, it's just a ride," she says infuriatingly. I ignore her presence and walk to the door, but she runs up next to me.

"I'm worried about you."

"Don't be," I tell her, softening my tone.

"Do you like it here? Are you happy?" she continues, the concern in her tone sincere.

I stop and face her. "Sweetie, let me find Elizabeth, and then we can have this discussion. Deal?"

She nods. "Okay."

"Good."

Luckily for me, Talon is out front, waiting for me.

"You ready to go?" he asks, getting into the club's black four-wheel drive.

I nod and look down at Faye, lean forward, and kiss her on

the top of her head. She's a pain in the ass, but she's right, she is growing on me. "Stay out of trouble."

"Find her," she says. "And be safe. I know you can do this."

Is she a motivational speaker now too?

I put my suitcase in the back and then slide into the passenger's seat. Loud music flares, but Talon lowers it. I spare him a thankful glance.

He grins as he starts to exit the parking lot. "Sounds like Faye's music."

I make a sound of agreement.

Talon laughs, then turns serious. "Are you sure you don't want me to come with you? You say the word and I'm there."

"I'll be fine. I'm just making sure the cops are doing everything they can. There's nothing you can do to help. Stay with your woman and your kid."

Talon has his own little family now: his woman, Tia, and her son, Rhett, who he's taken on as his own. Talon might have been the Wild Men president, but being part of the Wind Dragons seems to be working out for him really well. I've never seen him so happy.

"I know you can handle yourself. Just know that I'm here if you need me."

"I know," I say, and I do. "I really want to find her, you know? Even though I'm not keen on working with this cop."

"No shit," Talon says, groaning. "Fuck, never thought I'd see the day. Be careful. You know you can never trust them."

"I know," I say, leaning my head back against the headrest. "We're going to have to just deal with each other and work as a team, forget the cop and biker shit until we find Elizabeth."

"Easier said than done," Talon says, gripping the steering

wheel. "But you're right. I really hope you find her, brother. I know she meant something to you."

"Yeah," I say softly. "She did."

And she does.

Not finding her isn't an option.

She's sitting at the gate when I see her.

I drop into the seat next to her. She's wearing a blue top, jeans, and pink-and-black sneakers. She looks fuckin' adorable, and it annoys me. I shouldn't think she's adorable. I shouldn't think she's anything except someone I've called a temporary cease-fire on. We're on the same team for now, but as soon as we're done here, things will go back to normal. We'll step back onto our opposite sides and pretend we never knew each other.

"Finally decided to show up, hey?" she murmurs, not bothering to look up from the magazine she's flipping through. She doesn't have any polish on her nails—they're just short and blunt—but her fingers and hands are still pretty and feminine.

"It's a domestic flight, no need to be hours early," I decide to point out.

She glances at her watch. "Cutting it a little close, don't you think? I'd rather be early than take any chances. I want to get there as soon as possible."

Yeah, I almost missed the flight, but she doesn't need to know that.

"What are you reading?" I ask her, relaxing in the chair, stretching my legs out. "How to be a feminist in 2017?"

She smirks, but I don't get a rise out of her. She simply ignores me, which makes me want to push her more. Get a reaction out of her. What makes her tick?

What is she like in bed?

I shake my head as if that will get rid of that thought. Fuck, my mind doesn't need to go there. Nope, not at all.

"You going to be quiet the whole trip?" I prod, wanting her to speak. "Do we have a plan for when we get there?"

She closes her magazine, which is actually *Guns & Ammo*.

I get hard.

Fuck.

"We need to liaise with the local police there. They're expecting us. Well, at least they're expecting me."

"Didn't tell them you're bringing along an outlaw biker with you?" I tease, grinning at my own comment.

"No," she simply says, turning her body toward me. "I think I'm just going to surprise them with that one." Then she mutters under her breath, "I'm sure they'll be just as thrilled as I was."

I grunt in agreement. I can't pretend like I was looking forward to this, but that was before I saw her. I scrub my hand down my face. No. Her looks don't change the fact that she's a cop, and I can't ever go there. Not only would I never be able to trust a cop, but I'd lose respect in my world for fraternizing with the enemy.

"What, don't you like Faye?" I ask her, twisting her words around a little. "I'll be sure to pass on the message to the woman who is helping find your cousin when she doesn't have to."

Her eyes narrow to slits. "I wasn't talking about Faye, and you know it."

Her lips.

They're flawless. Heart-shaped and the perfect size. I'd like nothing more than to close the space between us and taste them. Why don't I ever want something that's good for me? I never seem to choose the easy route. Maybe easy is boring. Maybe I'm just a person who can never get what he wants without a fight.

I'm okay with that. I fought to leave the trailer park where I grew up, to become something, even though it may not seem like I became someone to be proud of, but in my mind, I did. When my mom was alive, she was so proud that I was in college. She never lived to see me graduate, but I know it would have been the happiest day of her life. Would she want me to be a biker instead of using those three degrees? Probably not. But it is what it is, and I am what I am. I joined the Wild Men right before I finished college. They became my family, and I never looked back, using any skills I gained in school as an asset to the club. I made them money with investments and playing in the stock market, shit like that. I didn't need to get a "real" job.

"We're going to have to get along until we find her," I say, offering her my hand. "Why don't we call a truce for now?"

We're here for one reason, and that's to find Elizabeth. Yes, I'm attracted to Johanna, but it's not like I'm going to act on it. I'm a grown man, and I can control myself.

I think.

She eyes my hand for a second before placing her small one in mine. "So I'm not a cop, and you're not a biker? We're just—"

"Ranger and Johanna."

She nods and lets go of my hand, even though I don't want

her to. The airline personnel call us to board, and I follow behind her, wondering what the fuck I'm getting myself into.

I'm not a small man, so when I see that Faye put me in business class, I send her a little prayer of thanks. Johanna sits right next to me, and even though we just declared a truce, I kind of wish she was seated somewhere else, because she's a distraction I'm trying to avoid, and it's hard when she's so damn close. I guess I better get used to it though. Still, if we were in economy I'd be pressed up against her, and now we have space between us. I catch her glancing over at me but pretend that I don't notice it. Maybe I should pretend I'm asleep or something. Fuck it, I'll just watch a movie. I'm about to put on my headphones when she speaks.

"Ranger?"

"Yeah," I say, turning my head to the right and looking into her eyes. Her beauty hits me. Fuck, she's stunning.

She wrings her hands together, then winces. "I'm not a very good flier."

I sit up straighter. "What do you mean you're not a good flier? Do you get sick?"

"Sometimes," she admits, the color leaving her face as the plane starts to move. "I usually just feel nauseous and drowsy. Light-headed."

I undo my seat belt, get up, and crouch in front of her seat. I know I'm not meant to, and I'm about to get told off, but I can't exactly leave her to suffer. Fuck the rules. "You're only mentioning this now? Isn't there some motion-sickness medicine or something you can take?"

"No, no, I'm fine," she says, forcing a smile. "I'm only telling you in case I pass out."

My eyes widen. "Pass out? Fuckin' fuck, Johanna! Should I call a flight attendant? I'm sure they'll have something that will help you."

She shakes her head. "I'm fine. I shouldn't have said anything."

She waves me off, even though I can see she's not feeling well. She's clearly stubborn.

"Excuse me, sir, but you must be seated and have your seat belt on for takeoff," a flight attendant tells me. I sit back down but ask her if she has anything that can help Johanna, who, from the side, denies needing any kind of assistance. The attendant fusses over Johanna for a little while, gives her some water and a bag, in case she needs to be sick. Johanna convinces her she's fine, so the attendant leaves us alone.

"You're not fine," I growl, narrowing my gaze on her. As the flight ascends, I can see a sheen of sweat appear on her brow. I wait until the stupid seat belt light is off, then return to her side. She doesn't even react to my nearness, just keeps her eyes closed and her head back against the seat. Getting tired of her shit, I undo her seat belt, lift her up in my arms, and lift her into my lap.

"Ranger? What are you doing?" she asks in a soft voice. She must have a killer headache, because she seems so disoriented, nothing like the feisty cop I met at the café. She doesn't even try to move from my hold, something I'm sure she'd have done if she were feeling normal. I sit back down, with her cradled in my lap, rubbing her back gently. She presses her cold, clammy face against my black T-shirt, so I start to give her a gentle head massage, hoping it helps with the tension. It must work, because she relaxes against me, her body going limp. Soon after, she falls asleep on me, her soft snores making me grin. Just who is this woman in my arms? Not just her job—who is she, other than a cop? If all of that was peeled back, to the very essence of her, that's what I crave to know. I, too, close my eyes and try to sleep. I don't think we'll get much rest after this flight, so I should take advantage of it.

I pretend I don't enjoy the feeling of having her in my arms.

I pretend I don't like it, and I sure as hell ignore the way it makes me feel.

I'm good at that, turning off my emotions. I can go cold as ice, make myself feel nothing.

It's the best way to be.

SIX

S HE sleeps like a baby the whole flight, until we get told by the flight attendant that she has to return to her seat for landing. She doesn't look at me after she wakes, probably shy, or embarrassed, I don't know which. Maybe she's ashamed to have been so close to a biker without a gun aimed at him.

Or maybe it's me with the issue.

I keep an eye on her as the flight lands. I see her dig her nails into her palm, and I want to help, but I don't think she'd appreciate the offer right now. If she wants my help, I wish she'd ask, but I know she won't. Reality has hit, which means she must be feeling much better than before, when she was so out of it that she didn't care whose arms she was in. Feeling helpless, I watch as she tries to keep herself calm. When we land, I see the relief play out on her face, and I feel it too. Since neither of us has any carry-on bags, we exit the plane quickly. We walk side by side in silence, and it's only when we're standing at baggage claim that she speaks.

"Thank you, for what you did back there," she says, exhaling roughly. "You didn't have to. And to be honest, no one has taken care of me like that before, so yeah . . . thank you."

"Don't mention it," I say. She moves to grab one of the bags, so I lean forward and carry it before she can.

"Thanks."

I simply nod my head, grab my bag when it comes around, and then walk through the exit with her to hail a cab. I open the cab door for her, then put our suitcases in the trunk, wondering when exactly I became gentleman of the year. She gets in the back, while I get in the passenger seat to give me a little space to clear my head. The driver is chatty as fuck, which is both annoying and welcome at the same time.

"Business or pleasure?" he asks after I tell him the name of the hotel we'll be staying at.

"Definitely business," Jo says from the back, sounding tired but still managing to muster a dry tone.

Jo? Since when is Johanna, Detective Chase, just Jo? Great, now I've given her a fuckin' nickname.

The cabdriver and I discuss everything from weather to politics before we reach the hotel. When we get there, I pull out my wallet just as Jo shoves a fifty-dollar bill in the middle of the driver and me, her outstretched hand waiting for someone to take it. With a shake of my head, I tell the driver to ignore her, which he does with an amused smirk.

"Seriously?" she says, sounding annoyed. "Ranger, take it, don't be ridiculous."

I pay the driver and tip him, ignoring her money, and then get out to unload our suitcases. Taking one in each hand, I walk toward reception, but then stop and wait for her, realizing that I'm being a little rude.

"I can carry my own suitcase," she grumbles, trying to take it from my hand.

I sigh, glancing down at her face. "It will go easier and quicker if you just let me do what I have to do. Why don't you go and check us in?"

"Did you print out the reservation?" she asks, going through her handbag as if looking for it.

"No," I say, brow furrowing. "I assumed that you would."

"Why, because I'm female, I'm meant to be the organized one?"

"Yes," I say, wondering if Faye printed it out and put it somewhere for me. Sounds like something that she'd do; she usually thinks of everything.

Jo makes a sound of frustration and walks to the reception desk. I stare at her ass in those jeans as it jiggles with each angry stomp she takes. She can get as angry with me as she wants as long as I get to enjoy that view. She returns a few moments later and hands me my key.

"We're right next door to each other," she says, nodding toward the elevator.

"Okay."

We get inside the elevator together and she presses the button for level five. I look down at my key, which reads ROOM 538. When the elevator stops, I carry the suitcases out and walk toward my room.

"I'm here," she says when we pass the room before mine. She uses her key to open the door, and I carry her suitcase inside for her.

"So what's the plan?" I ask, taking a look around her room. It is nice. Spacious. I know Faye chose the place, so I wouldn't expect anything less, but we don't really need nice rooms. We won't be spending much time in the hotel.

"Get some food and some sleep, and we'll start early tomorrow morning. How about six a.m.?" she suggests, sitting down on the bed. "I'll catch a cab to the car-rental place, and then I have to stop by the police station."

Great, just great.

"Well, while you do that, I'm going to go have a look around the area she was last spotted, speak to the locals, and see what I can find out," I say, glancing around her room once more. "Anyway, good night."

"Good night," she says softly, leaning down to pull off her sneakers.

I back out of the room, dragging my suitcase behind me, and close her door. I'm about to call out for her to remember to lock it, but she's a fuckin' cop, and I don't think she needs to be told. Instead, I head next door to my own room, place my suitcase in the corner, and then fall back onto my bed. I barely fit on it, but I manage. I really hope that coming here was the right decision—that we can find out where Elizabeth is. I close my eyes and dream about one of the last times that I saw her.

"I can't believe the vacation has come to an end," she says, closing her eyes and letting the sun hit her face. "Back to reality. I'm going to have to find another job now, and save money until I can afford my next adventure."

"You could go to college," I suggest, adjusting myself against the tree trunk.

"Maybe," she says, shrugging her shoulders.

Another girl from the tour, Jane, spots us, and comes to sit down.

"Hey, Cam. Hey, Lizzy. Am I the only one feeling sad that this is our last day?"

I grin, knowing how much she hates being called Lizzy. I tell her that her name's too long, so she can't blame people for shortening it, but she says she doesn't care. Her mother named her Elizabeth after her grandmother who died in childbirth, and that's what she likes to be called.

"You're definitely not the only one," Elizabeth replies, sighing deeply. "All we'll have are our memories." She smirks in my direction. "And maybe an STD for Cam."

"Hey," I say, swatting at her leg. "I can't help it if the women think I'm fuckin' irresistible."

"They definitely think you're something," she mutters under her breath, but a smile plays on her face. She never brings up my reputation from high school, and I appreciate that. Half the women here wouldn't want me if they knew where I came from. They see who I am now, not who I was, and I like that. I thrive off it. I like Elizabeth. In fact, I wish we'd been friends back in school. I could have used a friend like her. Then again, maybe I'd have dragged her down with me, ruined her reputation around town. Yeah—I guess things happen for a reason. We were meant to be on this trip together. I've learned from her, and I hope she's learned from me.

"Yes, they think I'm good-looking, and amazing in bed."

Jane stands up, brushing the grass off her ass, and says, "Well, I'll leave you guys to it, then."

We watch as she departs. "We scared her off."

"You did, you mean," she says, laughing. "I hardly spoke."

"Maybe your silence intimidated her."

"Maybe your talk of how amazing you are in bed made her feel *awkward," she fires back, nudging me with her foot. "Or maybe you already slept with her, and that's why she wanted to run away."*

I haven't.

At least I think I haven't.

"Yeah, yeah. We should probably pack our shit and get ready to fly out," I say, standing up and offering her my hand. She takes it, and I pull her up. "The end of this adventure."

"But the start of another one," she says, smiling.

She's always smiling.

Elizabeth Chase is sunshine, rainbows, and butterflies, and I'm not used to that. Sometimes I don't know how to deal with it. I've never been friends with someone like her. A good girl. Someone who sees the positive in everything. I hope we remain friends after this. She lives several hours away from me, but we can still keep in contact.

"Let's go," she says, nodding her head toward the hostel.

I follow behind her.

SEVEN

Johanna

ORDER room service for dinner and assume that Ranger does the same, because I don't hear from him again for the night. I feel so embarrassed when I replay the flight in my mind. I've never been a good flier, but that flight was a whole other level. My head felt like it was going to burst, the migraine and nausea were that bad. Why did it have to happen in front of him? I don't want him to see me as weak. I don't want anyone to see me as weak. I cradle my head in my hands and groan. Oh well—it happened, and Ranger was infuriatingly sweet about it. No one has looked after me like that. No one. Handed me some painkillers and rubbed my back or something? Sure. Picked me up and cradled me like I was fucking precious? Like he wanted to take the pain away for me? Like he was experiencing my pain—that's how much it felt like he didn't want me to suffer?

Definitely not.

He's a take-control kind of guy, this Ranger. I'm used to being around alpha males—in my line of work it's kind of a given, but there's something about Ranger that takes it to a new level. He's just . . . silently powerful. I don't even know how to explain it, or him. Even in my short time around him, I can tell he's different from any biker I've ever met. He's nothing like I thought he was going to be.

When I found out I was going to be working alongside bikers, I have to admit that I was confused and angry. I didn't see how bikers could help me in any way, probably because all the ones I've met have been good-for-nothing criminals, and I didn't understand why they'd have anything to do with Elizabeth's case. It makes sense that Faye was brought in, because of her connections with the feds, but it's almost like these guys are the exceptions to every rule I've been taught as a police officer.

Ranger though, I didn't see him coming. When I'm around him I forget who he is . . . and to be honest, I kind of forget who I am too. I shake my head, as if that will clear my mind of his craziness. Ranger is going to have to act as my partner while we're here, working together to find Elizabeth, and that's it. Look at me, overthinking things just because he did something nice for me. Travis would have looked after me. Maybe not pulled me into his arms, but he would have made sure I was okay. At least I think he would have.

This probably shows just how I've been treated by men in the past. I haven't had a man cook for me, or ever truly been spoiled before. I don't know anything about love, or romance, or dating. All I know is work, family, and friendship, which isn't a bad life at all. My job might not be safe, but my personal life is. I take risks every day as a cop, but I won't take them with love. It's just not worth it. I've never been lucky in love. A few lukewarm relationships, but no real connection that left a lasting impression on me. I'm married to my job and that's just how it is. I've accepted it.

Then why does it feel like I'm reminding myself?

I wake up early, jump in the shower, turning the water to as hot as my skin can take, then get dressed. Ranger didn't want to come to check in with the local police, but it's something I need to do, both because I have to let them know I'm in their territory and because I need their help. I gave them a call to tell them about the tip, and they told me to come in and see them. The more people we have looking, the higher our chances are for finding her. I don't bother with any makeup, just rub some lotion into my skin and run my fingers through my hair before rushing out the door. I walk to Ranger's door and consider knocking to wake him up, or to see where he's going to meet me today, but he's a grown-ass man and he has my number.

I shake my head and rush toward the elevator. I'm here for a reason, and finding Elizabeth is my only priority.

When the police here turn out to be helpful and cooperative, and tell me Elizabeth was seen on camera at a nearby gas station, I feel like today might be my lucky day. When I go to the gas station, I talk to the man who saw my cousin, writing down anything I think can be of help, even minor details. I view the footage of Elizabeth, which was taken only yesterday, and it's definitely her. She looks disheveled, her normally perfect hair wild, her shoulders slouched, her posture telling me what I need to know.

She's terrified.

But it is her. She's alive.

She walked inside the gas station with a man staying closely behind her the whole way. She grabbed a few things, bottled water and snacks, and then he pays for everything along with his gas. I can see her glancing around, as if looking for an escape, but then the man whispers something in her ear and she stills.

He looks tall, and built, with broad shoulders, muscles, and dark hair, but I never get a good look at his face. She is tiny compared to him, the contrast between them striking. The two of them exit and head for their car. I write down the make and model, and the license plate number, then head back to the police station to run the plate and get any information I can to track this car and its owner down. It's clear she's being held against her will. Was it just a case of wrong place, wrong time?

I send Ranger a quick text telling him to meet me at the station. He's going to hate that, but he came here to help me, and he needs to suck it up and do what needs to be done. Adrenaline fills me at the thought of being a step closer than I was yesterday to finding Elizabeth. I turn off the radio, needing silence to think. What's the best way to approach this? Go in guns a-blazing, or with just Ranger until we can figure out the situation? My phone rings and I know it's him, so I pull over and answer it.

"Tell me everything, now," he says into the phone. He's rude, but right now, I don't care. We don't have time for niceties.

"She's alive! Saw her on the gas station camera footage from yesterday. Saw the man she was with. I have his license plate number and I'm on my way to the station to locate it."

"I'll get in a cab and be there ASAP," he says, then hangs up.

I throw the phone on the passenger seat and pull back into the driving lane.

And then I smile.

My baby cousin is alive, as of yesterday. One year younger— younger than me all the same—and she's still alive. I can only hope that they haven't hurt her, and that I can find her before anything else happens to her. I remember her face and how proud she was when I graduated the academy. Never did I think I'd be using my skills to find her. Never did I think there'd be a situation I wasn't sure I could save her from.

She needs to be okay.

And I want whoever did this to her to pay, either with their blood, or with life behind bars. I really want anyone that has hurt my family to suffer.

Maybe I'm more like Ranger than I'd like to admit.

Ranger storms into the station like he owns it, like it doesn't faze him to be here when I know it does. He probably feels as comfortable as I would in a motorcycle clubhouse—he's in enemy territory.

"What did you find?" he asks, ignoring everyone and everything else around us. "Do we have anything to go on? An address? A name? I'd like to know who the fuck I'm about to kill."

My eyes flare. "Can you not yell that out? Pay attention to where we are, Ranger," I hiss.

"Yet you're not telling me not to do it," he adds, crossing his arms over his chest and staring me down with those amazing hazel eyes. "Because you know the fuckers who took her don't deserve to breathe our air."

"The courts will deal with them," I say, even though silently I do agree with him. "They can suffer behind bars. Unfortunately for us, I tracked the car but they've already dumped it. It was stolen anyway, so we have nothing except the location where they left it and a description of the man. I'm getting them to do a sketch of him right now and we're going to plaster his face everywhere."

"Fuck," Ranger grits out, rubbing the back of his neck. "Did you search the car for prints or DNA?"

"Doing it as we speak," I say, shifting on my feet. "Waiting."

It would normally take longer, but because of me, they're doing it quickly.

Ranger's hands tighten into fists. "At least she's alive, you know?"

"I was thinking the same thing," I admit quietly. I wonder why he's so passionate about this case. I always just assumed he was here because of Faye, maybe protecting her, but is there more to it than that? Is he just a good man? Or maybe something similar happened to someone he once loved, or something like that. Maybe he has a hero complex. I'm curious about him, I have to admit.

"They'll call us the second they get the results. Do you want to go back to the hotel in the meantime, or hang around here and wait?"

He glances around as if only just realizing where he is, and says, "Not staying here, but I don't want to sit in the hotel playing the waiting game either. Is there any way I can see the footage of her before we leave though?"

I nod and lead him into one of the rooms, gesturing for him to sit.

Then I press PLAY and let him see my cousin and her kidnapper.

EIGHT

Ranger

WHILE we're waiting on the DNA results, we head to a café just down the road from the police station. There's no point going anywhere too far because we'll just have to rush back, and we both need to eat something. I skipped dinner last night, I wasn't feeling hungry, but I saw that Jo had ordered room service, by the tray left outside her door in the morning, so at least she ate. While she was doing her own thing this morning, I went out and tried talking to some locals. They either know nothing or are too scared to talk, but either way, there was no information to be found. When Sin texted me last night with a number, I have to admit I was surprised. I had no idea the WDMC had a chapter out here, but he told me I can go to them for anything, and I feel relieved that I have men at my back should I need them. I'm hoping that we can find this asshole's fingerprints or DNA from the car, then we can track him down and deal with him. He is the lead to finding Elizabeth. I don't care what I have to do, I'll do it. I'll torture him to find out her whereabouts if I have to. Seeing her on that video . . . it was hard to watch. My mind is now running wild with all the shit that could have been done to her, and it's making me want to kill someone.

A waitress approaches, smiling warmly at both of us. "What can I get you both today?"

"I'll have a coffee, please," Jo says, scanning the menu. "And a ham-and-cheese croissant."

"Excellent," the waitress says, making a note. "And for you, sir?"

"I'll have a coffee too, and the bacon and scrambled eggs. Thanks."

She writes that down, then tells us that the food won't be long. I glance across the table at Jo, whose eyes are already pinned on me. Today she's in tight jeans and a white T-shirt, and her hair looks like she's run her fingers through it several times, almost like she's just been fucked. Even with no makeup on, she's stunning. A natural beauty—something very rare in today's day and age.

"So you're her cousin," I say, leaning back in the booth. Elizabeth never mentioned much about her family, just her sister, so I have no idea how many cousins she has, or if she's close with them, so I decide to ask. "Are the two of you close?"

Jo nods, sadness flashing in her blue eyes. "Yeah, we're close. We went to different schools and everything, but family is important to us. We always kept in contact, and saw each other whenever we could. She used to live a few hours away, in a small town, but I saw her the weekend before she went missing, actually. She'd just moved, five minutes away from my house. I helped her move all of her furniture in."

So that explains why Elizabeth was at that biker bar—she'd actually moved to my town. I wonder what brought her to the city. Right now she's probably wishing she'd stayed in our sleepy hometown, which makes me sad, because that place is a shithole. This is not the introduction to city life she needed.

Our coffee appears, and the two of us go silent until the waitress leaves.

"Do you have a boyfriend?" I blurt out, realizing I have no idea if she's taken or not. She's not wearing a wedding ring, although I have no idea why it matters to me.

It doesn't.

I'm just curious.

"Nope," she says, eyes on her coffee. "Why do you ask?"

"Just wondering," I say, picking up the tiny cookie next to my coffee and popping it into my mouth.

"Not every man can handle a cop as his girlfriend," she admits, shrugging. "Tried a few times, it never really worked out. I've been single for a while now, and I'm okay with it. It's not like I have much free time anyway."

But what about sex? I wonder. She can't pretend that she doesn't miss having a man's hands on her, a man's mouth on her pussy, licking at her clit until she screams. Then again—it's been a while for me too. I shift on my seat, my cock hardening at the thought of Jo spread before me as I have my mouth on her. Fuck. This is not what I need to be thinking of right now.

"How about you?" she asks, bringing the mug to her pretty lips. "No girlfriend?"

I shake my head. "Nah."

"How come?" she asks, putting the mug on the saucer and tilting her head to the side. "You're a good-looking man, and women dig the bad boys."

"Are you stereotyping me?" I ask, lips twitching. "Finding a woman isn't hard, but finding a good one is. Although it's not like I've been looking. I don't know if I'd make a good boyfriend, to be honest. I've never really had any long-term girlfriends." I pause and consider that. "Never met one who I wanted to keep."

"Keep? You make women sound like puppies," she says, smirking. "Maybe you just haven't met the right one yet. Or maybe there's no such thing as the right one, who knows. I think the people who stay together are the ones who make the choice to do so. It doesn't just happen, and you have to want it more than anything."

"That's not very romantic," I tease, loving listening to her voice her opinions. She's definitely interesting, different, and smart. Why does she have to be a fuckin' cop? Maybe that *is* what makes her so different though. Fuck, I can't win.

"My life isn't very romantic," she admits, ducking her head. "That's more Elizabeth's life. She's always dating, always just loving life, being social. I'm not really like that. I don't really like going out and meeting new people."

I can see Elizabeth being like that. When I knew her, she was shy, but she was always smiling, always up for an adventure. I can see her dating a lot, searching for romance and passion. She's a dreamer, that one. I, on the other hand, am a realist. And although Jo claims to be one, I think she secretly wishes she had that passion too. A woman who hasn't been treated right can claim they're fine without passion, but it's only because they don't know any better. I imagine a well-loved woman would thrive in the world, and be a reflection of her man's love and treatment.

But what the fuck do I know?

Actually, I'm probably a fuckin' pro after living in the Wind

Dragons clubhouse and observing all the couples, even Talon. They're all different, but the love is there—you can see it. I'm the only single one in the house, since Ronan just found a new girlfriend. I really am the odd man out. It doesn't bother me, exactly, it just makes me feel a little on the outside. Unlike in my old clubhouse, there are some nights where no one is in the clubhouse except me. That's not really a clubhouse at all. Do I feel lonely? Is that what this is? Fuck, I have no idea.

"You're an introvert at heart?" I guess. I know the type.

She nods. "I recharge when I'm alone, and being social drains me. At work it's usually just me and my partner, Travis, and I know him well, so it's fine. It's comfortable. With my job I have to be confident at all times, and speak to people on a daily basis, so I can do it. Just that if I had my way, I'd prefer not to socialize."

The only thing I focus on in that sentence is the name Travis.

Have the two of them ever fucked?

"Just how close are you and your partner?" I ask, unable to help myself.

Instead of getting offended and telling me to mind my own business, like I thought she would, she just laughs. "He's like family to me. He's good-looking and everything, but we don't see each other like that. I get asked to hook him up with women a lot. They rave about his 'very, very blue eyes.' Apparently they're hypnotic."

"That's more information than I needed," I mutter under my breath, making her laugh again. "So you don't . . . have anyone you're sleeping with right now?"

I can't take my eyes off her, especially when she laughs. I don't think I've ever been so attracted to a woman in my entire life.

"No," she says, ducking her head. "I'm not sleeping with anyone. How about you? Or do I even have to ask?"

"I think you'd be surprised," I say, gaze lingering on her upturned lips.

"Bikers have a reputation."

"So do cops," I add, smirking.

She rolls her eyes. "Don't act like you don't throw wild parties and women don't throw themselves at you."

I choose to ignore that comment, because it's true, although not for some time.

"I haven't slept with anyone in quite a while," I admit, licking my suddenly dry lips. "No one has really appealed to me."

"Oh," she says, eyes widening.

"Yes, oh." I grin, and then add, "Until now anyway."

She smiles, then looks down at her hands. "Sometimes I feel guilty for smiling, or for laughing. How can I laugh at all, when fuck knows what Elizabeth is going through right now?"

Her words bring me back to reality, sobering my thoughts. All of this must be tough on her too. But she can't really admit if she's struggling, because it would make her seem insensitive in comparison to what her cousin is going through. That doesn't mean her feelings aren't valid. She's a strong woman, and I can see that she's trying to hold it together. Yes, she's a cop, but at the end of the day she's still a person.

"You're doing everything you can to save her, Jo. And you're not giving up on her, and you won't. I won't either. That's everything. It's okay to laugh; in fact, it's required. It's hard on you too, and you need to do whatever you have to do to make it through this."

It's the first time I've called her Jo out loud, but she doesn't even seem to notice. Maybe everyone calls her that.

"Yeah, I guess," she replies. The food arrives, and both of us dig in. I personally think she should eat more, but I don't voice my opinions. I don't think they'd be appreciated.

"So how did you get brought onto this case?" she asks, breaking the silence. "Is this something you do on the side or something? It's a little unusual, don't you think?"

I wipe my mouth with my napkin, then answer honestly. "This isn't something I do, no. And it's not something I'll be doing again. Faye asked me for my help, and here I am."

"Are you and Faye close?" she asks, looking interested.

"We haven't actually known each other for long," I say, wondering the best way to explain this. I never give out a lot of information about my club, and now isn't an exception, especially with her being a cop. I want to share everything with her, but I'd be stupid to tell her anything that could bite me in the ass later.

"Really?" she asks, tilting her head to the side. "Have you ever been . . . more than friends?"

"Definitely not," I say, unable to stop the laughter that escapes me. "She's been with her husband for a long time, the two of them are the couple of all couples."

Jo smiles, watching me. "She's a force to be reckoned with, isn't she?"

"That's an understatement," I say, lips twitching. "She grows on you."

"Like a fungus?"

I nod. "Like a fuckin' fungus."

She grins and takes a huge bite of her croissant.

Fuck, I'm in trouble, because that grin hits me right in my chest.

NINE

WHEN we get the call that the results are in, we rush back to the station. Jo looks over the paperwork while the man who handed it to her starts to explain. There were four different fingerprints on the car. He ran them in the database, and one belongs to the owner. Two belong to two other men. One belongs to Elizabeth. He found different DNA in the car, as well. So if we find a suspect, he can do a test to see if the DNA from the car matches.

"So we now have two names to work with," Jo says, glancing up at me. "Are you ready for this?"

I nod. "More than ready."

It's completely inappropriate, but I don't think I've ever been so turned on in my life as I am right now, watching Jo get ready for battle. Watching her check those guns, knowing exactly what she is doing, is making my dick strain against my jeans. She's in full professional mode, testing the weight of each gun in her hands, sliding knives into secret sheaths and making sure we have enough bullets. I don't even know what to say right now. All I can do is watch as she does her thing, hoping she doesn't see how it's affecting me. She tucks a knife inside her boot, then raises her head, her blue eyes landing on me, her blond hair falling over her cheek bone.

I've never seen someone so beautiful.

"All you're taking is one gun?" she asks, arching her brow. "Do you want any other weapons? I probably shouldn't be offering, but I want you to be protected."

I shake my head. "I'm not just taking one gun. I have these too," I say, flexing my biceps.

She makes a sound of amusement deep in her throat. "I don't think anyone else would joke in a time like this. We're about to raid someone's house," she says, straightening and flexing her neck from side to side.

"You obviously don't know Faye very well," I mutter, standing from the table I was resting on. She makes jokes at the most inappropriate times. "How many men are you bringing with us?"

"Men? You mean officers. Some of them are women—don't be sexist," she says with no heat in her tone.

I walk up to her, so our bodies are almost touching. "You know what I mean."

"No, I don't," she says, lifting up her little stubborn chin. "Why don't you explain it to me? And why don't you stay in the car and let the cops handle this? You might just get in the way."

I lick my lips, ignoring her ridiculous comment, wanting nothing more than to taste her lips. Yes, it's probably the worst timing in the history of the world, or is it? Who knows what could happen in there today? Well, nothing to her, because I'm going to protect her with everything I have, but what if something happens to me? What if this is the only chance I have?

Fuck it.

I place my hands on her hips. Her eyes widen, but she doesn't say anything, so I continue. I lift her in the air, so her face is level with mine, and her arms come around my shoulders, so naturally, like they're meant to be there. Then, I kiss her. Softly at first, testing my boundaries with her. I don't know what she's thinking. I don't even know if she likes me, but I fuckin' like her, so too bad. She tastes like strawberries, her mouth so soft and perfect that I hope she never stops kissing me. When she wraps her legs around my waist, holding on to me completely, I'm in heaven. I let my hands roam over the curve of her ass, groaning as the kiss deepens, becomes hungrier and more desperate.

Kissing her is the best decision I've ever made.

It's me who pulls away, because I don't want another cop to come in and see this and then give her shit. They might lose respect for her and not treat her the same, and then I'd have to do something stupid to defend her. I rest my forehead against hers and tell her, "After this is all over, I'm taking you out on a real date. Old-school style."

"Are you telling me or asking me?" she says, sounding breathless.

"Telling," I say, grinning and kissing the corner of her mouth before putting her back down onto the floor.

She looks a little dazed, and she confirms it when she mutters, "What just happened here?"

What happened was, she just became mine.

But I'll let her figure that out for herself.

Ten of us storm inside the house. Never once in my life did I think I'd be working with a team of police, but here I am, and if it saves Elizabeth, then I'm perfectly okay with it. I had to compromise and promise them I'd stay in the back, out of their way. I get that I don't know anything about their rules and regulations, but they're stupid to underestimate me. I'm an asset and they should utilize that, not make it a point to tell me that they don't want or need me here.

We kick in the door and enter the house, fanning out to cover all the rooms. "Put your hands up!" one of the officers yells when he comes across a man sitting on the couch in the living room. He puts his hands behind his head while two of the cops keep their guns trained on him. In any other situation, I'd have felt bad for the guy. He was just sitting there, trying to enjoy a beer, now he's on his knees on the carpet wondering where he went wrong in his life. I stick with Jo, watching as each room is searched. No one else seems to be in the house, and the man they have is not the one on the gas station footage with Elizabeth, but that doesn't mean he's not connected in some way, or that he doesn't know anything. We can't miss any little details here, because something small could lead us to find her. If I'm given an hour alone with this man, I can find out everything he knows, without a doubt. However, I don't think the cops would approve of my methods, and they're the ones running the show.

For now anyway.

I'm walking down the hallway when I feel something under my feet, something different from the rest of the flooring, like there's something under the carpet. I stop, pressing down hard on my feet, then test the area around it. It feels different.

"Jo!" I call out, bending down and touching the carpet with my fingers while she turns around and retraces her steps back to me. "There's something under here."

She pulls the knife from her boot and hands it to me. I cut through the carpet and sure enough, there's a trapdoor under there.

"A secret basement?" I guess, ripping up more carpet to expose the entire door. When I touch the carpet near the skirting of the wall, I realize I didn't need to cut up the middle, because I could have actually just lifted the carpet up from the side. It was just very well concealed. I share a look with Jo, who calls some of the team over. I lift open the door, and it makes a loud bang as it falls backward against the floor, exposing the opening. I look inside, but all I can see is darkness.

"Hello?" I call out. "Is anyone down there?"

"We're here to help," Jo calls out, which I realize is a smart move, because if any women are down there, I doubt that they'd want to hear a man's voice right now.

When I hear a woman yell out, "Help!" Jo and I share another look.

Fuck.

"I'm going down," she says, looking to one of the cops. "There's a ladder. I just need a light."

If she's going down, so am I.

One day soon I'd love to say that line in a completely different context.

We're both handed flashlights.

"Let me go down first, just in case," I tell her softly so only she can hear. "Okay?"

What if there are men down there? What if it's a huge drop? Too many what-ifs, and I don't fuckin' like it. I've never liked a woman like this before, and I'm sure as fuck not going to lose her when I've just found her.

I don't wait for her answer, I just head down there. The ladder is wobbly, and I'm sure my weight isn't helping, but I make my way quickly, then turn the flashlight on.

The sight before me has me wanting to kill someone with my bare hands.

There are three women here, all of them in separate cages.

Cages. Like they're animals. They're all dressed in white, and they all look like they could use a shower. Disheveled, dirty, treated like they are worthless.

And none of them is Elizabeth.

"Hey, it's okay," I say, trying to appear nonthreatening. "The police are here. You're safe now."

Jo comes down the ladder, and I help her when she reaches the end, placing my hands on her hips until she reaches the floor. When she turns and sees the women, she curses under her breath.

"Come on," I tell her softly, holding her hand and walking over to the first cage. It's locked from the outside with a latch, but the bars aren't big enough for the women to be able to break out themselves. I open it, but when I reach inside for the woman, she flinches away. "I'm going to carry you out of here. Is that okay?"

She doesn't reply.

She doesn't do anything.

I look to the woman in the third cage, who is watching us warily but is very alert. "Will you let me help you?"

She nods. I open her cage, and she comes out. I carry her in my arms and walk to the ladder. "Do you think you can climb up? It's all cops up there, so don't be scared, all right?"

"Okay," she whispers, and starts climbing up the ladder. I wait until she reaches the top, then turn to see Jo has coaxed the first girl out and is carrying her in her arms. The woman is about her size, but Jo carries her like she's a child. How strong is she?

"I'll carry her up," I say, because there's no way Jo can do it.

"I can do it," Jo says, shrugging me off and heading up the ladder. I watch her for a few seconds, then turn to the third woman, lifting her over my shoulder. I look around the basement, making sure there's no one left behind. The cops can do a more thorough sweep for anything else that may help with this investigation.

I climb up the ladder, glad we are able to save these three, but also wondering if Elizabeth is in a cage somewhere right now, waiting for someone to come and save her.

Fuck.

What type of man does this to a woman?

I can't even comprehend the evil some people have in them, but it makes me fear for humanity.

And that's coming from a biker.

TEN

Johanna

WATCH as the women are taken away in ambulances, while the man we found in the house is led in handcuffs to the back of a police car. He hasn't said anything so far.

"We need to raid the next house, now," I say to Ranger. "Before they figure out we're onto them and they move any other women they may have."

It's obviously some sort of human-trafficking operation, which was of course my worst fear, and it looks like it's a reality. One of the women told us about how she was told she would be sold off to the highest bidder. As a cop, I know things like this happen, but I never would have thought something like this could happen to someone I love.

It's a hard pill to swallow.

The rest of the team head to the next house, while Ranger and I stay behind with the forensic team. If Ranger hadn't noticed the trapdoor, we never would have found those women. A whole team of police, and it was the biker who saved the day.

I don't know how to thank him, or if I even should, but all I'm feeling right now is grateful that he's here. He's a good man to have around, that's for sure, even though he keeps trying to protect me from things I'm used to doing.

Yes, I'm a woman, but I can do everything a man can do. I train to make sure I'm strong and can lift heavy things; I know how to fight, so I can protect myself even in a hand-to-hand combat; and I can handle weapons as well as any man can. At the same time, it's kind of cute that he's being all protective and chivalrous, because I'm definitely not used to it.

The biker has a heart.

And that kiss. I absently touch my lips, remembering the way his mouth felt on mine. I don't know what's happening between us, and I know I said I'd never have anything to do with a biker, but when he kisses me like that it's hard to remember reason. It's hard to remember anything.

While it hurts that my cousin wasn't here, three women are now saved, and that's a start. I'm hoping that the man we arrested can give us the information we need to find her, or that the second raid proves to give us more information, maybe even lead us to her. Either way, we're onto something good here. I feel like we're so close I can taste it.

"Can they check his call history and maybe interview the people he has contact with?" Ranger asks, his mind still working on ways to bring these assholes down.

"Yes, don't worry, Ranger, everything will be looked into," I assure him. "We are the police, you know. We've got it all under control." I step closer to him and lean my head on his arm. "You were so good in there, by the way."

"So were you," he says, wrapping his arm around me so my

head is now touching his stomach. "We make a great team." He pauses, then adds, "Travis better look out."

I can't help but grin at that. "I'll have to give him a heads-up."

I've never been so lighthearted in such serious moments before, and I know it all has to do with him. Normally I'd be feeling down right now, replaying events in my head, just being really harsh on myself, but with Ranger here going through the exact same thing with me—I don't feel so alone. I don't even know how to explain it, other than that he seems to bring out a side in me I didn't know existed. With Travis, we'd just go our separate ways after our work is done, and I don't know how Travis deals with it, but I tend to go into a zone where I overanalyze everything. Ranger being here with me is changing the way I handle the aftermath of the situation.

You just met him, and he's a fucking biker.

Ahh, right. That little chestnut.

Then why aren't I stepping away from him right now? Why didn't I stop the kiss? Why can't I stop thinking about the kiss? I look at his lips, then clear my throat.

"I need a shower. Let's go back to the hotel and wait for more calls," I tell him, stepping away, breaking our contact. But then, he offers me his hand, and I take it. I don't question it, I just do it because it feels good, and it feels right. I don't listen to the voice in the back of my head. I don't have time to listen to it.

We still have more work to do.

Once this is all over, I'll worry about it then.

I'm fresh out of the shower and sliding on my black silk pajamas when there's a soft knock at my door. I know it must be

Ranger, but I still peep through the hole, watching him standing there. It's about ten o'clock at night, and I know that inviting him inside right now will be a very dangerous thing. Maybe he just wants to tell me something? Maybe I'm making excuses for what I secretly want to happen anyway. Did I just actually admit that to myself?

I unlock the door and open it. "Hey."

"Hey," he murmurs, looking down at my pajamas. "Can I come in?"

"Sure," I say a little warily, opening the door wider and stepping back. "Is everything okay?"

"Yeah," he says, closing the door behind him. He sits in the chair by the desk, and glances up at me. "Today was intense."

"It was," I agree, sitting down on the edge of the bed. The second raid came up with nothing, and still no sign of Elizabeth. The man from the first house is now in custody, but he's not talking.

"Do you think they'll let me interrogate him?" he asks, dead serious.

"Probably not," I say, feeling amused. "Let's see how the detectives do first before we offer our services."

"We?"

"You think I don't want a piece of him too?" I say, arching my brow. "And if you're going in there, so am I."

"Why?" he asks, studying me. "I'd rather you not see that side of me."

"She's my family," I fire back, brow furrowing.

"And she's my friend," he says, surprising me.

He knows Elizabeth?

"Why didn't you mention anything about that before?" I ask. "How do you know her? Is that why you came on this case?"

It all suddenly makes sense. He isn't here because Faye made him, or because he has some kind of hero complex. He's here because he knows Elizabeth and cares about her. I rack my brain, wondering if she's ever mentioned a biker, or if I've ever heard the name Ranger before, but come up with nothing. We didn't grow up living near each other though and went to different schools, so she knows a lot of people I don't.

"You didn't ask," he says, playing it off. "We used to be friends. We actually went to high school together. I haven't seen her in years, but when I saw her photo I knew I couldn't just sit back and do nothing. So, yes, that's why I'm here. This isn't just personal for you—it is for me too. Trust me, I wouldn't be here otherwise. You might be her blood, but that doesn't mean that I care any less. I won't rest until she's safe."

We share a look, a moment of understanding passing between us. Neither of us will quit until we have her back; we're both on the same wavelength. I never thought I'd have something in common with a biker, but here we are, in my hotel room, basically partners. It goes to show that you never know where life will take you. All you can do is hold on for the ride.

"If you hadn't found that trapdoor today . . ."

"But I did," he says, moving his gaze from me to around the room. "I should be tired, but I'm not. Do you want to watch a movie or something?"

My eyes widen at the offer, taken aback. "Ummm, sure," I say, handing him the remote. "Why don't you choose something?"

Is he going to watch on the bed with me? Is this appropriate? We did kiss—it's not like that's appropriate, but I don't regret it either. I don't know what to think or say, so I just move to one side of the bed and watch as he puts on the TV and selects a movie channel. When he moves to the bed, on the other side, I hold my breath. He, on the other hand, acts like this is something we do every day. He makes himself comfortable lying on the bed, flicking through the channels again when apparently the one he chose wasn't entertaining enough.

"Any requests?" he asks, not paying me any attention. He still has his shoes on, so his feet are off the bed, but every other part of him is flat on the mattress.

"I'm easy," I reply without thinking, then cringe when I realize what I just said. "You can watch whatever you want; it's fine."

Nice save.

However, Ranger doesn't let it go. "Are you?"

"Am I what?"

"Easy?" he asks, lip twitching. He finally looks from the screen to me. "Because I don't think you are."

"Really?" I say, turning my body toward him. "What am I, then? Have you already figured me out in the little time you've known me? I must be pretty simple, then . . . hmmm?"

He throws his head back and laughs. "Fuck, Jo. You're not simple—no woman is—but you definitely aren't. You're strong, yet you have a soft, vulnerable side that I want to protect. You don't know what you want. You think that you don't need anyone else, but you do. You love hard. You love everyone hard except yourself. You—you just get by, working yourself into the ground and not giving yourself what you need, what every fuckin' human needs."

I blink slowly. "I don't need anyone else. I've gotten on just fine, thank you. I don't need love, or an epic romance, or whatever else other women want, because it's not in the cards for me. I haven't even had sex in over a year!"

"Do you make yourself come?" he asks, scanning my face and waiting for my reply.

I swallow. "Ranger. I feel like we need to have a talk about boundaries."

"I have none," he says, shrugging, his expression blank. "Now answer the question."

"Yes, I do," I say, cheeks heating. "I'm a grown-ass woman, what do you think?"

"I think that you have needs."

"That I can take care of on my own," I say, lifting my chin.

Ranger licks his lips, then replies with, "You don't miss someone holding you? Kissing your neck? Someone's mouth on your pussy? A vibrator can't replace that connection, that pleasure. The truth is, I haven't fucked anyone in a while, because I'm sick of meaningless fucking. I did so much of it, and it got old really fast. Without a mental connection, I get bored. So, I've been waiting. Waiting for someone worth fucking. The difference between me and you? I know what I'm missing, I'm not in denial about it. I never thought I'd meet a woman who actually held my interest, but I always hoped to. I'm the only single man in the whole MC now, you know that?"

"Really?" I ask, eyes flaring. "All the women must want you, then, if it's only you who is available."

"Is that supposed to be a compliment?" he asks, lips turning down. "It didn't sound like one."

"As if you don't know that you're good-looking," I say, feeling bold. "Women must throw themselves at you."

I shouldn't be feeding his ego, but we're both being completely honest right now. This conversation isn't about anything but the truth—like he said, no boundaries. No filters. Just being real. So I'm not going to hide behind anything.

He isn't.

He ignores my comment and says, "Come here."

"What?" I ask, tucking my hair back behind my ear.

"Come here," he repeats, lifting his arm out.

I scoot over on the bed until I'm within reach. He pulls me into him, so my head is on his shoulder and I'm wedged into the crook of his arm.

"Much better," he says softly, then returns his attention to the TV. While surrounded by his warmth, I realize that what he said is right. Sure, I miss sex, but I miss this more. The contact, the affection and just the feeling of being close to someone. Damn him for being right, because I was doing so well convincing myself otherwise. The worst part is, I think I only crave these things being near him.

I don't think I've changed my opinion on things—I think that *he's* changed it. Because I don't want to cuddle up to anyone, it's just him—being like this right now, I don't want to move. It feels perfect. How did this happen exactly? And so quickly? If I don't want this, I need to back away now, before we're in too deep. Before I probably end up hurt, or with regrets.

Ranger-size regrets.

I notice him glance down at me, but he doesn't say anything, he just returns his gaze to the TV screen, where an Adam Sandler movie I've never seen before is playing. I bury my face in his black hoodie, taking in his scent, closing my eyes and just enjoying the moment. And that's how I fall asleep.

ELEVEN

Ranger

FREEZE when I walk out of the bathroom to find Jo pointing a gun at me.

"Oh fuck, it's just you," she says, lowering the weapon and touching her free hand to her chest.

"You spooned me all night and forgot about it?" I ask, feeling offended. She rubs her eyes, still looking half-asleep.

"I forgot where I was for a second," she murmurs, sliding out of bed. "What time is it? We better get to the station."

She puts the gun down and starts walking to the bathroom but then stops, and starts to stare at my bare chest, blue eyes widening as they roam up and down my torso and back.

"What?"

"When did you get half-naked?" she asks, eyes now glued on my abs. I absently run my hand down them, and her eyes follow the movement. I don't think she's even blinking. I try to hide my smile, amused and pleased that she finds my body so appealing. This is definitely a good thing, and one I plan on using to my advantage.

"In the middle of the night. It was hot with you pressed against me," I explain, picking up my T-shirt and hoodie from the floor. I leave the hoodie on the bed while I put on my T-shirt, purposely flexing as I lift my arms up. Her eyes widen even further, if possible, and are as big as saucers. "I'm normally cold at night because of the air-conditioning."

With my arms through the T-shirt, I pull it down over my six-pack slowly for effect.

Jo clears her throat, but she doesn't look away. When I let go of the material, she raises her eyes to mine. "We fell asleep watching movies. Nothing happened."

"I know," I say, taking my hoodie in my hands. "I was there. Who are you trying to convince here? We didn't do anything wrong."

"We spooned," she says, cheeks going pink. "This isn't what we're here for, Ranger. We're here on a mission, and I don't know how this is happening."

"Like you said," I tell her, taking a step toward her and lifting her chin up with my finger. "Nothing happened. Don't over-think this."

I graze my thumb across her cheek, and her eyes flutter shut. She likes me touching her, and I like touching her. What's the issue here? She's Jo, and I'm Ranger, nothing more and nothing less, like we both agreed before we got on the plane. So what's the problem? What's stopping me from sinking inside of her once we're done with our day, holding her close every night? Does she just see me as her enemy, no matter what she agreed to? Or does she feel guilty, thinking that she shouldn't be able to enjoy herself until Elizabeth is found?

"Okay," she whispers, turning her face into my hand. "I

won't. While we're here, there are no rules, right? Nothing else exists. We aren't our labels, we're just us."

"Jo and Ranger," I reiterate, eyes softening. "It's just us, trying to find Elizabeth, but that doesn't mean we can't enjoy ourselves when we're off duty. Life is short, Jo. You never know what can happen."

"I know," she says, looking away. "But finding her is the priority."

"I know."

And I do. But when we're alone, Jo clouds my mind. All I can see is her. It's not wrong for me to admit that.

She takes a step back, her expression going blank. "We need to get to the police station and see what we can find today. Time is running out, Ranger."

I know this, but when we get back here this evening, after we've exhausted ourselves, I want her in my bed. Or me In hers—I'm flexible.

I head to my room and jump in the shower as fast as I can.

Time to see how the interrogation went.

"They might as well offer him a doughnut and ask him if he wants a fuckin' massage," I mutter, watching through the window as the detectives question the man. They're being so fuckin' gentle with him, it's like they're interviewing him for a job or something.

"What do you want them to do?" Jo asks, glancing sideways at me. "Punch him in the face every time he doesn't answer a question?"

"To start with," I say, my hands clenching to fists as I picture the women in the cages, the looks of hopelessness on their faces.

"He's given only two names so far, and what's the bet they're the bottom of the barrel? We need something on him so that he's more scared of us than whoever it is that he won't name. Does he have any kids?"

"You want to threaten his children?" Jo asks, jaw dropping open. "We're police. We don't do that shit."

"I'm not a cop," I point out, stretching my neck from side to side. "No rules apply to me here, Jo."

We share a look.

I can see her weighing her options. We have a loophole here and we'd be stupid not to use it. Police ethics and rules don't concern me, and I'm here on behalf of Faye and therefore the feds' approval. I give Faye a quick call, and she's with me on this one. No one can really say shit. Fingers will be pointed if it comes out, but I'll just fuckin' deny it. It will be my word against his. Why should he even have any rights after what he's done? Those women didn't have any. They were treated like shit, like possessions. Why shouldn't I be allowed to put some fear into this man, put him under pressure so we can save more women and hopefully find Elizabeth?

Then she surprises me by saying, "Let me see what I can do."

I turn to watch the man while she leaves the room, planning my course of action. When she returns and nods at me, I crack my knuckles in preparation.

Time to shine.

"So, you have a son," I say, sitting down across from him. I don't look into his eyes, I just clean the gun in my hands.

He watches every action, probably wondering how to handle this.

"You threatening my kid?" he asks, jaw going tight. I see him eyeing the tattoos on my arm. "What if I want to see my lawyer? I don't think they'd appreciate hearing that I'm being threatened by the cops."

"I'm not a cop," I say, flashing my teeth at him. "It's just you and me in here."

"I'm not giving you any names," he says, looking away. "I'm going to be doing time anyway. It won't change anything."

"Will change a lot of things actually," I say, looking up at him. "Have you heard of the Wind Dragons MC?"

He nods, eyes going wide. "What about them?"

I grin evilly. "I'm one of them. You don't care about your wife and your son? I have no problem killing them, you know." I'm lying. I'd never hurt a woman or child, ever. But the WDMC reputation is useful to me right now. "Maybe your wife knows something. Should I get the cops to bring her in for questioning too?"

He looks me right in the eye, searching for whether I'm being serious or just bluffing. I stare back, daring him to test me. He swallows, his throat muscles working.

"They're innocent," he says, licking his lips. "My wife and kid. They didn't know anything that was going on. They don't know—"

"Yet they might have to pay for your mistakes," I say, sliding my gun into the waist of my jeans. "There is nothing I won't do to find out what kind of operation you're running, and if you don't help me, I'll make sure your family pays the price. Don't fuckin' test me. I have no boundaries, and I have no problem killing. You have five minutes to give me a name. The name of the man at the top of this whole operation, or you'll have no one left who cares about you. There will be no one to visit you in prison, because they will all be dead."

"He'll kill me," he says, looking on the verge of tears now.

Fuck.

"He won't know it was you," I say, even though I'm sure "he" will probably figure it out. That's not really my problem. The schmuck shouldn't have gotten involved in human trafficking. He's obviously not a man with a conscience, or maybe he cares only about himself and his family, I don't know. Either way, if I have to choose between him and innocent women probably being sold off—it's not his life I'm going to save.

He mutters two words.

A name.

"If you're lying to me . . ."

"I'm not," he swears, looking down at his hands. "Please, just leave my family alone."

I leave the room, and walk right into Jo.

"I'm on it," she says, hanging up the phone she was on. "We're looking into him."

"Good," I say, nodding. "We need to take him down."

"A SWAT team is assembling as we speak. You did well in there. How did he know you'd seriously do it though? It was just words, you didn't even use force."

"I guess one beast recognizes another," I say, shrugging it off, but the truth is, he saw my tattoos. If he knows what they mean,

he knows I'm not one to fuck around with. I wonder if he rec-
ognized my newest tattoo, the Wind Dragon I have on my forearm, to prove that I'm telling the truth. Either way, I just hope
that the name he gave is the breakthrough we need.

No more fuckin' around.

TWELVE

Johanna

WE spend the entire day looking for this man who is supposedly in charge, and come up empty. He's not in the system and has no priors, but we have his name, address, pictures of him. Problem is he's obviously gone into hiding. We lost the element of surprise, and who knows where he could be now. His face is all over the news, in hopes that someone sees him. After exhausting all resources, I have to wonder if we ever will find my cousin.

It's midnight by the time I fall onto my bed, feeling tired and extremely disappointed. I feel like crying. I haven't cried since she went missing, because I'm the police officer. I'm the strong one. I kept telling my family that I will bring her home, and I made myself believe that I could . . . but what if I can't? How can I live with myself? I'm mentally beating the shit out of myself when there's a knock at the door. I open it, not really paying attention, knowing that it's Ranger. He takes a look at my face, then pulls me into his arms, kicking the door closed with his foot and rubbing my back with his large warm hand.

"Hey, it's okay," he rumbles as I bury my face in his chest. I don't cry in front of people, because I don't like to be seen as weak, but right now I can't hold it back. I burst into tears. He lifts me into his arms, carrying me like a bride, and lays me down onto the bed, with him still pressed against me. "Don't cry."

His comment makes me cry harder, big, heart-wrenching sobs. "Where the fuck is she?"

"Did you think it was going to be easy to find her?" he asks, his voice gentle. "It's not. We're going to have to push, and we're going to have to fight, but we'll get there, all right? I know your heart's in it, Jo, but you need to stay strong. Pretend this is just another case. You need to shove your emotions aside right now so you can think with a clear head."

"I know, I know," I say, compelling myself to stop crying. Fuck. Why does he have to see me like this? The first man I've found myself attracted to in forever. Who would want to sleep with this mess? I just cock-blocked myself. And I admitted to myself that I *do* want to sleep with him. Fucking great. It hits me just how close he is to me, how I can feel the warmth coming from his chest and how the delicious woodsy cologne he wears is hitting my nostrils. The way he's holding me, his hand still running up and down my back, comforting me. When's the last time someone comforted me like this? Him on the plane? Before that . . . I can't even remember.

Wow.

I need a life.

I try to stealthily blot my tears on his T-shirt. Luckily my nose isn't running, or snot would be all over his T-shirt too, and that would be embarrassing. I take a deep breath, and then slowly lift up my head. His hazel eyes are already on me. They're soft. They aren't filled with pity, because if they were I'd tell him to get out right now. He isn't judging me at all. They are filled with understanding. Compassion. I don't know where the hell Ranger came from, but I'm glad he's here with me right now.

I tell him as much. "I'm glad you're here."

"So am I," he says, flashing me a small smile. "It's okay to be vulnerable sometimes, Jo. There's beauty in it."

"You're never vulnerable," I point out.

He gives me a weird look. "I don't think that that's true."

We just watch each other, eyes locked.

I don't know how this happened, how I ended up being literally so close to him, but he's here, and it feels . . . right.

I must be losing my damn mind.

"Hi," I whisper, my voice croaky.

"Hi," he says back, pushing my hair gently off my face. "I think you needed that."

"I think I did too," I say, already feeling better. "I've held it all in since she went missing. I'm the strong one in the family, so I had to hold everyone together, you know?"

"You shouldn't have to feel that way," he says, lips tightening. "You're strong every day in your job, and then you have to come home and hold everyone together? There's only so much weight one person can take on their shoulders, Jo. You shouldn't feel like you have to be strong just because you're a police officer. You're still human. Don't carry that burden for them. Why did you want to become a cop anyway?"

"My mom was one," I say, shrugging. "It's all I ever wanted to be, ever since I was a little girl. I saw her as a superhero growing up. What about you? What did you want to be?"

He frowns, going silent for a few seconds before answering. "I don't know. I didn't have the best childhood. We didn't have much money, I grew up in a trailer and was known for being a troublemaker. The only thing I wanted to do was to get out."

"And you did," I say, imagining him as a kid living like that.

"No one knew the real me, you know? They saw what they wanted, and I eventually ended up acting how they expected me to. They didn't know how smart I was—how I aced all my exams without studying, or that I'm good with numbers. They just saw a boy from the trailer park."

My eyes widen. I know Ranger is smart, but just how smart are we talking?

"You did what you had to do," I say, wanting to reach out to him, but I refrain.

"I did what was best for me," he says, shrugging his shoulders. "And you need to do the same. You can't worry about everyone; you can't save everyone."

We stare into each other's eyes, and I wonder what he's been through to say that. He's got a whole MC at his back; I'm sure they'd help him if need be. Can he relate to this? He's right though, there hasn't been much give-and-take in my family relationships recently. I've been giving everything I can, and they've been taking. I even gave Elizabeth's sister, Helen, some money because Elizabeth normally does. Is it guilt? I don't know. I like to take care of the people around me, but no one is really there to take care of me. If I fall, I fall alone.

Fuck, when did my life become so depressing? But, how can I even complain about it with what has happened to Elizabeth?

It all comes back to the guilt. I'm a policewoman. My cousin is missing and everyone is relying on me to find her, but my harshest critic is myself. *I* won't be able to live with myself if I don't find her.

"I know," I say, resting my head on his chest once more. "Why is everything so hard?"

I've never whined about anything, but for once being vulnerable doesn't feel so bad, because it can bring people closer.

Ranger clears his throat and mumbles, "Because you're so fuckin' beautiful."

Wait, what?

When I scoot closer to him and feel his hardness pressed against me, I understand his comment.

"Oh," I say softly. "Ohhhhh."

He's hard.

And he thinks I'm beautiful.

Even after I just cried on him, and opened up to him.

And did I mention that he's hard?

I bite my bottom lip, then lift my head up and look at him once more. "Ranger?"

"Yes," he says, licking his bottom lip. "What do you need from me?"

"Why haven't you kissed me again?" I ask, feeling bold.

"I was waiting," he murmurs, eyes darkening.

"For what?" I whisper, feeling a little dazed.

"For the right moment."

My gaze lingers on his mouth, the tension between us heightening. Unconsciously, I lean closer to him, and then he does the same. As our lips touch, it's like a starting gun is fired, because suddenly, we're all over each other.

My hands are in his hair, which falls out of its binding, the soft locks running through my fingers. His hands wander to my ass, lifting me to straddle him as he lays flat on his back, our lips still fused. He kisses me so deeply, I can taste the hunger on his tongue, the need fueling his desire. He wants this badly, just as I do, and the fact that I can feel it fires the heat behind my passion. His hands squeeze as he ends the kiss, only to kiss down my neck, making me moan at the sensation.

Suddenly, I'm rolled over onto my back, and his lips are slammed back down on mine. I can feel his hard cock pressing into my thigh, straining against the soft material of his gray sweatpants. His fingers skim my lower stomach, lifting the silk of my pajamas as he removes my top. I lift my hands for him as he bares my stomach and then my breasts, exposing pebbled nipples just begging for attention.

"So pretty," he murmurs, licking his lips before bringing his mouth to suck on one nipple, and then the other. My eyes close on their own accord, my hands threading through his hair, encouraging him. He starts to kiss down my tummy, just near my belly button, then farther down, until he hits the waistband of my silk pants. Pulling them down, he hums his approval when he sees I'm not wearing any panties, then continues kissing his way down my right thigh. I help him take off the pants with a flick of my ankle, my eyes fluttering open as he slowly spreads my thighs, then peppers kisses up the inside of my left thigh.

"Ranger," I whisper, wanting more than anything for the torture to be over, for his mouth to be where I crave it most. He lifts his head, hazel eyes filled with lust and smugness, then brings his tongue to my pussy, licking my center.

Fuck.

THIRTEEN

Ranger

I DON'T know how we went from her crying to me going down on her, but I'm not complaining one bit. Her pussy is shaved bare, and so fuckin' pretty, it would be rude for me not to have a taste. I don't know the last time she had an orgasm, but I'm going to give her one to remember. I ignore my throbbing cock and focus on her pleasure, sliding my tongue over her clit. She raises her hips, and makes soft moaning sounds, so I increase the pressure with my tongue.

"Ranger, I'm going to come," she whispers, her thighs trembling. Fuck. She's amazing. So responsive.

Perfect.

I continue to flick my tongue over her clit, the way I'm learning that she likes it, and insert a finger inside her. It sends her over the edge. She cries out as she comes, and I enjoy every second of it—the sound she makes and just watching her writhe in pleasure while I continue to taste her, dragging out her pleasure as long as I can. She pushes my head away gently, so I lift my head up and look at her, lying back, her eyes heavy, a sated, satisfied smile playing on her heart-shaped lips.

This is a moment that I will never forget.

I move up the bed, leaning over her and kissing her lips. She lifts my T-shirt, her fingers running up my back, then mutters, "Your turn."

My cock approves of this.

I slide off the bed and pull my T-shirt over my head, throwing it on the floor. My sweatpants and boxers soon follow, and then I'm standing there naked before her. I let her take me in, knowing she likes what she sees by the wide-eyed stare she gives me. She bites her bottom lip as her gaze reaches my cock, which is proudly jutting out, just waiting for her attention.

"Fuck me," she mouths, and I can't help but smile.

"I plan to," I reply, grinning as I sit on the bed, roll her over to her side, spooning her from behind. "Are you on the pill?"

She nods. "Yeah, I am."

"I'm clean," I tell her, hoping that she'll let me fuck her bareback. "And I got tested and haven't been with anyone since."

"Okay," she says, reaching behind her to stroke my cock. "I want you to fuck me, Ranger. I trust you."

Those words are like music to my ears.

Turning her head toward me, I kiss her again, while my hand wanders down and starts to play with her clit. She's still wet, dripping from her orgasm. I take my cock in my hand and gently slide into her from behind, my lips still attached to hers. I've never wanted to kiss someone so much before, which is new for me. I don't usually kiss that much during sex, because it feels too personal, but with Jo, there's no such thing. I want to be as close to her as possible. She feels amazing, her pretty pussy squeezing my cock as I slide in and out. She moans into my mouth as I continue to play with her clit, wanting her to come, over and over again. I slide out of her and lay back, pulling her on top, wanting her to ride me so I can watch those tits and stare at her face. I want to take her in every position possible, and I plan to by the end of the night.

She takes my cock and slides herself down on it. I sink my teeth into my lip, watching her as she lifts her hips up and down, owning it. I sit up and take her face in my hands, kissing her lips and thrusting upward, fucking her. She feels so fuckin' amazing, and now that I know what I've been missing out on, I know I can't . . . no, I won't, give this up. She comes again, and I can feel it, her pussy squeezing even tighter, the ecstasy playing on her face turning me on even more. When I can see that she's come back to herself, I roll her over onto her back with me still inside her, and thrust in and out, deeper and harder, until I come, my face buried in her neck as I whisper her name. I wipe the sweat from her brow and kiss her lips gently, then the apple of her cheeks. I take in her expression, and something inside me does a little flip when I see the small, sleepy smile on her face.

"You okay?" I ask, sliding out of her.

"Perfect," she replies, pulling me back down so I'm pressed against her. "Don't go anywhere."

"I wasn't going to," I say, already wanting her again as her nipples touch my chest. "Do you want anything? Some water?"

"No," she says, placing a kiss on my neck. "I'm okay. I don't want to move right now."

"You don't have to, because I'll get whatever you want for you."

"The only thing I want I already have," she says, yawning. "Which is you right here."

Fuck.

She falls asleep soon after that, but I stay wide-awake, replaying those words over and over in my head. Did she mean them? Does this mean that this is more than a onetime thing? Or will she wake up and turn ice-cold? Or worse, what if she regrets us being together? I don't know how I'd take that, to be honest. I might not have known this woman long, but I've been drawn to her like no other from the very beginning, and every new thing I find out about her I like. I *want* to know everything about her. I want to protect her, and I don't want another man even fuckin' breathing in her direction. I've never felt possessive about a woman in my life, and I don't really know how to handle it, but she's just going to have to deal.

She's mine, and I don't fuckin' care what I have to do to keep her.

I exhale as I let that sink in, realizing that that's what I've decided.

She's mine.

I kiss her forehead, and eventually fall asleep with her wrapped safely in my arms.

The next morning, when I open my eyes, Jo is gone from the bed and I can hear the shower running. I woke her up early in the morning with my mouth on her, and then fucked her until we both came before falling asleep again. Curious to see how she's going to react, I get out of bed and walk into the bathroom, taking the partially open door as an invite. I just watch her for a second, water cascading down her body, her blond hair stuck to her face. I love the shape of her figure, and I harden at the sight of her. Fuck, I hope she has no idea just how much I want her, because I fear the intensity will scare her. It fuckin' scares me. I've never cared before, and, for the first time, I don't know how to deal with this. I really just want to go caveman on her ass, throw her over my shoulder and take her back home, but we still have Elizabeth to save and a fuckin' operation to take down.

"You just going to stand there watching me, or are you going to join me?" she asks without turning around. I open the glass door and step inside—the hot water on my skin just what I need. Jo moves over, my large presence shadowing her body. Silently, I reach for the soap and wash my body, then wash hers too, any chance or excuse to touch her.

She calls me out on it.

"If you want to touch me you can, you know," she says in a husky tone. "You don't have to wash me."

"I like getting you all soapy," I tell her, which is the truth. We don't really have time to be messing around like this right now, but it's 5:00 a.m., and we're running on practically no sleep, which is our fault and no one else's, so we need to suck it up today and be on the ball. When we leave this shower, reality is going to hit. Everything about us is going to have to be pushed from our minds, our focus on Elizabeth, so I'm going to enjoy this moment while I can.

"I wasn't sure how you were going to act this morning," I admit to her. "I didn't know if you were going to regret what happened."

"What? You fucking my brains out last night and giving me

four orgasms?" she says, turning her head to me and flashing a cheeky smile. "I don't regret anything, Ranger. And I'm not going to regret anything else we do together."

I grin. "Good, because I'm going to want you again. And again."

"Me too," she admits, running her fingers down my wet chest. "I'm not going anywhere."

"Me either," I say, running my thumb along her plump lower lip. Water from her hair drips down her cheeks, and I wipe it away. "I want this. I want you."

"You have me," she breathes, and in this moment I think she knows what I've known all along.

That she's mine.

We finish up in the shower, and then I do a run to my room in a towel to brush my teeth and get dressed.

Time to be badass.

FOURTEEN

"Jo," I say quietly, nodding my head at the man standing in the corner of the room, a black hat on his head.

"I know," she replies, not looking up. She keeps her eyes on her drink. "How do you want to handle this?"

I look around the bar, taking in the exits and playing out the possible scenarios in my head. "I think you should go to the bathroom, or out the front, and call for backup. If he tries to leave, I'll stop him."

"Okay," she says, waiting a few moments and setting down her untouched Scotch-and-Coke before standing on her tiptoes and kissing me, then casually walking to the ladies' room. I keep an eye on our suspect without making it obvious, nursing my own drink, pretending I'm here just for that.

We've been tracking this man all day. We got an anonymous tip that he was staying in a house just down the road. Now all we have to do is get him before he escapes again. I won't admit it to her, but I'm concerned Jo will get hurt when we try to bring him in. I mean what if he tries to take her as a hostage or something? Fuck. So this is what the men have to put up with every time something goes down, the fear that comes with caring about someone? I don't know how they deal with it. How did Sin keep it together when Faye was kidnapped?

A woman in a red dress approaches me, and it honestly can't be at a worse time. I don't want to draw any attention to myself right now, and if I reject her, she might do just that. I can't lose visual of the suspect.

"Hello, handsome," she purrs, scraping her teeth up her bottom lip. I notice that she has red lipstick on her teeth too. "How about a drink?"

Women don't even wait for men to offer to buy them a drink nowadays; they just suggest it, apparently.

"I'm actually here with my girl," I tell her, forcing a smile. "You are very pretty, but I'm going to have to decline."

I glance back at the corner of the room. He's still here. Unfortunately for me, so is the woman.

"Where is she, then?" she asks, running her hand down my arm. I stare at it in distaste. I really, really don't want to be dealing with this right now.

"Right there," I say, nodding my head toward the bathroom as Jo reappears, heading straight for me. The woman pouts, then walks away, and Jo quickly reclaims her seat next to me.

"A fan of yours?"

"Something like that," I tell her, waiting for her to instruct me on how we're going to handle this.

"They'll have the place surrounded within minutes," she says, looking straight forward.

"Are they coming in or are we taking him down?" I ask, placing my hand on her nape and squeezing gently. "Tell me what to do here, Jo."

I'm not letting this man go. He's our only lead right now, and I'm not letting this opportunity slip through my fingers.

"We don't move until they come in," she says in a calm voice. "We don't want him to grab someone as a hostage, or anything like that. The squad is going to come in and take him down."

She's only just said those words when the door opens and eight police come storming in, guns in their hands. Everyone drops to the ground. Jo and I move toward the door, behind the men, watching while the suspect is arrested. I have to admit that it feels like I'm doing less than I could. Yes, we're the ones who located him, but we could have taken him down ourselves just as easily. This way is safer though, and I guess they know what they're doing. We watch him being put away in the cop car and then drive back to the police station ourselves.

"I have a good feeling about this," Jo says, nodding. "He has to give us something, anything that can help find her."

"We'll find her," I say, reaching my hand out onto her thigh. "Don't worry about that."

She turns her head to me, her eyes smiling. "I sure hope so, Ranger. I sure hope so."

I kick down the locked door and walk into the house, looking left and right. I turn into one of the hallways, opening and searching each room as I go. I find her in the third room. There are eight women in the room, all huddled together in the corner. I see her straightaway, right in the middle, dressed in a white nightgown that leaves nothing to the imagination. They've obviously tried to give them a virginal, ethereal appearance, although the look on their faces is anything but. They all stare up at me with scared eyes, staying silent, waiting to see what I want. I can only imagine what they've been through. Elizabeth has a black eye, and I want to kill whoever has struck her. The police step in behind me, taking in the scene, and I feel Jo's presence at my side; I hear her gasp. I know the police didn't want me here, but I walked in anyway, before them. If they want to give me shit for it afterward, I don't give a fuck; they can shove their protocol right up their asses. I take a step toward Elizabeth, who seems to be seeing me but not really seeing me. I say her name, and she shakes her head as if clearing it. I come closer to her, and the other women move backward, up against the wall, away from me.

"Elizabeth," Jo whispers, stepping forward and crouching down in front of her cousin. She reaches out her hand but Elizabeth moves away. It's like she doesn't recognize her own family, like she doesn't know where she is or who she is anymore. She's locked in her own hell. They've broken her.

The police start going to the women, assuring them that they're now safe. I lift Elizabeth in my arms—she comes willingly—and carry her outside to the waiting ambulance. Jo is crying silent tears next to me. I know she just wants to hold her cousin, to be there for her, but right now she's not in a good state. I wonder if they'll let us take her home after she's checked out by a doctor. I don't know what the protocol is, and I don't know what will be the best course of action for her either. On the bright side, we found her, and she will never have to experience anything like this again. I look down at her face to see her looking up at me, and she mouths one word.

Cam.

"I've got you," I tell her softly, pushing her long hair off her face. "The doctor will have to look at you, okay?"

No reply, but she doesn't object as she is placed on a stretcher. She does, however, grab hold of my arm so I can't move very far. Jo stands on the other side of her, speaking soft words to her, and I feel like I'm intruding on a moment.

"You'll have to go to the hospital and wait until the doctor has seen her," the medic tells us, wheeling the stretcher into the back of the van. I look to Jo, seeing how she's taking it, and as soon as the van doors shut, she melts into my arms. She's shaking. I don't know if it's relief that her cousin has been found, or if she's sickened with what she's witnessed today, but I lead her to our rental car. We need to get to the hospital, because Elizabeth needs to be around people she knows, she needs her family and friends to support her.

"I'll drive," I tell Jo when she tries to slide into the driver's seat.

She nods absently as I lead her to the other side and open the door for her. She gets inside the car and I close the door, then get in and head to the hospital.

"How are you feeling?" I ask her, running my thumb along her knuckles. "Are you okay?"

"Did you see how they were all sitting there?" she asks, looking straight ahead. "On the floor. Wearing the same white dresses. How sick are these people?" She turns her head and looks at me. "Do you think she will ever get past this?"

Probably not right away, but I don't say that. What I do say is, "She's strong."

"Yes, she is," Jo murmurs, leaning her head back against the rest and closing her eyes with a sigh. "It's over, yet at the same time, the battle is just beginning."

I couldn't have said it better myself.

Who knows what they subjected those women to? The thought makes me want to beat the shit out of something, or someone. The fucked-up thing is there will always be operations like this around, and if one is taken down, another will just start. Elizabeth was all sunshine, rainbows, and butterflies, but the Elizabeth I saw today has a hollowness in her eyes that sent shivers down my spine. We found her, but she might already be lost, and I think that that's something Jo needs to be ready for. You don't come out of something like this the same person. She was kidnapped; taken across country and held captive, like a slave; locked in a room. They made her not a person but a possession. And I refuse to think of the other fucked-up things they may have done to her, because I will end up in prison for murder.

FIFTEEN

Johanna

THE pain, the tightness in my chest won't ebb. I always knew I'd find her, but I never thought about what it would be like when I did. I hope she's okay. I hope she will be okay. My heart is broken for her, and I just don't know what to do in this situation. What if she doesn't want me to stay with her? I take comfort in Ranger's hand in mine as he softly runs his thumb over my knuckles and down my fingers. I don't know what I would do if he wasn't here, if I had to do all of this alone. I'd probably be more of a wreck right now, if that's even possible.

"What do we do now?" I ask him, puffing out a breath. "Wait until she's allowed to leave, then take her home to heal? I need to call my family, they're all going to want to fly here as soon as possible."

"I think that's probably the best," he tells me, tone gentle. "She will need everyone she loves around her right now. If they can get here on the next flight, that would be good. I think she might need some time to deal with what happened. I don't know how she will react. I guess we're going to have to wait and see, but either way, yes, her immediate family need to be here."

I pull out my phone and send out a few texts, telling everyone that we found Elizabeth and they need to get here as soon as possible, and to call me if they want any further information. When we get to the hospital, it's hectic. There are people with cameras out front; I have no idea how the media found out about this so fast, but they're really on it.

"This will be the hot story for the week," I say in a dry tone, not liking that this whole thing is going to go public. Not only will Elizabeth have to handle so much, now she's going to have to deal with the media backlash, and the fact that everyone will know she was kidnapped and sold into human trafficking.

"Come on," Ranger says, taking my hand and leading me through the doors, then down the hall to the emergency room. "Do you think they'll even let us back there right now?"

I look around, at all the medical staff rushing around, and wonder the same thing.

"I'll go ask about her at the front desk," I say, letting go of his hand and approaching the receptionist. I can feel Ranger at my back as I give Elizabeth's full name and ask when I'm going to be able to see her.

"Are you her family?" the lady asks, looking over some documents.

"Yes, I'm her cousin."

"She was only just brought in," the lady tells me, pushing her glasses up on the bridge of her nose. "You can take a seat, but it's going to be a bit of a wait. The doctor needs to see her, run some tests, and run a psych evaluation on her."

"Is that necessary?" I say, even though I know it is.

She nods. "It just depends on your cousin and what she wants and needs right now. I don't think they'll let you in there for a while, unless she's demanding to see you."

"We'll wait," Ranger says, resting his hands on my shoulders. "Let's go sit down, yeah? I'll grab you some coffee and something to eat."

I don't feel very hungry, but coffee sounds amazing. He leads me to a vacant seat, and I practically drop into it.

"Any requests?"

"Just coffee please," I say, glancing up at him.

"Okay," he says, pressing a kiss to my forehead before walking toward the café in the hospital. I watch him disappear, then check my phone and reply to a few texts from family members. I need to keep reminding myself that at least she's safe now. That's what matters. I can't change what happened, but at least she's away from that hell; she's safe. We can get through the rest together. Ranger reappears with a giant cup of coffee in his hand, and I take it from him gratefully. "Thank you."

"You're welcome. Anything you need, you just ask, okay? I've got you," he says, sitting down next to me, holding his own cup of coffee.

"Likewise," I say, resting my head on his arm. "She's your friend too, this isn't only about how I'm feeling. I just wish I could take the pain away, you know? I need to be strong for her, but it's hard. I don't know what to expect."

"We need to talk to her," he replies, kissing the top of my head. When did we start acting like a couple? Why does it feel so natural? I don't know, but I don't want it to go away. I'm not a woman who has ever relied on a man before, but right here right now, I need Ranger. I don't think I'd ever admit that out loud, but it's true. I need him here. He knows how to handle every situation, and he knows how to take care of me. He'll know how to take care of Elizabeth too; I know it. It's so different having someone like him around. I don't always have to lead now. I don't always have to take control of a situation, and I don't have to be the strong one for everyone. That doesn't mean I'll ever be weak, it just means I can relax a little more knowing that for the first time in my life, someone actually has my back, physically and emotionally.

An hour passes, then two and three, and eventually I fall asleep wrapped in Ranger's arms. I don't know how much time passes, but when he wakes me up and tells me we can finally go in and see her, I stand up and follow behind the doctor.

"Let her know that you're here," the doctor says. "It's up to her if she wants you to stay or leave."

He opens the door and we both walk in. She sits propped up in her bed, her face pale and her eyes tired.

"Hey," I say, walking over to her and taking her hand.

"Jo," she says, squeezing my hand. "You're here."

"Of course I am," I tell her, brow furrowing. "Our family is on the way. Everyone has been so worried about you."

She then looks over to Ranger, her eyes widening.

"I thought I imagined seeing you," she says to him.

"No, I'm here," he says, sitting down beside her on the other side. She reaches her hand out to him, and he takes it.

"I wanted to see you again," she says, looking down at their hands. "But not like this. How were you there?"

"I've been helping Jo look for you," he explains, looking toward me. "We flew here when someone sighted you."

She turns to Jo and lays her head back. "Thank you for bringing Cam with you."

Cam?

My eyes dart to Ranger, and in this moment, I know I've fucked up. No. This can't be happening to me.

No. Surely not.

He can't be.

I didn't know his name, until now. Why didn't I ask his name? I just called him Ranger, like I assume everyone else does. I didn't put two and two together. How did I miss this?

You see, Elizabeth has an old friend named Cam who she always talks about.

Her one who got away.

The so-called love of her life.

The same man I'm currently falling in love with.

Ranger keeps looking at me like he's wondering what's wrong, because he doesn't understand that knowing who he is to Elizabeth has a huge impact on me. Elizabeth—my cousin who was just kidnapped and God knows what else—the woman who once told me that she thinks her old friend Cam was the only man she could ever truly love.

Does she want to be with him now? I can't tell her what happened with him. The way she's looking at him right now, like he's the light at the end of her tunnel, is making my stomach drop, and not in a good way. Is that how I look at him? I absently rub my chest, trying to ease the sudden pain I feel there. I should be concentrating on her, not him. How fucked-up is this?

"We better get going," Ranger announces, his eyes on me. "We'll be back in the morning, Elizabeth. I think your family will be here by then."

She grabs on to his arm. "I don't want you to leave, Cam. Can't you stay?"

I feel like I'm going to be sick.

Ranger again looks to me for help, but I just shrug and say, "You should stay."

I kiss her cheek and tell her to rest, before leaving the hospital room without saying anything further to Ranger. I actually feel like a monster for all the feelings and thoughts running through my head right now. What kind of person am I?

He's mine.

She needs him now though. I don't think that Ranger has feelings for her, otherwise he wouldn't have slept with me, but this is still a complicated situation.

I'm down the hallway when Ranger calls out my name and jogs up to me, stopping me by gripping my upper arm. "What's wrong? I saw the look on your face."

"Nothing," I say, forcing a smile. "She needs you now, Ranger. We'll talk later."

"Yeah, but I need you," he says, brow furrowing. "Stay. Don't go back to the hotel alone. We can share the extra bed in her room."

He really doesn't get it. He doesn't see how she feels about him, and how awkward that would be right now. I don't think she needs to be any more hurt than she already is. It's selfish of me to take Ranger away from her, if he is who she needs to get through her ordeal right now.

"She didn't ask me to stay, Ranger," I point out, smiling sadly.

I crook my finger at him until he lowers his head, then I kiss his cheek. "She wants you, and we need to give her whatever she wants. I'll call the fam and see what time they're arriving so I can pick them up from the airport."

"Are you sure?" he says, frowning. "I don't want you driving alone."

"I'm fine," I say, rolling my eyes.

"I'll meet you back at the hotel in the morning, then," he says, scanning my face. "Text me and let me know what your plans are, all right?"

"I will," I say, turning around and walking out of the hospital, feeling sad and resigned.

SIXTEEN

Ranger

"REMEMBER the time we went swimming, I think it was in Croatia?" she says, with her eyes closed. "The water was so clear that you could see the bottom, and you said that was the only reason you were going in."

My lip twitches. "Not much of a fan of the ocean."

"I remember," she replies, yawning. "I always think about our trip. I think it was one of the best times of my life."

"It feels like a lifetime ago," I say, then decide to ask a question of my own while she's being so chatty. "Did they hurt you while you were taken?" I ask her, and her eyes open. "I mean besides . . ." I point to her black eye.

"You mean did they rape me?" she asks, pulling the sheets up her body. "No, Cam, they didn't. We were going to be sold off at an auction—none of us were touched in that way because then we'd be damaged goods, you know?"

I exhale in relief. "So why did they hit you?"

"I tried to escape," she explains, staring at the wall straight ahead. "You know what's funny? I actually would daydream about you coming to save me. That's why when I saw you, I thought it was another dream. I didn't think you were actually there."

"Jo wouldn't have given up until you were found. She was so determined to save you, Elizabeth."

Which is why I'm a little confused about the sadness I saw on her beautiful face. She knew Elizabeth and I were friends, so I don't get why her face dropped, like something hit her, some kind of realization. Was it because Elizabeth wanted me to stay and not her? I don't know what it is, but I want to get to the bottom of it right away. I don't like the thought of Jo being out there overthinking everything. I understand that things changed the second we found Elizabeth, our little bubble popping and becoming reality, but now we need to face it. And I want her still to be in my life when we get home. I really fuckin' hope she wants the same, or I'm about to have a war on my hands to make her see that we're meant to be together. I don't give a fuck how pussy-whipped I sound: I've never felt like this for a woman, and I'm not about to let her walk away.

"I know, she's so amazing," Elizabeth agrees, eyes softening. "She's a great cop. I knew she would be looking for me."

"Can I ask you something?"

"Sure," she says, shrugging. "I'm not a delicate flower, I'm not going to freak out if you ask me something."

She is in a delicate situation, even if she doesn't realize it. I'm wondering if she's going to get some kind of post-traumatic stress disorder, or something like that. I don't think anyone can come out of this unscathed, even someone as strong as she is.

"Why did you go to that biker bar in the first place? And alone at that?"

Her eyes flare as she turns her head to look at me. She's quiet for a while before answering me. "I went looking for you, Cam. I had no idea where you were and I couldn't find you, but remember when you called me a year after our trip? You told me you were about to start prospecting for a biker club. I wanted to find you, and "biker" was the only clue I had. Your number was cut off, and you'd moved. You never called me again, and I waited for you to, but you didn't. It's like when you became a biker you forgot all about me."

I stand up, unintentionally knocking the chair backward. "Are you fuckin' serious? You went to a biker bar trying to find me? Asking questions and then they kidnapped you? Why the fuck would you do that, Elizabeth? Did you ever think that I cut everyone off for a reason? I don't exactly live in a life where I can have civilian friends without them being dragged into trouble."

"It had been years, Cam," she says, scowling. "I wanted to see you. Is that so bad? It's not your fault I was in the wrong place at the wrong time. But you asked a question and I'm answering it. That's why I was there."

I scrub my hand down my face. "After all these years you decide to come looking for me, and then this happened? Fuck, Elizabeth. This is the reason the only people I care about are in the same lifestyle as me."

"So you don't care about me anymore?" she asks, sounding hurt. "I thought we were friends. Friendship doesn't just go away, Cam. You obviously cared enough to come looking for me with my cousin, who is both a cop and a stranger to you."

She was just a cop and a stranger, but now she's a lot more than that. I don't know how to break it to her that, yes, of course

I care about her, but I didn't exactly think of her a whole lot over the years. She was just a friend that I had and lost, which isn't exactly an unusual occurrence for me. My friends and family became the Wild Men MC, and now I've even lost them. Talon is the only man still standing.

"Of course I care about you," I say, lying back on the spare bed. "You never mentioned Jo to me before."

"We didn't really talk about our families," she says, yawning and covering her mouth with her hand. "You especially didn't want to, remember?"

No one would if they came from where I came from, but I guess she's right. We lived in the moment; we didn't really discuss the past. We got to know each other in other ways: what we liked to eat; what we liked to do in our spare times. I know she likes the beach, apple martinis, and to dance all night long to any music the DJ plays. That's what I remember the most from that vacation.

"I guess you're right," I murmur, turning my head to look at her. "Do you need anything?"

"No, I'm good," she says, then lowers her tone. "I feel tired, but it's like my body won't let me fall asleep, like I'm scared to or something. Like it will take me back there."

I instantly sit up, walk to her bed, and take her hand in mine. "I'm here, watching over you, and you know I won't let anything happen to you. Sleep, Elizabeth."

"I'll try," she says, closing her blue eyes, a shade darker than Jo's. When she falls asleep, I send Jo a text, asking her what she's doing, and then send one to Faye too, with two words:

Mission complete.

My phone rings instantly, and "What You Need" by The Weeknd fills the room. I answer it quickly, not wanting to wake Elizabeth up.

"Hey," I say softly.

"'Mission complete.' That's all I get, really?" Faye says into the line. "Tell me everything. How did you find her?"

I give her a quick rundown of everything that happened since I arrived here. Well, not everything, but everything to do with finding Elizabeth.

"You and Jo did so well, Ranger," she says, sounding both excited and impressed. "How is Elizabeth doing?"

"She's okay," I say, glancing over at the woman in question. "Her family will get here tomorrow, so I'll probably come home in a day or two."

"Sounds good," Faye says. "We miss you. Even Clover's been asking where Uncle Ranger is."

My heart warms at that. I know that all the Wind Dragons have really tried to make me feel welcome in their MC, even though I don't seem to be fitting in as well as Talon has. They're good people, and Faye is an amazing woman.

"I'll be back soon enough," I say, tone gentling. "But I'm done with your heroine shit, Faye, all right? No more cases. I'm going back to dealing with biker shit."

"Fine," she grumbles, saying 'bye, then hanging up.

I'm not being fair. If it wasn't for Faye, I probably wouldn't have met Jo, and the cops might not have found Elizabeth in time, so I don't have any regrets. I just don't want to return to the clubhouse only to have Faye dangle another file in my face. I'm going to leave this shit for the professionals . . . unless Jo needs help with something.

Knowing me, I'll probably want to check on her and make sure she's okay when she's doing something dangerous, which is probably going to be twenty-four hours a day, seven days a week. Yeah—talk about a full-time gig. The thought makes me smile. I'd like to be around her that much. I check on Elizabeth once more, then allow myself to get some rest.

SEVENTEEN

Johanna

STEP into the room quietly, coming to a stop as I see them to-gether. Elizabeth has moved from her bed onto the one Ranger is on, and her head is on his arm. I don't really know what to say or do right now, and I don't want to wake them, so I slowly leave the room and turn to Helen.

"She's sleeping."

"I'll go in quietly," Helen says, eyes red like she's been crying. "I just need to see her."

"Okay," I say, touching her arm. "She's in there with Cam."

"Cam who?" she asks, brown eyes flashing with confusion.

I realize that I don't even know his surname.

"I don't know," I admit, wincing. "The guy she met overseas years ago."

Helen's eyebrows rise. "Cam, as in her old friend and so-called love of her life?"

I cringe—I can't help it. To me, he's not Cam the love of her life, he's Ranger, the man I've become so close with in such a short amount of time. There's a connection with us, and I don't know how I'm supposed to turn my back on that, especially when I've never experienced it before. In fact, before meeting him, I would've denied a connection like that could even exist. I actually let my guard down with him, and I don't want to put it back up, but realistically I might have to.

"That's the one," I say, unable to keep sadness out of my tone. "They're asleep."

"I won't wake them," she says, silently making her way into the room. I sit down in the closest chair and wonder how the hell I'm meant to deal with this right now. Seeing them together like that . . . knowing she has feelings for him, is a hard pill to swallow. I don't want to see her hurt. But I don't want to see Ranger with any woman other than me. I don't know what to think; I'm all over the place. Maybe now that reality has hit, he thinks that all bets are off and we're back to being a cop and a biker? I guess I won't know what's going on in his head until he tells me. There's no point guessing. He said he wanted to come with me last night, and he texted me too, and I doubt he'd have done that if he thinks we're done.

Helen walks out and sits down next to me with a sigh. "She's still fast asleep. Cam's awake though; he was asking if you're here yet."

I decide to change the subject. "I wish your parents could have made it."

Elizabeth and Helen's parents are much older, and live in a retirement village. They weren't able to fly in because of their health, but Helen and our uncle and aunt did.

"I know," she says, sounding tired. "They've been worried

sick about her and can't wait for her to be brought back home. Jack and Shane have been so worried too."

Jack and Shane are our other cousins. I look up as the door opens and Ranger walks out.

"Hey," he says, eyes scanning me from top to bottom. "Did you manage to get any sleep?"

I nod, straight-out lying. I didn't sleep a wink, and no one can blame me.

"You met Helen, Elizabeth's little sister, right?"

He nods, and gives her a brief glance but then brings those hazel eyes right back to me. "I'm going to go back to the hotel and shower and change. Are you going to be here?"

"Yeah, I'll be here. My aunt and uncle will be here any moment."

"Good," he says, shifting on his feet. "Can we talk for a second before I go?"

I ignore Helen as she looks at me, nod, and stand up, walking with him toward the exit.

"I missed you last night," he says, ducking his head. "When are you going to fly home? I'll book us our flights today."

My eyes widen slightly as we step outside and stop and turn to face each other. "I'm not sure, depends what the doctor says, you know?"

"We need to have a talk, Jo," he says, looking me in the eye. "I know things are different now, but I don't want them to change between us." He makes a sound of frustration and glances around. "I know this isn't the time or place to talk, but I just need to know that you're not going to shut me out."

He turns and takes my hand in his, then leans down to kiss

my forehead. A tender kiss full of promise. The thing is, I can't give him what he's asking for, and I need to explain that to him. I might have to shut him out. He's right: we do need to talk and this isn't the time. I want to be honest with him though. I'm not one to play games, and I'm not going to start now.

"Can we talk later? When I get back to the hotel maybe?"

He nods, relief flashing on his handsome face. "Yes, that sounds good. Have you eaten? I'll get us something for lunch. And don't lie to me, it doesn't look like you got much sleep last night."

I roll my eyes at him. "I slept enough."

"According to who?" he asks, arching a brow. "If you're not going to fuckin' take care of yourself, I'm going to do it for you."

"Is that right?" I ask, feeling amused. "Well, I'm not going to say no to some lunch, since I haven't eaten since early yesterday."

He scowls, but I know he hasn't eaten either.

"You must be hungry too."

"I'm fine," he says, eyes softening. "Come to my room when you get back and food will be waiting for you. Just text me when you're leaving the hospital."

"Okay," I say, smiling at him.

"Go back inside," he tells me, nodding to the entrance. "I don't want to leave until I know you're in there."

I try to hand him the car keys, but he shakes his head. "No, I'll take a cab so you can drive back when you're ready."

I wrap my arms around him suddenly, burying my face into his T-shirt and closing my eyes. He returns the gesture, and for a moment I can pretend like it's just me and him, with no other issues around us to deal with. I open my eyes and pull away, glancing up at him. He cups my face with his palm, then gives me a soft kiss, full of promises to come. I flash a small smile at him before walking back inside. As I approach her room, reality hits me again, and I picture how happy Elizabeth was being cuddled with Ranger. She'd been smiling.

Shit.

A few hours later, I find myself knocking on Ranger's room door. He opens it quickly, freshly showered and changed into a black T-shirt and gray sweatpants that he definitely shouldn't wear in public, because I can see the outline of his huge penis. In fact, it's all I can see right now.

"I didn't know what you felt like, so I kind of got a bit of everything," he says, lifting the lid off the room-service trays. My tummy rumbles as I take in the burger and fries, chicken and rice, nachos and fruit platter.

"Which one do you want?" I ask him, eyeing the burger.

"Babe, take what you want. We can order more if need be," he says, sitting down on the bed and watching me.

"You're going to just sit there and watch me eat?" I ask, raising my brow. "Please tell me you already ate something and didn't go hungry waiting for me."

He simply shrugs, and his silence speaks wonders.

"Ranger, eat," I command, then change my tone and add a "please."

He smirks and picks up the nachos and starts eating, while I grab the burger I've been eyeing and take a huge bite of it. I sit down next to him, and the two of us eat in comfortable silence for a while.

"So should I call you Cam now?" is how I start the conversation, licking the ketchup off my fingers.

He looks at me, as if surprised by the question. "You can call me that if you like, but everyone I know pretty much calls me Ranger."

"Your parents call you Ranger?" I ask, curious to find out more about him now that we have the time.

"My mom passed away," he says, standing up and putting the empty plate on the tray and picking up the fruit. "And my dad left us when I was three. Kept in contact for a while, but we lost touch, and I have no idea where he is now. My family is the MC. Talon is my family. Shayla and the rest of them. And they all call me Ranger."

"How did you get the name?" I ask him, wondering how MCs choose the road names of their members. "And who is Shayla?"

He chuckles before he replies. "When I started prospecting for the Wild Men, I was actually working as an assistant ranger. They found it amusing, and the name just stuck. I've been Ranger ever since."

I can't hold back the bubble of laughter that escapes me. "That's actually a pretty cute story. I have to admit I wasn't expecting that answer."

"What did you think? That I killed a ranger or something?" he teases, making me laugh again.

"No, I didn't think that at all," I say, shrugging.

"And Shayla is Talon's cousin," he says. "Talon loves the shit out of her, and we get on really well. We're family."

"Sounds like you have quite the family," she murmurs. I nod in agreement, then change the subject.

"Now about that conversation," he says, lifting a strawberry and bringing it to my lips. I take a bite as he says, "I want you," and almost choke on the piece in my mouth.

He grins, and pops the next strawberry into his own mouth, while I try to think of what to say next.

And come up with nothing.

EIGHTEEN

Ranger

"I WANT you too," she says after she chews and swallows. But I feel a *but* coming on.

"But?" I prompt.

I'm not going to accept any buts.

I don't like the serious look that takes over her beautiful face. "There's something you need to know, Ranger, but it's hard for me to explain because I don't know if it's my place to."

I have no idea what she's talking about right now. "Jo, you need to tell me what the fuck you're talking about, because I've got nothing here."

Did she not want to be with me anymore? Is she embarrassed or some shit? Maybe it's because some of her family members are here now. Or maybe she wants to concentrate on making sure Elizabeth gets back on her feet before she jumps into something—which is a valid concern I guess, but I'm still not going to let her use it as an excuse. Whatever she wants to do, I can do it with her. I can help her.

Her phone starts to ring just as she opens her mouth, so she flashes me an apologetic look, then picks up.

"Hey," she says into the line. "Yeah, he's here with me." She pauses, says okay, and then hangs up.

"She's asking for you," she says, reaching over and taking a slice of pineapple.

I feel like I'm missing something right now. I tell her as much.

She sighs and brings her baby blue eyes to me. "Elizabeth used to talk about you, you know."

My eyes widen. "What did she say?"

"Just about your trip and how great you were," she says, chewing thoughtfully. "She called you Cam, so I didn't put two and two together, but yeah, I did hear a lot about you."

"Okay, and?"

"And," she says, dragging out the word. "Did you ever have any feelings for her?"

Oh fuck. Now I see where this is going.

"We're just friends, Jo. That's all we ever were," I say, brow furrowing. "Is that what the problem is? You think that you're trampling on her toes, or is this an insecurity thing?"

She looks like she wants to kill me with her bare hands. I look down to see her little hands closed into little fists, and her eyes are filled with a fire I've never seen coming from her before.

"Please tell me that you did not just say that," she asks between clenched teeth. "You think this is about me being jealous? This has nothing to do with that, Ranger. My cousin just went through a fucking ordeal, and I had no idea that you were the

Cam she kept talking about, or I never would have slept with you."

"Why not?" I ask. "Just because I was friends with your cousin years ago? Because she seems to need me now for some reason? I don't know why she seems to want me near her—maybe she feels safer? I don't know, Jo. I care about your cousin, and I'll be here for her if she needs me to be, but it's you I want to be with. I hope you're not just looking for excuses because you're scared . . . I know this isn't exactly what you'd hoped for, and I know we don't have an easy path ahead of us, but I don't give a fuck. I think you're worth it, and I hope you feel the same way about me."

There it is. All my cards laid out on the table, no games, no messing around. She said that I'm never vulnerable, but in this moment I am.

When she doesn't reply, I bring my hand to her jaw and look her right in the eye. "Tell me I'm worth it, Jo."

"You're worth it," she says. She opens her mouth to say something else when her phone rings again.

"We better get going; we can talk more about this later," I say, leaning forward and kissing her lips. "But the bottom line is, whatever shit happens, we'll sort it out, all right?"

She nods and kisses me this time, harder than I kissed her. I smile against her lips, happy that she's not acting off anymore, that she's back on my team. On *our* team. She ends the kiss, flashes me a smile, and stands, ready to go back to the hospital. I stand and take her hand, bringing it to my mouth and placing my lips on her knuckles. We share a look, a moment, something passing between us.

I let her know that I'm all in, and she acknowledges that fact. It's not exactly what I want from her, but it will do.

For now anyway.

"Are you flying back with me?" Elizabeth asks. She looks much better today, color in her cheeks and a sunnier disposition. Maybe seeing her family did her some good, or maybe she's just realizing that she's safe now. I'm not naïve enough to think that it's going to be all good now for her, but she's definitely heading in the right direction, I think. She's looking forward to going home, and that's something.

I look to Jo as I answer her question. "I'm flying back whenever Jo is, so if she's flying with you, then yes."

Elizabeth glances at Jo. "Okay."

"I need to head into the station today," Jo says, looking at her watch. "Tie up some loose ends. After that I'm ready to fly out whenever. Depends on you, Elizabeth, and how you're feeling."

"I'm ready to go home," she says to Jo, wrapping her arms around herself. "I just want this whole nightmare to be over, you know? I want to be at home, back in my own bed."

Jo nods, eyes softening. "I know, sweetie. If the doctor says it's okay, I can book all of our tickets to fly out tomorrow. We need to make sure the media doesn't get wind of it though, because the news stations are dying to cover this story, and they're going to be all over you."

"They'll want me and the other girls to do an interview or something, right?" she asks, raising her eyebrows. "Yeah, I'm definitely not ready to do something like that. I just want to crawl under my covers and sleep for a year. Helen will be at home with me, so I won't be alone." She brings her eyes to mine. "And, Cam, you can drop in if I need some company, right?"

I nod. "Sure, I can check in on you."

"Great," she says, a slow-spreading smile appearing on her face. "If I get the go-ahead, then we can leave tomorrow morning."

"Sounds like a plan," Jo says, standing up. "I better get going, I'll be back here in a few hours. Is there anything you want on the way, Elizabeth?"

"I'll get Cam to text you if I think of anything," she replies, flashing Jo a grateful look. "Helen brought me some clothes and shoes and stuff, so I'm good in that area. Maybe I'll want some nonhospital food though, like a giant burger and fries or something."

"I'll be waiting for your text, then," Jo says, then turning to me. "I'll be back soon."

"Okay, drive safely," I tell her, watching her as she leaves the room. When I turn back to Elizabeth, her eyes are already on me, slightly narrowed.

"You two seem to have gotten pretty close," she says, looking contemplative. "You're a biker."

Amusement fills me. "Yes, I am."

"And she's a cop."

I nod. I know all this. What I don't know is why she's pointing it out.

She licks her lips and looks down at her hands. "Cam, the reason I went looking for you wasn't just to say hello. I wanted to tell you that . . ." She clears her throat, then looks up at me, blue eyes boring into me. "Did you ever think that maybe we'd have been perfect for each other? We got along so well and we had the best time. I don't think I'd ever laughed so much in my life. I know I was different back then, I was more shy and inexperienced, but I'm older now. Wiser. And I always think about what would have happened if we gave us a chance." She pauses, smiles, then adds, "You're kind of the one who got away for me."

The one who got away? As in . . .

Everything suddenly clicks. Jo's behavior, Elizabeth's behavior . . . fuckin' everyone's behavior.

Fuck. She thinks she's wiser? She went into a biker bar by herself asking questions about me. That's not wise. Unless you're Faye fuckin' Black, you don't pull that shit. I run my hand over my head, then rub the back of my neck. This woman has just been through hell, she's vulnerable, and she's someone I don't want to hurt. How do I tell her that I've never thought about all the things she just said? That after I met Jo, no other woman will measure up?

I don't even know how to explain that without sounding fuckin' crazy, even to myself. I just saw her, I wanted her, I got her, and now I'm trying to keep her. I don't want anyone else. There's nothing wrong with Elizabeth, but I never really thought about her in that way. She didn't leave the impact on me that I apparently left on her. Yeah, we had good times, and, yes, I will always care about her, but it's only friendship. I like her. I more than like Jo. How do I explain this?

"We were always just friends, Elizabeth," I say in a gentle tone, hoping that it softens the blow.

"Really?" she asks, sounding incredulous. "Cam, I—"

"Friends," I repeat, reaching out to take her hand. "I care about you. You're an amazing woman, but—"

"Wow," she says, moving her hand away and staring straight

ahead. "Did I just make up everything between us then? Yes, we were friends, but we were always friends who had the potential to be more. If we both want it, we can be amazing, Cam. You've never given us a chance. I want to take that chance so I don't have to always wonder what could have been. Just think about it. I think we'd be great together."

She's been through so much, and I don't want to contribute to any more of her pain or upset her, but she doesn't seem to be understanding that I don't want to, and will never want to be with her in that way.

What the fuck am I supposed to do now?

NINETEEN

"**C**AM?" She softly says from behind me as I walk toward the door and stop. "Where are you going?"

"Nowhere," I say, turning around. "I'm not going anywhere, Elizabeth, I'm just thinking."

"About us?" she asks boldly, sitting up in her bed and adjusting the sheets. "Say something, Cam."

I grit my teeth and return to the bed. Do I mention Jo, or will that just hurt her and cause shit between them? I don't want to do that, but I don't want to fuckin' lie. I know how upset Jo will get if Elizabeth lashes out at her, and she might not even want to have anything to do with me after that. Fuck. That isn't an option. Not being with Jo isn't even a fuckin' option. Maybe we can keep things between us a secret for now, until Elizabeth realizes that we're not meant to be. Maybe she'll get over it soon. I don't know; I need to talk to Jo about all of this. I'll let her decide how to handle this so she can't throw it in my face later. I also know very well how jealous women get. I don't peg Elizabeth as the malicious type at all, but honestly, you never know.

After everything that's happened . . . I also don't know her that well anymore. Time changes people. I've definitely changed since then.

"I feel safe around you," she continues to speak. "Don't take that away from me right now, Cam."

And when she puts it that way, what the hell am I meant to respond with? I'm itching to leave this room, but I know I can't do that to her. I decide to just say, "If you need me, I'll be here," and leave it at that. I will be here if she needs me, whenever she needs me, but Jo will be by my side too, where she belongs.

I watch her break eye contact, then she lets out a breath and nods. "Okay."

I feel relieved that she's letting it go, and try to change the subject. "Your sister looks nothing like you, by the way."

"I know," she says, her body language relaxing. "She looks more like my mom's side of the family. I spoke to my parents on the phone today. They're so upset they couldn't fly here."

"How old were they when they had you and your sister?" I ask, wondering just how old they are that they can't fly.

"Mom had me when she was thirty-eight, and Helen when she was forty-two."

"Pretty late," I say, wondering how it affected their family dynamics.

"I know," she agrees. "I'd never have kids that late. I think midthirties will be my expiration date."

"Expiration?" I repeat, smirking. "Don't worry, you have some time until then."

"Do you want kids someday?" she asks, tilting her head to the side.

"I haven't really thought about it," I answer honestly. "I guess so. It depends on the kind of life I'm living at that point."

She nods like she understands, but I know she doesn't. I don't know what I'm going to do with my life when I return home. I love the Wind Dragons, but for some reason I don't feel like I belong there. I don't think I belong in an MC anymore, and I don't know what to do, or where to go. I can either stay there and see how it goes, or I can leave and see where life takes me. I have my education to fall back on, and maybe I can finally put it to use. I need to explore a new path in life.

Although, I won't be going anywhere without Jo. I wonder how she'd feel being on the back of my bike. Fuck. I can't wait to get her on there. Maybe I can talk her into taking a little trip with me.

When she returns to the hospital room I'm still thinking about her. It's like she never leaves my mind. She stays and chats with Elizabeth for a while, and even brought her food even though Elizabeth didn't end up asking for anything. My baby is thoughtful, that's for sure. I wait until we get into the car before I bring up what happened tonight.

"I understand now," I say as I pull onto the main road. "The reason why you were so weird about the Elizabeth thing." I cringe when I remember asking her if she was jealous. "What do I do?"

"What did she say to you?" Jo asks, eyes going wide. "I don't know what to tell you to do. She's just been rescued, and I don't want to tell her that I accidentally slept with the guy she thinks is her soul mate."

"She said that?" I say, suddenly feeling a little claustrophobic. "Fuck. I really didn't see this one coming."

"Stop being so hot," Jo grumbles under her breath, making me grin.

"I think it's just the Chase girls who think that," I say, unable to help myself. When I see her scowl, I add, "What? Too soon?"

I take her putting the music louder as a yes. "Controlla" by Drake fills the car, and I turn it down a little, glancing at her from the corner of my eye. "She'll get over it. I think we just need a little time before we tell her that we're together."

"We're together?" Jo asks, voice going higher. "Since when?"

"Since I first laid eyes on you in that biker bar," I say, smiling and bringing my hand to her thigh. "Stay in denial all you want, I don't mind. I know the truth and that's all that matters."

She releases a breath, acting put out, but I don't miss the small upward curve of that beautiful mouth. "The whole situation is out of control."

"We'll rein it in," I say with confidence. "Let's get her back to her normal self and see where we go from there. I don't want to see her get hurt any more than you, but, babe, I truly have no idea where this soul mate idea came from. We were close friends, yes, but never did I think those words would be falling from her lips."

A memory hits me, and I push it away. That's not something I want to deal with, because if it comes to light it's going to bring a shit storm along with it. I squeeze Jo's thigh and move my hand down to her knee.

"There's also the cop-and-biker thing to deal with," she adds, sighing.

"One problem at a time," I say, then ask, "Are you hungry?"

"No, I'm good. Are you?" she asks, staring at my profile.

"Not for food," I say, pinning her with a hungry look before returning my gaze to the road.

She shifts on the seat, then reaches her hand out to rest it on my pec. "What exactly are you hungry for, then, Ranger?" She purrs in that hot-as-hell voice of hers.

I run my hand up the inside of her thigh, wishing she was in a skirt instead of jeans. Still, I run my fingers over the material covering her pussy. She spreads her thighs for me. I like a woman with a little bit of wild in her, and I'm fuckin' thrilled that she's not telling me to get my hand off her right now. If she were wearing a skirt I'd slip my finger inside her panties, and slide it inside of her. I'm about to undo her jeans button and see if I can get her to pull her jeans down a little bit when she stretches over and does the same to me, undoing my zipper slowly and then reaching inside to grab my cock.

"Fuck, Jo," I grit out, glancing down as her hand starts to stroke me, then raise my eyes back to the road. By the time I park the car at the hotel I'm so hard it's actually painful to put my cock back inside my jeans. I manage to get it in there, hard against my leg, and practically run to the elevator. When the doors close and we're alone, I push her against the mirrored wall and kiss her hard. I'm past the point of caring where we are, or who sees, I just want to be inside of her at this point. I cup her face and press myself against her, wanting her to feel how she makes me feel. Her hands go under my T-shirt, running up my back slowly. I lift her up, and her legs wrap around me just in time for the elevator to come to a stop. I walk with her in my arms to my room, sliding the card in and then opening the door. No one saw us walk through the hallway, but even if they did, tough fuckin' shit.

I kick the door shut, then practically throw her onto the bed. She bounces twice, laughing, watching as I put down my restricting jeans, which are currently my enemy, almost tripping on them as I try to get them off my ankles in haste. Jo starts laughing, which I ignore, removing my boxer shorts and lifting off my T-shirt.

"You won't be laughing in a second," I growl, grabbing her ankle and pulling her down the bed so her legs are hanging off. I undo the button of her tight jeans and start peeling them off her legs until they join mine on the floor, then slide off her white panties. I lick my lips as I take her in, lying on the bed, her bottom half bare. Her eyes are heavy as they watch me, silently letting me take my fill. I hope she feels beautiful right now, because all I see is her beauty. Her shapely legs, her pretty pussy that is just begging for attention, and the simple, sensual beauty in her face of a woman who is about to get pleased and knows it.

When a woman gets turned on, she forgets the usual things running through her head. The insecurities and the doubts. She doesn't think—she just feels. At least if the man is doing his job right, and trust me, I'm going to. I cover my body with hers and kiss her deeply, our tongues tasting each other, our skin pressed against each other. I lift up her top, exposing her breasts covered in a white cotton bra. I don't give a fuck that it's not some fancy shit. Jo looks sexy in anything. I gently bite down on a nipple through her bra and reach my hand down to play with her pussy at the same time.

I'm just getting started.

TWENTY

Johanna

I WISH I'd brought some sexy lingerie with me, but seduction wasn't on my mind when packing for a last-minute rescue trip. Ranger doesn't seem to mind though, going by the way he looks at me, like he wants to eat me whole. His finger slides inside me then, up to my clit, and I gasp as he starts to rub it in a circle. I've never been with someone who knows exactly how I like things, and who actually pays attention to my body language and works out what I need without me having to give verbal commands. Ranger never misses a thing. I never even knew a man like him existed. I remove my top completely as he kisses down my stomach, the stubble on his cheeks prickling my skin, but in a good way. He spreads my thighs and flashes me a dark look before lowering his head, his tongue on my flesh. I remember how hard I'd made him in the car and wonder how he has so much restraint to take the time to go down on me first instead of just slamming into me. Suddenly he stops and lays back on the bed. I think he wants me to ride him, but then he says, "Sit on my face."

I get up on my knees and move to straddle his face, facing

the same way as him so I can take him into my mouth too. I want to please him as well; I want him to love fucking me and to always want more. I lean forward and take his cock in my hands, stroking before lowering my head and taking him into my mouth as far as I can. I bob my head up and down, licking and sucking, his moans turning me on even more. He grips my hips and holds me down onto his mouth as I feel myself come, removing my mouth from his cock so I don't accidentally hurt him as I fall apart.

"Oh my god," I whisper, as Ranger keeps licking my clit, prolonging my release.

When he rings the last wave out of me, I'm about to crawl down and take him back into my mouth when he lifts me off him and rolls me over onto my back. He lies on me and slides inside of me with one deep thrust, his mouth slamming down as he slides in and out of me, almost desperately, and it's in this moment I know that his patience has come to an end. I score my nails across his back, not hard enough to leave any marks, then kiss down his jaw and suck on his neck. I want him to come, now, but I know he's going to want me to come a second time before he succumbs to his own pleasure. I know I'm right when he brings his hand down and starts touching my clit again.

"That feels so good," I breathe, allowing my eyes to close. I lift my hips to meet his, thrust for thrust, the two of us so in sync it's like we're made for each other. I open my eyes and look into his to find him already looking down at me, a sheen of sweat on his brow. I'd never admit this out loud, but he looks like a god right now, like a dark Adonis, his hair falling out of its restraints and framing his handsome face. It's not long before he has me coming again, but this time he joins me. He really was waiting for me to come once more before he allowed himself to do the same.

He rolls over onto his back with his cock still inside of me, so I'm on top of him. I push his hair out of his face and kiss him deeply. I can't pretend there's no emotion between us in the sheets, because there is. It's a part of what makes the sex so amazing, so addictive. It's that connection, the one thing everyone craves the most to find. I don't think I've ever felt a connection so strong as the one Ranger and I share.

It's a dangerous thing, because I don't know how far I will go to keep it.

He kisses my forehead and lingers there, while I close my eyes and wonder how the hell this happened. I have no logical answer for it. We were meant to be enemies, yet we fit together like the pieces of a puzzle. I don't really know him, yet I know him so well. So many contradictions. The only thing I know is that right here, with him, is a place I don't want to leave or lose.

"I'll be happy to get home tomorrow," he says, moving his lips back to mine. "I want you in my own bed."

"At your clubhouse?" I ask, wincing. "I don't think I'll be welcome there, Ranger."

He laughs softly, then says, "It will be fine. I've got another house I could always move into if it's an issue for you."

I pause, suspicion taking over me. "How did you pay for the house? What illegal operations do you guys do anyway?"

I don't expect him to tell me, but he should probably know that I'm not okay with it. It goes against everything ingrained in me. Am I going to have to turn a blind eye to all this shit?

"Relax, Jo. I make money from stocks and investments. All legal. I can show you, if you don't believe me. And I have enough money for both of us to never work again from this day forward. Anywhere you want to travel to? Hawaii? Portugal? We can leave tomorrow."

I roll my eyes, but I'm kind of impressed he's been able to do so well for himself. If he's telling the truth, and he did all this on his own, he must be a very intelligent guy, which I've seen for myself. I'm sure his start-up money came from the club though, but I can't really use that against him, can I? He is who he is, and I am who I am. I don't know how it will work, or if it will, but it's worth the try. He's worth it.

"I have to go back to work," I say, amusement filling me. "Rain check on Hawaii."

"Done."

I lay my head on his chest and close my eyes. I don't want to ruin this moment by letting any guilt hit me, but I do feel it. Elizabeth is going to hate me, but I'm too far into this now, and Ranger doesn't feel that way about her anyway. Does that make it okay? No, but why should both of us not have him? I run my hand down the side of his stomach, feeling his rigid muscles. I'm hoping she forgets about her infatuation over him and just concentrates on getting better. I never would have done this if I knew who he was, and that is the honest truth. I'm not a bad person, I don't think, and I value loyalty and honesty above all else, so this is really killing me.

Yet I can't stay away from him.

That's pretty fucked-up in itself. If there is any time to bail, now would be it, before we return home and bring each other into each other's daily lives. Lines will be crossed, and someone is going to get hurt. Elizabeth doesn't deserve to be hurt any more than she has, she really doesn't.

"Stop thinking so hard," Ranger says, kissing the top of my head. "We'll sort it out, okay? And don't even think of being some fuckin' martyr and leaving me because of it. It won't work. I'll just keep coming after you." He pauses, and I can hear the smile in his voice as he adds, "I do like a challenge."

"I just feel like such a bad person," I try to explain to him.

"You're not," he says instantly, his hands roaming to cup my ass. "And if you leave me, then you'll hurt me. So that's not even an option."

"You can handle it," I mutter, sighing softly. "The difference is, I don't think she can."

"We just need a little time," he says, sounding so sure that I want to believe him. "We'll keep us to ourselves for now, and when the time's right, then everything will be fine."

He makes it sound so easy. Stressing isn't going to fix anything though, so I try to push everything out of my mind and just enjoy the feeling of my skin against his. I haven't had something like this in so long, I forgot how good it can be. Bikers . . . who would have thought?

"Can we stay at my house instead of the clubhouse?" I ask him, my mind going back to that.

His chest shakes as he laughs. "You already planning sleepovers, Jo?"

"Apparently I am," I grumble, kissing his chest. It's like my common sense fails me when he's involved. He makes me blind, weaker and stronger at the same time.

I don't know how that is.

But I think I'm done trying to figure it out.

TWENTY-ONE

"HAVE you been talking to other women?"

"Yes . . . but it's not important."

I ignore the couple sitting next to me as we're waiting to board the plane, and their ridiculous argument. What did he mean it's not important? I look at Ranger, who is watching my facial expressions and smirking. I narrow my eyes and silently warn him that I don't care how big and bad he is, if he ever says that to me, my gun will be drawn. He laughs, which garners Elizabeth's and Helen's attention.

"What's so funny?" Elizabeth asks, looking between the two of us. She and Helen are seated opposite us. Our aunt and uncle caught the earlier flight home because there weren't enough seats left on this one.

"Nothing," Ranger says, looking over his boarding pass, a smile still playing on his lips. The two girls watch him, both intrigued, but for different reasons. Helen is probably fascinated by the man who has her sister so enthralled, while Elizabeth is probably wondering if Ranger is the same man that

Cam was. I look away from all three of them, and pay attention to my phone. It's so easy and natural for me to be around Ranger, for us to laugh and joke and tease, and with them here I feel like I shouldn't do that. It's a tell. They shouldn't know how close we are.

It makes me sad that I have to hide the first good thing to happen to me in a long time, but there's no alternative. I can't be selfish. Not yet. There are more important things that need to be handled first. We all board the plane, and I count down until I can be home.

After we get Elizabeth settled, Ranger and I head back to my house. Luckily for us there were no cameras or TV crew at the airport, and we were able to quietly get out of there with no one noticing us. I watch him as he walks inside and looks around my house, wondering what he thinks of it. It's nothing fancy, a three-bedroom two-bathroom brick house that I've owned for a year and a half. It's home. I've decorated it sparsely, and there isn't much clutter or bright colors. It's tidy, simple yet classic. At least that's how I think of it.

"There's beer in the fridge if you want," I offer, putting my thin jacket down on the countertop. Ranger sits on one of my stools and shakes his head.

"No, I'm okay, thanks."

Feeling tired, I let him pull me onto his lap and bury my face in his neck. "So it's all over now, hey?"

"I guess so," he murmurs, kissing my forehead. "I have to get back to the clubhouse and check in with everyone. When do you have to go back to work?"

"Officially tomorrow, but I'll drop by the station in a bit too," she says, yawning. "Do you want me to drop you at the clubhouse, or will they run out with guns the second they see my squad car?"

"Don't you have a non-police car?" he asks, sounding amused. "Perhaps we should take that so the men aren't running around and flushing the drugs down the toilet when they spot your car."

I playfully slap at his chest. "That better be a joke. Yeah, I have another car, I hardly use it though. My life is pretty much work and home."

"Are you inviting me to sleep over tonight?" he asks, nibbling on my earlobe. "I'll bring dinner for us. And then if you're good I'll take you for a ride on the back of my bike. I think it's time the two of you met."

I roll my eyes at that. "Okay, sounds good. Do you need to leave right now?"

"No. Why, what do you have in mind?" he asks, wiggling his eyebrows.

"One-track mind."

"When it comes to you, yes," he agrees, placing his lips against my neck. "You're just too sexy, and you smell so good, and fuck . . . you're perfect."

"No one is perfect," I correct, but still smile at the compliment. If anyone were close to physical perfection it is him. He's the perfect one, well, minus the whole biker thing, but that's a part of him too. "And I don't have anything in mind . . . except maybe a shower."

"Hmmmm," he rumbles, kissing my neck. "A shower with you sounds good. I know it's kind of selfish considering the circumstances, but I'm so happy to be alone with you."

I feel the same, but I don't voice my thoughts. Instead, I jump off his lap and take his hand, leading him to the bathroom that connects to my bedroom. Our clothes drop onto the tiled floor, and we step inside, water cascading down our bodies.

Maybe this won't be so bad after all.

I'm on top, riding him hard and fast, lifting my hips up and down in a rhythm that has him on the verge of coming.

"Fuck, Jo," he grits out, teeth clenched, watching me. I lift my hands to my breasts, pinching my nipples and using my knees to push myself up and down on his hard cock. I can feel my orgasm building, and I know it's going to be amazing. I move my hands to rest on his chest, and am about to lower my lips to his when my phone starts ringing. I ignore it, trying not to let it ruin the moment, allowing myself to kiss him through the sound. It eventually stops and Ranger rolls me over and continues to thrust inside of me, taking control. His lips have moved down to my neck when the phone starts to ring again, but this time it's his. Why didn't we both put our phones on silent? I never really thought about it, and what if there's an emergency? Right now, I don't even care, I'm so close to coming and really, really need to be pushed over the edge. His phone stops ringing, but then mine starts again.

"Fucking hell," he groans voicing my frustrations. "They're not going to stop, whoever it is." He slides out of me and storms over to my phone, picking it up and looking at the caller. "It's Elizabeth."

We share a look.

He passes me the phone and I quickly answer it. "Hey, is everything okay?"

"Where's Cam?" she asks, sounding worried. "He won't pick up his phone, and I was wondering if he could come and stay with me tonight. I don't want to be alone."

Which is completely understandable. But why him? "What about Helen?"

"She's around," she says, voice going soft. "But I'd rather Cam be here too, you know? I know I'll be safe then."

"Okay," I say, looking at Ranger, standing there naked in front of me. "I'll tell him."

"Thanks," she says, then hangs up the line.

"She wants you to stay over there tonight," I say, putting my phone back down on the table. "She said it will make her feel safe."

Ranger's expression flashes with frustration but also with understanding. "Can't you come with?"

"She didn't invite me, Ranger," I say, getting back into bed and covering my naked body with my white sheets. "Should I take you to the clubhouse now? Then you can do what you have to do and see all your friends before you go to her house."

"Yeah, all right," he says, getting back on the bed with me and pulling the sheets down. "But if you think we're going anywhere without both of us coming first, you have a lot to learn, Jo."

I smile when his lips slam back down on mine.

TWENTY-TWO

Ranger

"WELCOME home, Ranger!" Faye says, smiling widely as she runs into my arms. "How's our hero of the week?"

"All that and the title only holds for a week?" I ask, raising my brow. "Tough crowd."

She throws her head back and laughs, auburn hair bouncing. "You know it. You gotta do more than fly across the country and save women from human trafficking to hold the title for longer."

"I'll remember that," I say in a dry tone. All the women come and hug me, welcoming me home, except Anna, who gives me a small wave and knows how to hold a mean grudge. Once upon a time Talon had ordered me to kidnap her and bring her back to the Wild Men clubhouse, and I did so, but I also knocked her out to do it. She remembers it like it was yesterday. To be fair, Talon wasn't too fuckin' happy with me either, but hey, I got the job done.

"Men are all outside," Faye says, nodding her head. "We didn't know what time you'd be getting in, since you didn't tell us." She purses her lips. "Even though I texted four times to ask. But we cooked a welcome-home dinner for you."

"Thanks, Faye," I tell her, flashing the women a grateful smile before walking outside. Talon is the first one to greet me, pulling me in for a hug.

"Thank fuck you're home, brother," he says, grinning. "Good to have you back."

The rest of them surround me, slapping me on the back, all smiles.

"You did well," Sin says, nodding his head, looking impressed. "You should be proud of what you've done."

I shrug and look out over the grass and playground, not wanting them to make a big deal about it. "What have I missed?"

"Absolutely nothing," Tracker replies, stretching his arms up over his head to touch the patio roof. "Businesses are running smoothly, and everyone and everything else has been quiet. Arrow has decided we're going to open up another club, so we're looking for a new location."

"You say it like it's a bad thing," I tease, pulling a chair out and sitting down. The others do the same.

"Could use a little excitement," Tracker agrees, smirking. "But you know what they say, be careful what you wish for."

Sin scowls in his direction. "Think we've had enough excitement to last us a lifetime."

Arrow lifts his pint of beer. "Ain't that the fuckin' truth? Could write a book on all the shit that's happened here over the years."

"Lana probably has," Tracker adds, taking a swig of his own beer.

"She'd have more than enough material," Vinnie says, running a hand over his bald head. "It's kind of nice that things have slowed down now. Don't worry, when the time comes to kick ass we'll be more than ready."

Rake rubs his flat stomach. "No one better get a fuckin' beer belly."

We laugh.

Irish nods his head to Arrow. "If anyone is getting a beer belly it's going to be the prez here. He's the oldest."

Arrow taps his stomach a few times. "This old man will still take your ass down in the ring any time, Irish."

"Challenge accepted," Irish fires back.

I check my phone, wondering what Jo is doing right now. I can't say no to Elizabeth, but the situation is a little bit fucked. Maybe I can talk her into being okay with having the men do checks around her house at nighttime, or something like that. What am I gonna do if she tries to kiss me or something? It's really fuckin' hard to reject someone who has been through what she has. Not only that, it was me she went looking for in the first place, otherwise she'd never have been inside that biker bar. At the same time, Jo is my first priority, and I don't want her to feel uncomfortable. She wants Elizabeth to be happy, as do I, but I won't do it at her expense.

"Everything all right?" Talon asks, studying me.

"Yeah," I say, scrubbing my hand down my face. "Elizabeth doesn't want to be alone tonight, says she doesn't feel safe."

"Is that the real reason she doesn't want to stay alone tonight?" Talon asks, frowning. "I guess it's understandable—she wouldn't want to be alone and you're her friend, but she has a family to look after her, right?"

"Apparently only I will do," I say, avoiding his gaze. "I don't know. I saved her, maybe she just feels safer with me there to protect her."

"Her cousin is a cop," Sin points out. "If anyone should be protecting Elizabeth, shouldn't it be her? I mean, sure, maybe because you're a big, scary biker that might make her feel safe . . . but more than likely—"

"She just wants to fuck you?" Rake crudely supplies. "Maybe she sees you as her hero. Knight in shining armor. Women love that shit. You should probably just bone her, it would be rude not to."

I groan and rest my elbows on my thighs. "I'm not boning her. But I can't exactly say no to going over there, now can I? I'll try to show her it's safe now, and tell her that we can drive by her house at night as a precaution or something."

"Not me," Tracker mutters under his breath. Rake slaps the back of his head playfully.

"Whatever you need, we have your back," Arrow says, nodding at me.

"Thanks," I say, standing up. "I should get there before my phone starts ringing again."

Talon cringes; he knows I don't do clingy. I usually need my space, and I like my alone time. Jo seems to be the exception to that rule though, and I know that means something. She means something. The men don't need to hear about it just yet though. I need to make sure she's not going anywhere first, and to break the news to Elizabeth when she's in a healthier place.

"They closed the bar down, by the way," Talon notifies me before I walk inside. "The biker bar where they took her. Whole operation has been shut down. Faye made sure of it."

"Does she think she's the heroine of the week, then?" I joke, clapping Talon on the back and walking inside. I pass the women in the kitchen on the way out and make a stop as I smell the food. I can't exactly leave without eating when they made everything for me. "Smells delicious."

"Have a seat," Bailey says, smiling at me. I sit down and they pass me a plate. I start piling food on it, from homemade sausage rolls to quiche, wondering what Jo is having for dinner.

"You guys spoil me," I say, taking a bite of a spring roll. I groan and dip it in some sauce. "So good."

Faye sits next to me and watches me eat. "How is she doing?"

"She wants me to go stay with her tonight," I say, chewing and swallowing. "She doesn't feel safe."

"That would be expected," Faye says, sadness hitting her hazel depths. "I'll pack up some food for you to take to her, then. Will anyone else be there?"

"Her sister, Helen, and Jo," I say, thinking that even if Jo isn't going to be there I can drop off some food to her on the way.

"Three plates coming up," she says, then adds, "By the way, this is just finger food, not the actual meal, so save some room."

My eyes widen. "Fuck me, you guys went all out, didn't you?"

She grins, flashing her straight white teeth. "Steak with mushroom sauce, mashed potatoes, corn, salad, and garlic bread."

I place my hand over my heart. "If you weren't married, you would be right now."

"To you?" she asks, laughing. "I don't think the cop would like that very much."

I stop chewing and narrow my eyes on her. "What are you talking about, Faye?"

She waves her hand in the air. "Oh please, I know sexual tension when I see it. You couldn't take your eyes off her. She's a babe, so I get it. What happened with that, by the way? Did you bone—? You so did! You're hot, as if she could have resisted that, biker or not."

"Did you just have a whole conversation with yourself?" I ask, continuing to eat.

"Yes, she did," Shayla says, kissing my cheek and then sitting down on the other side of me. "We missed you around here. You're not going to leave again, are you?"

"Tonight? I have something to take care of. In general? Nope, I'm done playing hero. I'm going to leave that up to Faye."

Faye rolls her eyes but stays silent.

Anna sits down opposite me, green eyes narrowing slightly, but she stays quiet. I love fucking with this girl. Every time she's around it's always a good time.

"Staying out of trouble, Anna?" I ask, reaching for another sausage roll. "Any recent kidnappings?"

"Nope," she replies, pursing her lips. "No one else has been stupid enough to try."

"Or smart enough to succeed."

"Remember the time I beat you in beer pong?" she says, smirking. "We should have a rematch. So I can see your face when you lose again."

"How long are you going to bring that up?" I ask, scowling. I really don't like to lose.

"How long are you going to bring up the kidnapping?" she fires back, crossing her arms over her chest.

"For as long as you still hold a grudge about it."

"So forever, then?"

I nod. "Guess so."

"Can you come and hang out tomorrow?" Shayla asks, brown eyes pleading with me. "We can watch *Supernatural* and binge eat." She looks at me stuffing my face. "Again."

"If you bring Jordan with, then it's a date," I say, referring to her and Vinnie's young daughter. I'm not much of a baby person, but Jordan is adorable. She's a part of Shayla, and Shayla is Talon's cousin, so she's like family to me.

"Deal," she says, smiling widely.

"Speaking of," I say, glancing around. "Where are all the kids?"

"They're with a sitter tonight," Faye explains. "We haven't really had a night with all of us together in so long, we thought we'd try to organize one."

I still. "And now I have to leave. Fuck, I'm sorry. Should I call her and tell her to expect me later?"

"And leave a scared woman waiting while we're sitting here stuffing our faces and having a few drinks?" She shakes her head. "Definitely not. You go, don't worry about it. We're just happy to see you and feed you." She stands and adds, "I'll pack up the food for all of you."

"Thanks, Faye," I say, genuinely meaning it. She cares about everyone so much, and it's plain to see.

"Do you want us to come with you?" I'm surprised when Anna offers. "I mean, maybe we can distract her or something. She might enjoy some female company."

"Her sister is there," I explain, pushing the plate away, now full. "I think she just wants to feel a little safe, you know? I told her I'd be there for her, so I'm going to be. I'll let her see that it's over now, and those men can't hurt her."

Faye places two giant trays on the table, filled with food for half-a-dozen people. "There you go."

"Thank you," I say, looking around the room. "To all of you."

"We take care of our own," Anna says, flashing me a little grin. "Plus, apparently you're some kind of hero."

"Apparently?"

She shrugs. "To me you'll always be the man who knocked me out and kidnapped me. Sounds more like the bad guy than anything else, but to each his own."

I throw my head back and laugh. That does sound more like me.

TWENTY-THREE

"**W**HAT are you doing here?" she asks as she opens the door, sounding surprised but pleasantly so.

I step inside and close the door behind me. "I brought you some food so you don't have to cook, and I was also hoping to get you to come along with me to Elizabeth's."

She's wearing tight-fitting black sweatpants and a tank top and I momentarily get distracted, before offering her one of the trays. "The women cooked up a storm, and I wasn't sure if you had anything planned for dinner."

She takes the tray and wrinkles her nose. "Which women made this for you, exactly?"

Does she think we have club whores cooking for us? The Wild Men always did, but there are none that I've seen at the WDMC because everyone has an old lady except for me. And if club whores could cook this, well, they'd probably become old ladies. I don't say that out loud though.

"Faye and the other old ladies cooked. A welcome-home

thing for me. You can meet them all if you like," I say, following her as she heads into the kitchen.

"Tell them I said thank you, please," she says, placing the tray down on the table. "That's very nice of them, and of you for bringing it to me. Are you always this thoughtful?"

I don't think I've ever even been called thoughtful before, but I'll take it. "I could be."

"I appreciate the food, but if Elizabeth wanted me there, Ranger, she would have asked me. She didn't, so I'm assuming she doesn't. Trust me, I wish you were staying here tonight, but we can just wait until tomorrow night."

"Okay, that sounds reasonable," I grumble, coming up behind her and wrapping my arms around her. I nuzzle her neck and say, "I'm going to be thinking about you the whole time."

"How do you know that?" she asks, letting her head stretch to the side to give me more access to her slender neck.

"Because it's all I seem to be doing lately," I admit with full honesty. No games, just the truth. I kiss her cheek, then bring my hands to rest on her hips. "Can I come over in the morning?"

"I'll be leaving for work pretty early," she says, but smiles at me.

"I guess I'll have to get here pretty fuckin' early, then," I reply, not fazed. My phone starts vibrating in my pocket and I can only guess who it is. "I better get going, babe. Text me or call me anytime if you need anything, or if you just want to chat, yeah?"

She nods. "Will do. Thanks again for the food."

She walks me to the front door, and I kiss her before I leave, a lingering, hungry, passionate kiss. I let the kiss tell her that I'd rather be here with her than doing anything else right now, and it's important to me that she knows it.

"Lock the door," I say, ignoring her eye roll. I grin as I walk to the car, forgetting that she can damn well protect herself, but still. I wish I could have ridden my bike, but bringing her food meant that I had to sacrifice that. It's okay though, because I'll get to ride tomorrow, my bike and Jo. With a smirk playing on my lips I drive to Elizabeth's house.

I really wish Jo was here, I think to myself as I watch Elizabeth stroll around the kitchen in nothing but a silk robe. Has she always been like this? I don't remember it. I remember her laugh, her good humor. The way she'd tease me about everything and anything. She was always so bubbly. It's almost like I have to get to know her all over again. But this new woman—I don't know if it's because of the abduction or because time has passed—is not the Elizabeth I knew. It's actually kind of weird.

"What movie do you want to watch?" she asks, sitting down, the silk split, exposing her thigh.

"Whatever you want," I tell her, glancing around her house. "I'm actually going to do a security check of all the doors and windows, maybe install some new locks if you need them."

"Okay," she says, nodding. "Now? I'll choose something and wait for you."

"Okay," I say, standing up. "Where's Helen?"

"She's staying at her friend's house," she says, shrugging. "They have some assignment to do."

I nod and walk up the stairs of the house, wondering what the hell I'm getting into. Did she ask Helen to go? Or is it me being paranoid right now because I don't want to fuck shit up with Jo? When did my life turn into a fuckin' soap opera?

I do a check of the house, testing the locks, and then walk

around the perimeter. Honestly everything looks pretty good, with the exception of two windows I want to put new locks on just to be safe. Maybe a dog will make her feel safer? Like the ones the Wind Dragons have. I particularly like Tracker and Lana's German shepherd. By the time I make it back to the couch, she's sitting there with a bowl of popcorn and the remote in her hand, waiting for me.

"Everything looks good," I tell her, sitting down. "Just two windows that I'll fix up tomorrow."

"Thanks, Cam," she says, pressing PLAY on the movie. I'm not in the mood to watch anything, but I guess I have no choice. It's going to be a long night. I pull out my phone and send a text to Jo.

I miss you. What are you doing?

She replies after a few minutes.

In bed watching TV. She doing okay? I miss you too.

I glance up at Elizabeth to find her watching me.

"Are you going to watch the movie or be a phone snob?" she teases, and for a moment I simply wish I was snuggled in bed with Jo, watching whatever she is. I bet it's better than what Elizabeth has picked for us, some college movie. I reply to Jo to try to prove my point.

What are you watching? Yes, all good.

My phone beeps instantly.

Supernatural.

Fuck.

See? She really is perfect for me. There couldn't have been a better response. Meanwhile, I'm sitting here watching some other crap.

What season?

I put my phone down on the couch and grab some popcorn from the bowl, shoving a few kernels in my mouth. I feel like I'm at a sleepover, and not the kind I'd enjoy. Elizabeth's watching the movie, ignoring me, for which I'm grateful. She doesn't seem scared. I'm being an inconsiderate, selfish asshole here, and I know it, but if she was scared she has so many options, so much help that can be offered to her.

"How are your parents doing?" I ask her, hoping that they can relax now that their baby girl is home safely.

"They were so happy to hear from me," she says, shaking her head. "Mom was crying, it was pretty hard to hear, you know? I never really thought about it from their point of view, but if Helen or someone else I cared about went missing it would be hell on earth. They sounded so tired, like they hadn't been sleeping or eating. It was hard. I said I'd head out to visit them when I was feeling up to it."

My phone beeps.

Season ten. Why? Are you going to give me shit about it?

"It would be rough for any parent," I tell her as I write back to Jo. "Yours is a story with a happy ending though, and most people don't get those."

Why would I give you shit about it? I fuckin' love that show.

"Yeah, you're right," she agrees, nodding. "I have to look on the bright side, I'm safe now. I can't let what happened hold me back. It could have been a lot worse, and I know it. I wasn't raped, although I would have been if they'd sold me off before you guys found me. I know I'm lucky—trust me, luckier than so many other women who have been in that situation. It's just so fucked. I can't understand how someone can do something like that, treat other humans that way, and live with themselves. They're just pure evil."

"They are," I agree, sinking deeper into the blue suede couch. "And I'm glad we made a difference by saving you girls and tearing the operation down, but this kind of thing is something that will be an ongoing war."

"You're right," she murmurs, moving closer to me. "Maybe I could turn a negative into a positive and try to help somehow."

And there's the Elizabeth I know. "I think that's an amazing idea," I say as my phone beeps again.

Dean or Sam?

Dean or Sam? Is she serious right now? I should spank her ass. Not for asking that question, which I find amusing, but just because I want to.

Ha-ha very funny!

I'll bet she's a Sam woman though. Tall, longish hair, yeah—she'd be all over that. I smile to myself and turn my attention back to the movie. Elizabeth takes this chance to lay her head on my shoulder. I look down at her, but she's looking ahead and doesn't make any further movements, so I let her be. As long as no boundaries are crossed and she doesn't think that we'll ever be something, then all will be fine.

I just hope that she doesn't hate Jo for being with me.

TWENTY-FOUR

Johanna

"YOU look different," Travis says, eyeing me from head to toe.

I look down at my uniform, wondering what the hell he's talking about. "How so?"

"I don't know," he says, a puzzlement flashing in his eyes. "You just do, but I can't pinpoint what it is."

"Well, when you figure it out, let me know," I say, amusement filling me. I smile and continue walking down the street next to him.

He clicks his fingers. "That's what it is. You're smiling. Why are you smiling so much?"

I stop in my tracks and turn to him. "Excuse me, I smile."

"You do now," he says, eyes narrowing. "Are you seeing someone?"

"Oh, so only a man could put a smile on my spinster face?" I joke, rolling my eyes. I'm so not telling him anything. Especially that the man putting that smile on my face is a biker. Do I seem happier now? Did I not smile at all before? Ranger came over early this morning, around six, and woke me up in a way that I'll never tire of. He also spanked my ass when he was taking me from behind, and now it stings a little every time I sit down. Jerk. Okay, I secretly loved it, but he doesn't need to know that. It's much more fun that way.

"Yes," Travis says, smirking. "You don't want to tell me? Fine. But for the record, I'm happy for you. If he hurts you though . . ."

"If he hurts me I'll take him down myself," I say, stopping when we arrive at our police car. "You driving?"

"Yes, ma'am," he says, opening the driver's door. He stops and looks up at me. "By the way, Jo. It's good to have you back."

I grin. "Good to be back."

It is.

And my life is now better than ever.

When I arrive home from work and see what I assume is Ranger's bike there, butterflies appear in my stomach. How long has he been here? I see him sitting on my front porch, and I grin when I notice he's actually fallen asleep, his face pressed against his palm. I unlock my front door, then sit next to him and just watch him for a second. He looks so peaceful when he's asleep. I put my hand on his back, shaking gently.

"Ranger?"

His eyes open instantly, and he smiles slowly, wrapping his arm around me. "Babe. How was work?"

"Let's start with why you're having a nap on my porch."

"I didn't know what time you were finishing and you didn't answer my text, so I thought I'd drop by, and when you weren't here I was just going to wait for you. Must've dozed off."

I touch my pocket where my phone is, then pull it out. It's on silent and there are a few missed messages. "I didn't even bother to check. How was your day?"

"Good," he says, checking me out in my uniform. "Better now. This is the first time I'm seeing you in your uniform."

"And?"

"And," he says, grinning devilishly, "I think it's time we head upstairs. Except it's me that's going to use those handcuffs."

I roll my eyes as he stands up, suddenly awake and eager, offering me his hand.

"You must be hungry. Want to go out and get something to eat?"

I take his hand and he pulls me up. "You went from wanting to handcuff me to wanting to take me out for food?"

"Can't let my baby go hungry," he says, leading me to the door.

"It's unlocked," I tell him, earning me a scowl.

"Why is it unlocked?"

"I just unlocked it two seconds ago, relax."

He opens the door for me and gestures for me to go inside, then walks behind me into the kitchen. I never realized how small he makes my kitchen look until right now. He's such a tall, broad-shouldered man, and my kitchen is kind of small and dainty-looking.

"I'm not hungry now; I can wait until dinner. Unless you want something? I can make you something," I offer. He's obviously used to women cooking for him, which, if I'm being honest, kind of annoys me. I don't know how the men are treated in the clubhouse, and don't get me wrong, I have no problem spoiling my man, but I don't know what he's going to expect.

Going by his actions so far, I don't think I have anything to worry about, but you never know these days.

"Only hungry for one thing right now, babe," he says, licking his lips. "Never thought I'd find a cop uniform so fuckin' sexy, but you surprise me at every turn."

Feeling playful, I grin and start running to my room. He chases after me, grabbing me by my waist and throwing me in the air and over his shoulder.

"Do not even think about slapping my ass," I growl at him, making him laugh.

"I didn't even spank you hard, and it happened like twice. Didn't take you for the dramatic type."

"I have a sensitive butt." I pout. "And I've never been spanked before, so excuse me for being a little dramatic about it."

He throws me on the bed. "Did you like it though? Because you were wet." He pauses. "Really wet. But if you say you don't like it, then I'll never do it again."

He waits, watching me, arms crossed and eyebrow raised.

I say nothing.

He throws his head back and laughs. "You shy all of a sudden, Jo? You've sat on my face but this you're shy about?"

I purse my lips. "I'm not shy, I just don't want to encourage you. Who knows what you'll come up with next."

"You'll love it. Admit it or I'm not going to go down on you right now."

My eyes widen. "You using sex as a weapon, Ranger?"

He laughs harder, falling onto the bed. "Yeah, I am. You don't tell me if you liked it or not, I'm going to take this huge dick away from you, teach you a lesson."

"I deserve that dick," I announce, huffing. "And you like fucking me too much, so it's an empty threat."

"Someone is cocky today," he says, resting his arms back behind his head, eyes dancing with amusement. "But you're right, I do love fucking you. In fact I seem to like everything about you."

The humor of the situation fades into something else, something much scarier. Deeper.

Something real.

Something worth fighting for.

I lick my lips, the tension between us building, the air thickening.

"Ranger?"

"Yeah?" he asks, his heavy-lidded gaze pinning me in my place. "Do you have something you want to say to me?"

"Nope."

"You're stubborn," he states, lip twitching.

"You not strong enough to handle me, biker?" I tease, starting to undress. His eyes lower to my fingers as he watches me pop each button.

"Oh, I can handle you," he says with easy confidence. "I'm here right now, aren't I?"

I smirk, shaking my head at him. "We haven't even had our first real fight yet. We'll see how you so-called handle me then."

"You'll probably go all silent and withdrawn, and try to walk away. I'll chase you down and drag you home like a caveman, and then we'll talk it out until everything is right in your world again, followed by the best makeup sex. What do you say? I'm kind of looking forward to it now," he says, winking at me.

He makes light of everything, but I like that about him.

Before I met Ranger, I was treading water, gasping for air. Just looking at him stirs something inside of me, something I never thought was in the cards for me. Such a surprise, a wonderful one. One I don't really know how to take. One that I'm scared will disappear the second I look away.

I know we have obstacles and nothing will be perfect. My cousin might hate me. Ranger may even hurt me in the end, but it's a gamble I'm willing to take. If I'm guarded all the time, if I don't take a chance, then nothing in my life will change. I'll continue to live for others and not for myself, and I will never be happy. I'll never have anyone who loves me, a connection, an understanding, and I crave all these things just like the next person. It's hard to find someone to trust these days—it's like everyone is replaceable to everyone, and I can't stand that, so I kept to myself.

No one ever caught my eye, and to be honest, no man ever made the effort to break through my wall and to get to know me. I wasn't easy, so I wasn't worth pursuing. Ranger saw me and wanted me right away. He took everything I threw at him without so much as a blink and pushed through my guards. But what happens now that he's in?

"Well, keep annoying me and I'm sure it will happen," I say, sliding my shirt off, exposing a black lace bra. I had no sexy lingerie while we were away looking for my cousin, and he didn't seem to mind, but now that I'm home I can put in a little more effort. It's not just for him: *I* feel sexier, and it's a powerful feeling.

I remove the rest of my clothes and stand there naked, bold and confident in front of him, while he still lies there, hands behind his head, eyes darker than I've ever seen him.

"Come here," he demands.

And this time, I don't argue.

TWENTY-FIVE

Ranger

"SO you fixed locks on her windows yesterday, and today she texted you again asking you to come over?" Faye asks, throwing a knife into the target. "Are you going to go? If she's really scared, why don't you ask her to come and stay in the clubhouse? It's not like the old days where we had heaps of shit to hide. We could bring her in for a while."

"I can ask her," I say, shrugging. "Maybe she'll go for it."

"And then you can spend more time with Jo."

I don't know how Faye ends up figuring everything out—it's like she has a tracker on everyone. Nothing escapes her.

"I feel like a bastard because that's exactly what I want to do," I admit, picking up a knife from the grass and giving it a try. I hit the target, but not the bull's-eye like she did. She sends a smirk in my direction and my eyes narrow. I don't like to lose. I've never trained in knife throwing before, but it looks like I'm going to have to do a little practicing. I can't let a woman have one up on me, although I'm smart enough to not admit that out loud, especially in the presence of the woman next to me.

"You're in that new stage," Faye says, pushing her hair out of her face. "All you want to do is be with that person."

"When does that stage end?" I ask, curious.

"I'll let you know when I find out," she says, winking at me.

I hide my grin, picking up another knife. I can only hope to have something like what she shares with Sin. The two of them are a power couple, and strong in a way where they haven't changed each other. Nothing but pure love, acceptance, and understanding. If I didn't see it for myself, I'd never have believed it existed. That type of trust and loyalty is something I never thought I'd get, but that was before I laid eyes on my blond bombshell.

"I'll run it by her, see what she thinks."

Although I have the feeling the answer is going to be a no if she finds out I plan to spend my nights with Jo.

"She obviously just wants you around. If she was actually scared, she'd call Jo or go and stay with family," Faye says, glancing at me out the corner of her eye. "What's the deal, Ranger?"

"Does this stay between us?" I ask, even though I doubt she and Sin have any secrets between them.

"Always."

"She doesn't know about me and Jo and we don't know how she's going to take it, because apparently she's been talking about me over the years," I try to explain. "But she called me Cam, and Jo only knew me as Ranger."

Faye's eyes widen and she freezes mid-throw. "So Elizabeth has a thing for you, Jo didn't know, fell for you, and now you guys are too scared to tell Elizabeth because she's vulnerable and you don't want to hurt her?"

"Something like that," I admit, cringing. "It gets worse. Apparently the reason she was at that damn bar in the first place is because she was trying to find me."

Faye's expression loses all of her usual good humor. "Are you kidding me? How did she think that was safe? She's clearly stupid. Or a stalker. I'm glad you aren't choosing her. She wouldn't fit in here."

I don't think I really fit in here either, but I keep that to myself.

"She made a mistake," I say, having no idea why I'm standing up for her. I guess I feel sorry for her. At the end of the day, she's still my friend, and the reason I met Jo. I don't want to hurt anyone, I'm not a dick, and Elizabeth has been through enough. Sometimes the situation feels like it's not a big deal, especially when Jo and I are alone, and at others it feels like it's something that's going to end very badly. It's fucked-up, is what it is.

What if Jo's conscience tells her that I'm not worth losing her cousin over? Or what if this whole fuckin' thing goes the other way and Elizabeth doesn't care. Maybe she just needs a new man to be infatuated with.

I study Faye, knowing that if you want to scheme with anyone, it's her.

"I know that look," she says, turning to me and giving me her full attention. "What's the diabolical plan?"

I grin and say, "Maybe this weekend we could have a party."

"Go on," Faye says, waving her hand in the air, her expression one of interest.

"Maybe there could be some appealing men attending this party," I say, shifting on my feet. "And maybe one might interest a damsel in distress."

"I see," Faye says, lifting her chin. "Like Cinderella's ball, but with Elizabeth as the prime meat."

"Did you just say that?" I ask, wondering where she comes up with this shit. "Do you know any prime meat? All the men here are taken."

"Yes, I did just say that," she says, stepping closer to me. "I think the idea can work, but look, she just got kidnapped and shit, so let's not be insensitive."

"You just called her stupid and a stalker," I point out.

"Let's not bring up the past," she says, scowling at me. I'm starting to wonder if Faye is legit crazy. "Why don't we give her a bit of time and then pull the biker sausagefest idea? I think I have a guy in mind. He's a total babe, all the women think so."

"Okay, plan on hold," I say, bending down to pet Colt, Shayla's dog. "I'm heading to Jo's. Tell the men to call me if they need anything. I'll drop in at Rift later tonight, Sin wants me to look over some accounts."

"I'll tell them," Faye says, sitting down on the grass to hug Colt. "Have fun, Ranger. Rock her world. Bring her over to the dark side!"

Her warmth at my back, her arms wrapped around my waist, now I know what heaven feels like. There's nothing better than sharing something you love with someone you can't get enough of, and Jo on the back of my bike has my chest puffed out. She belongs there, right where she is right now, holding on to her man. After I showed up at her house yet again, this time a little later so she was already home, she cooked me some dinner, and then we went on this ride. I can really get used to this.

With no particular destination in mind, we drive past the now-deserted Wild Men clubhouse, which kind of hurts, but I try not to dwell on it. Although Slice turned out to be a back-stabbing asshole, and the rest of the men were older and kind of useless, they were men I shared a lot of times with, good and bad. They were family. I thought the Wild Men were a strong MC, but I was wrong. The proof is in that empty building filled with memories and what could have been.

My phone keeps vibrating in my leather jacket, and I know it's Elizabeth, but she's going to have to wait until after I've spent some time with Jo. Helen should be there with her, so it's not like she's alone. If anything goes wrong, she needs to call the police. Nothing will go wrong though, Faye has made sure of that, making sure anyone who would recognize Elizabeth is now behind bars, in hiding, or dead. I push her out of my mind and think about Jo, and where I think she'd enjoy me stopping. I contemplate taking her to the beach, but we end up at a scenic park with a lake that I've been to a few times before. I help her get off my bike, removing her helmet, and taming her short hair with my fingers. With the moonlight on her, she looks fuckin' beautiful, and I can't help but lean down for a kiss.

"Want to take a walk?" I ask her when I pull back. "It's pretty nice through there."

"Sure," she says, smiling and placing her hand in mine.

I return the smile and lead her down the path, wondering if this is considered romantic, or if I'm making a complete fool of myself.

Probably both.

"What did you think?" I ask her as we both sit down on a park bench overlooking the lake. "Did you enjoy the ride?"

"I did," she says, smiling. "I can see the appeal. I can't wait to get back on for the ride home. Maybe next time I can ride it myself?"

"What, on my bike?" I ask, eyes going wide. "No one else has ever ridden her before."

She rolls her eyes and playfully nudges me with her elbow. "Well, maybe I'll be the first, then, won't I?"

She's so small and dainty that sometimes I forget she's a bad-ass in her own right. She's a policewoman, a warrior, and probably already knows how to ride. No one has ridden my Harley before, but for her I might make an exception. She doesn't need to know that though—I'll make her work for it.

"We'll see," I mutter, but the thought of her on my bike kind of has me a little hard. I want to fuck her on that bike. I wonder if she'll let me. If I didn't have to get to Rift soon, I'd try to tick that off my list right now.

"I'll just buy my own bike," she announces. "We can have races."

"Did a woman of the law just say she wants to race with me?" I ask, laughing. "Fuck, you've been hanging around me too long already, Jo."

"I don't think it's illegal when I do it," she smirks, the little minx. "I'll just say I was chasing after you to arrest you."

"At least you acknowledge that I'll be in the lead," I say, nodding my approval.

"Of course that's all you got from that," she grumbles, reaching out and grabbing the lapel of my leather jacket. "You look good in this."

"Yeah? Pretty sure that's meant to be my line."

She runs her hand down the zipper. "Nah, I think you've got

the leather thing covered, Ranger. I've never even checked out a biker before, so I don't know why I'm so damn attracted to everything about you. I think it's just you, you know?"

Her simple words mean everything to me. It's the best feeling to know that I'm not in this alone, that she wants me as much as I want her. "Where did you come from?"

"I could ask you the same thing," she replies, ducking her head shyly.

I stand up off the bench and offer her my hand. She takes it and I lift her up, then let my hands run down her body to rest on those hips I love so much. I lean down and take her lips with mine, kissing her slowly, sensually. I like being with her, around her. It's enough. It's intoxicating and addictive. Satisfying. The squeals when I pull back, then lift her in my arms, throwing her over my shoulder and carrying her back to my bike. I sit her on it, then kiss her again, smiling against her lips.

I can't get enough.

I used to give shit to the men in the clubhouse, but now I so fuckin' get it.

And it's everything.

"I don't want to take you home, but I need to get my ass to Rift," I say, sighing.

"And then go to Elizabeth's," she adds, also sighing. "Can I ask you something?"

"Babe, you can ask me anything," I assure her, wanting her to be able to be open with her feelings with me. "What's on your mind?"

"Did she hit on you when you stayed there?" she asks, looking me in the eye. "It's clear she wants you, so did she try anything? I didn't ask because I figured you would've said some-thing, but when you didn't it kept playing on my mind."

My mind races with how to answer this with pure honesty. "She didn't try to touch me or anything like that. She wore a robe around the house, but maybe that's normal for her? Other than that she rested her head on my shoulder and that's it. Nothing happened and nothing will happen.

"I'll handle her, all right? If she does try something, I'm just going to tell her that I'm seeing someone, and that will be that. You don't need to worry about it, Jo. I'm yours, and that's not going to change."

Her response is to bring my face closer to hers with her hands on my cheek and to kiss me.

"Where have you been recently?" Talon asks, studying me as I sit at a desk in one of the office rooms in Rift, going over some numbers for the club's accounts. "I feel like I haven't spent time with you since you got back."

"I know," I say, pausing and looking up. "Do you have any plans tomorrow? Maybe I'll come over and harass you and Tia at your place."

"You know you're welcome," Talon says instantly. "You have your own room there, brother. You just haven't used it yet. Are you sure everything is all right? You seem distracted as fuck."

"Everything is fine," I tell him. "I've just been busy. And be-tween me and you . . . I'm kind of seeing someone. But we defi-nitely need to cut out some time."

"I knew it," he says, grinning. "Which one is it? Elizabeth or the cop? My vote is the cop."

"Why do you say that?"

"Because I know you," he replies, shaking his head, eyes smiling. "You never take the easy road, and you're attracted to anything different and unique. That's why you got bored with all the club women, didn't you? No challenge, too predictable, too expected. Everyone else was doing it, and you don't like doing what everyone else does."

"I'm that easy to figure out, am I?" I ask, studying him. "It's not a game with Jo, Talon. It's something else, I can't even explain it, but she's mine, and I'm going to do whatever I can to keep her."

"That sounds like a lot more than 'seeing someone,'" Talon says, tapping his knuckles absently on the desk. "She's a cop. You think you can make it work?"

I nod.

"Will it affect her reputation at work?" Talon asks, running his hand through his shaggy white-blond hair in thought. "What if they try to use her to take down the MC? Have you thought about all this?"

And that's why I didn't want to tell anyone about this. I don't want to hear it. Are his points valid? Yes. But I want what I want, and listening to logic, valid or not, isn't going to change my mind. This is between me and Jo, and no one else has any part of it.

"I have it under control, Talon," I say, wanting to get him off my back. I return my attention to the documents in front of me, hoping he leaves it alone.

"Ranger—"

"I know, Talon," I say softly. "Trust me, I know, but I'm not going to stop seeing her. If any problems arise, I'll fuckin' take care of it, all right? Right now I just need to figure things out, and I need to do that on my own. You gonna give me time to do that before you get on my case?"

His green eyes narrow, but then he gives me a slight head nod. "Okay. You need me, I'm here."

"I know," I say sincerely, letting my eyes show how much I appreciate it. "Thank you."

"I'll leave you to it, then," he says, tapping the table once more, then stepping away. "See you at my place tomorrow? Come for lunch."

"Sounds good," I say, giving him a chin lift. "Let me know if you want me to bring anything."

Talon walks to the door and opens it. "Tia will handle it, brother. She'll be happy to see you. Rhett too." I look forward to seeing them all tomorrow. He walks out and closes the door behind him.

Returning my attention to the task at hand, I finish up and then grab my jacket, ready to head to Elizabeth's. Checking my phone, I see two missed calls from her. I send her a quick text, not wanting her to worry, then get on my bike. Going to her house feels like a job, and I hate that it doesn't feel like two friends hanging out. I don't know what else to do though, except suggest Faye's offer, that if she's truly scared she's welcome to seek refuge at the Wind Dragons clubhouse.

I have no fuckin' idea what I'm doing with my life right now.

And the fucked-up thing? I don't even care if it means I can be with Jo.

TWENTY-SIX

Johanna

WITH my eyes closed, I run my fingers down the inside of his forearm. I like it when he's in bed with me. Just his presence—it's peaceful. I don't mind waking up to his knocks on my door early morning; in fact, when I heard them I woke up with a smile. Now I'm half-asleep, and he's next to me, doing cute things like running his hands through my hair and massaging my scalp, lulling me into a more relaxed state. My fingers graze his, and that's all I remember before I fall back into a deep sleep.

"How have you been doing?" I ask Elizabeth as I sit down at her dinner table. Everyone wanted to have a family dinner.

"Pretty well," she says, taking a sip from her glass of red wine. "I've been talking to a professional about everything, and it's helping. I'm going back to work next week. I want my life back. I don't want to be broken, I want to be whole."

"You should be so proud of yourself," I tell her. "For being so strong."

I know nothing about psychology, but I do know enough about post-traumatic stress. I've seen it over the years in the force. There are some things you can't come back from. They change you, the pain irreversible.

"You know, I never thanked you for everything you did to find me," she says, tucking her hair behind her ear. "Helen told me how you never gave up, how determined you were." She puts her glass down and pulls me in for a hug. "Thank you, Jo. Without you and Cam . . ."

"Don't even think about it," I tell her, rubbing her back. "It's over now. And I was just doing my job."

"You did more than your job and you know it," she says quietly, pulling back and smiling gently. "And you brought Cam back into my life. If there's anything I can ever do for you, please let me know."

I force a smile and reach for the bottle of wine, pouring myself another glass. I try to compartmentalize my life, but when she keeps bringing him up, it's hard for me to deal with what's going on right now. She's talking about Cam, but she doesn't know that he's my Ranger. The guilt hits me straight in the chest. She's going to hate me. It's gone so far that I don't know what to do, what to say, or how to bring it up. Do I handle it, or does he? Do we sit her down together? I don't know. I'm a terrible person. This girl is my blood, my family, and I'm continuing to be with Ranger behind her back. She deserves to know the truth.

"Hey, is everything okay?" she asks me, brow furrowing in concern. "You just drank that whole glass like we're at a frat party."

I wish we were at a frat party.

"I'm fine," I utter, glancing around the room. "I'm going to grab some water from the kitchen. Do you want anything?"

"No, I'm good," she says, still watching me.

I stand up and walk into the kitchen, grabbing a glass and running some tap water from the sink into it. As I stare out the window into the darkness, I wonder what Ranger is doing right now. In this moment, I know that this can't go on. I don't want to go home alone tonight while he comes here to look after Elizabeth. I can't do it. The whole truth has to come out. I can't keep going from feeling like I'm on top of the world to feeling like the worst person in it.

This isn't me.

Feeling impulsive, I send him a quick text, telling him that we need to talk.

"You okay?" my cousin Jack asks me, coming to stand next to me.

"I'm fine," I say, turning to look at him. "Just tired. How's everything with you?"

"Not bad," he says, concern still etched on his face. "Just busy with work, I'm sure you know how that is."

"Yep," I say, forcing a smile. "You still out breaking hearts or what?"

He puts his hand on his chest. "I'm hurt you think that of me, Jo. I can't help it if I'm a favorite of the ladies."

I roll my eyes, turning to face him. Jack is a baby at nineteen, and a total heartbreaker. If you look into those brown eyes though, you can tell he's an old soul. "I hope you're using protection."

He starts laughing, leaning on the counter for support. "I'm not going to get anyone pregnant, don't you worry."

"The pullout method doesn't work," I advise.

He tries to keep a straight face. "And how do you know that?" He rubs my stomach. "Secret bun in the oven?"

"No," I say, playfully slapping his hand away. "That's how your mom told me she got pregnant with you."

He stills, cringing. "I could have lived without knowing that, Jo. Thanks, really, thanks. I'm going to get myself a drink."

He exits the kitchen, leaving me giggling to myself.

Is everything okay?

I stare at my phone. Is everything okay? I have no idea. I reply and tell him I'll text him when I get home, and ask if he's free to come over so we can talk face-to-face.

Of course. Text me and I'll be there.

Elizabeth and Helen walk into the kitchen, and I hear the end of their conversation. "We're just getting to know each other again. I don't want him to feel sorry for me, I want him to want me."

Fuck.

So that's her plan. I think I've been in denial, thinking that just maybe she wanted him around as a friend. Total denial, and it's been easy because I haven't seen her that much. But now, here in her house, hearing her talk about him, I realize that we've been handling the whole thing terribly wrong.

Shit.

"So you guys haven't kissed or anything?" Helen asks, sounding surprised. "You make me leave the house every time he comes over and you haven't even kissed? I might as well be here watching movies with the two of you, then."

And this is my breaking point.

I make it through the rest of the night, distracted, but pretending everything is fine. I reply, I smile, I socialize, but when I make it to my car, I let the reality of the situation hit me.

I'm not going to cry.

Elizabeth will get over it eventually, right? It's not like she's in love with him. Sure, she's made soul mate comments, but that's just a theory, isn't it? Can you love someone who never loved you back? Can you love someone you've known for only a short period of time?

I don't believe in instalove. No, I *didn't* believe in instalove. I don't know if I'm in love with Ranger or not, but I know this is something. I don't want to hide the fact that we're together. I don't want to have to hide anything. The whole situation has gotten out of control, and it needs to be reeled in.

What scares me the most is that more than my cousin being angry at me, I don't want to lose him.

I'd never admit that out loud.

I put the radio on full blast, trying to block out my own thoughts, but it doesn't help. At this point, I don't think anything can.

He's already there when I get home, and I didn't even text him. He opens my car door for me and offers me his hand. "Are you okay?"

"Yeah," I say as he closes my door. I press the button to lock the car, then walk to my front door. "I just spent the night with Elizabeth and heard her talk about you. I don't think I can do this anymore, Ranger. I feel like the shittiest person, even though I didn't really do anything wrong. I think the worst part is the lying. I should have just told her right away."

But she'd just been rescued. How was I meant to tell her I'd slept with the guy she thinks is the one for her? There's no way I could have, but the longer this goes on the more she thinks she has a chance with Ranger. Isn't it worse to let her think that?

Ranger says nothing about my rant; instead, he takes my keys from me and opens the front door. I walk inside and turn on the light, flopping onto the couch and staring at the blank TV. He sits down next to me, and takes my hand into his. "What do you want me to do? I'm glad you're telling me how you're feeling, Jo, but don't ever say that you can't do this anymore."

I lick my dry lips and turn to look at him. "I don't know what we should do, but not doing anything is only going to make this worse, Ranger. I feel so fake, sitting there with her while she talks about you like you're hers. She's my cousin. And she's been through hell. How can I add to her pain? I've been so selfish, and I just don't see a way out of this. Why don't we just cool things for a little until we can sort it out? Maybe she'll meet someone and forget about you. . . . I don't know. . . ."

He looks at me like I've lost my mind. "Cool things? What the fuck does that mean exactly?"

I look down at our hands and say, "I don't know, Ranger. I just don't know anymore."

"We're supposed to be in this together. When shit gets hard, we're meant to band together and handle it. Not run. You really don't get it, do you, Jo?"

He stands and leaves.

And I'm left feeling like shit.

TWENTY-SEVEN

Ranger

PICK up my glass of whiskey and swirl the amber liquid around before taking a sip.

"Long day?" Shayla asks, sitting down next to me.

"Something like that," I say, ignoring as my phone vibrates with Elizabeth's calls. It's not her I want to call me right now, but I know that Jo won't. She's upset, and I get it, I do, but we're in this together no matter what. She can't run every time something upsets her, unless it's into my arms. I want her, she wants me, why does it have to be more difficult than that?

"Want to talk about it?" she asks, watching me as I pour more whiskey.

"Not really," I say, turning to her. "Do you think that if a relationship is too hard, it isn't meant to be?"

She thinks it over, before shaking her head. "No. I think that sometimes you need to fight for what you want, to make your own fate. It just depends on how badly you want it. Sometimes what you want isn't what you need, or what's best for you. It all depends on the situation, Ranger."

"I want her badly," I say, looking into my glass like it has the answers to all of my problems. "And I know I can make her so happy, you know? It's not a selfish want. I could make her the happiest woman in the world."

"But she doesn't want that?" Shayla asks.

"I don't know. Shayla, is it always like this?" I mutter under my breath, the alcohol doing its job, my mind going hazy. "Maybe I don't deserve someone like her."

Shayla slams her hand down on the table. "Bullshit, Ranger. You're a catch. You're good-looking, educated, badass, and you're funny. I'll give you a moment to feel sorry for yourself, since you just had a fight and you're upset, but that's all I'll allow."

I reach over and tug a lock of her silky dark hair. "Did you just tell me off?"

"Yes."

"She's so fuckin' beautiful, Shayla. Perfect. She's mine, and that's it," I say, trying to explain my connection to Jo and failing miserably.

"There are plenty of beautiful women out there," she says in a soft voice.

"None like her though."

And that's the truth. I made it sound like her beauty is her main appeal, but that's not it. It's just one of the things that makes me want to be around her for the rest of my life. Vinnie walks into the room with Jordan propped on his arm, his eyes going straight to Shayla. "You ready to go, Shay?"

She doesn't take her eyes off me. "Yeah. Unless you want me to hang out for a bit, Ranger?"

"I'm good," I say, leaning over and kissing her cheek. "Go

and get that beautiful girl to bed. I'll talk to you tomorrow, okay?"

"Okay," she says, standing up.

Vinnie nods as I say good-bye. Left alone once more, I replay the last bit of the conversation with Jo in my head.

I want you more than anything, but not like this.

Does she think that I want it to be a secret? I want to scream out to the whole world that she's mine, but I thought we're handling the situation as delicately as we can, trying to do our best so Elizabeth doesn't get pushed over the edge. It's not that I think I'm such a catch that she will lose her mind over me, but she will see it as a betrayal, even though Jo isn't like that. Jo never betrayed Elizabeth, and we can't help how we feel about each other. We didn't choose it: it just happened. Jo doesn't want her cousin to hate her, but I'm sure Elizabeth will get over it. She will find someone else, move on, and realize that I'm not what she wants, but until she does have that realization, she might give Jo a bit of shit and make her look like a villain to her entire family.

Jo doesn't deserve to have to put up with any of that. I'd carry all the guilt, the entire burden if I could, but I can't. Fuck it, I need to talk to Elizabeth. If I'm being honest, there's a reason I've been avoiding it. I don't think I can avoid that reason anymore, because losing Jo isn't an option.

I don't know how it happens, but I end up at Toxic with Talon. He had to run in to deal with an issue between two of the bouncers, and drunk me asked him if I could tag along.

"We were supposed to run in and out, not sit here," Talon says, but then lifts his hand up to order some drinks from a passing waitress. "Two whiskeys and Coke, please," he says, then turns to me. "Not that you need any more alcohol."

"I think I do," I say, looking onstage at the woman dancing in front of me. I see her, but I don't see her, if that makes sense. She's dancing on the pole in nothing but a white thong, and her body is amazing, but it doesn't stir anything inside of me. I don't want to fuck her. Great, Jo's fuckin' ruined me for other women.

I read somewhere that once you feel a mental connection with someone, it's hard to go back to what you were used to before that. I honestly think that's what keeps a relationship going. You need the mental, physical, and intellectual connection. And you need friendship. No one wants to hurt their best friend. Great, now I'm a fuckin' philosopher or something. Although I do have a degree in philosophy, so maybe I'm qualified in my drunk rambled thoughts. In fact, I should write this shit down and turn it into a book or something. Our drinks arrive and I greedily swallow mine, while Talon watches me with a concerned look on his face.

"What happened?" he finally asks when the next girl comes up onstage. "I haven't seen you drink like this since the night you knocked out Anna and felt guilty about it."

"Don't let her know that," I grumble, leaning back and watching the redhead. Again, nothing. My dick doesn't even stir, it just sits there, uninterested.

Fuck my life.

"We had our first real fight," I tell him.

And then, something hits me.

We had our first fight, and I didn't handle it how I told her

I would. We didn't sit and talk it out. She had her say, I mentally disagreed but couldn't take how much her words hurt me, so I walked out and went home. There was no talking it out and there definitely wasn't any makeup sex, and now I feel kind of slighted. Why did I walk away? I shouldn't have. I should have been patient, sat down with her and spoken to her until we sorted it out. I should have calmed her down, told her that everything will be okay, because we're in it together.

But I didn't.

Fuck.

"So go and make up," Talon says, shrugging like it's no big deal. "Tell her you're sorry, then go and fuck her and remind her why she likes you in the first place."

"That easy, huh?"

"It's never that easy," Talon says, barking out a laugh. "But if it were, life would be boring, don't you think?"

"I think I could use some boring right now," I say on a sigh. I look down into my glass, surprised to see that it's empty. "Who finished my drink?"

"That would be you, Ranger," Talon says, chuckling to himself.

"Pony" by Ginuwine starts to play, and I fuckin' love this song, so I raise my arm in the air and cheer.

"Seriously?" Talon asks from next to me. He looks on the verge of laughter again, although I don't know why, but at least he's in a good mood. He's not a bad party buddy, that Talon.

"It's a classic," I point out, looking for another waitress. I'm too drunk to drop by Jo's house now, so I might as well go all out and get wasted tonight, then go to her tomorrow, when my head is clear. I texted Elizabeth and told her I couldn't make it tonight, but if she's feeling unsafe, she's welcome to stay at the clubhouse. She replied and said Helen is home tonight, so she's fine, and she hopes everything is okay with me. I find it a little ironic that she said she'd be fine without me, when if she was so before, maybe Jo wouldn't have been pushed to her breaking point.

Johanna.

I wish she were here.

I look up at the stage and cringe. Okay, maybe not *here*, here, but I wish I was with her.

Maybe I'll just go and see her now.

TWENTY-EIGHT

Johanna

AWAKE with a jump as I hear a banging on the front door. I grab my gun from my nightstand drawer and walk to the front door, barefoot, in nothing but my panties and T-shirt. When I turn on the light and look through the peephole I see Ranger standing there, looking disheveled. I quickly open the door and let him in.

"Good morning," he says, flashing me a lopsided smile. I can smell the alcohol on him from here, and I wonder where he's come from and how he got here.

"You didn't drink and drive did you?" I ask, scowling. "Or ride."

"Talon dropped me off," he says, closing the door behind him and locking it. "I wanted to talk to you, and it can't wait until tomorrow." He steps closer to me, but stops and leans against the wall for support.

"Talon dropped you here?" I ask, wishing I could have met the man I've heard so much about. "What, like a father dropping off his son at his girlfriend's house?"

Ranger smirks. "I found it hilarious too."

"Had a bit to drink, have you?" I ask as he wraps his arm around me and walks with me back to my bedroom. I put my gun away and watch as he removes his jacket and jeans and climbs into my bed.

"Just a bit," he says, resting his hands behind his head and watching me. "I missed you."

"So you decided to drop by at two a.m.?" I ask, lifting the sheets and sliding in next to him.

"Yeah," he says, snuggling into me. "We have some unfinished business."

"We do?" I breathe, laying my head on his chest.

I'm glad he came.

When he walked out of my house, I felt terrible. I wanted him to come right back, but I was too proud to say anything, and it wouldn't have changed anything. He didn't say much; he listened to me. He didn't argue against my points. He didn't agree either. He just nodded like he respected my wishes, said okay, and then left my house.

I don't think I wanted him to respect my wishes. Have I always been so complicated?

"Remember I told you what would happen after our first fight?" he says, kissing the top of my head. "We're going to talk it out. We're going to solve it. And then we're going to have the best makeup sex that ever existed."

"Bold claim," I murmur, licking my dry lips. "Do you want to wait until morning to have this talk? Maybe when you're sober and suffering with a hangover."

"I'm not so drunk that I don't know what I'm saying," he says, rubbing my back. "I shouldn't have left your house today. Your words hit me, babe. I didn't know how to handle them. All

I heard over and over was you saying that you can't handle being with me." He takes in and releases a deep breath, then lowers his voice to add, "I'm sorry."

I feel like he's not a man who apologizes often. "Apology accepted. I know it sounded like I was saying I wanted out, but I just can't see an alternative. I was upset. I shouldn't have said that I couldn't do this, especially when I don't even know if I meant it."

"I'll tell her that I'm seeing someone and, if she feels unsafe, to call me, but I'll make it clear that we will only be friends, and that will never change, okay?"

I nod my head against him.

"I don't want you to feel like you're in this alone, because you're not. If I could fix this for you I would, and I'm going to try to, okay? I don't want to be without you, Jo. It sounds selfish, and maybe it is, but I think I can make you happy. So don't take yourself away from me."

I close my eyes, letting his words hit me. "Okay," I whisper. "I won't."

"No running, Jo."

"No running," I repeat.

He lifts my face up and kisses my lips. Then against them he says, "Now it's time for the making-up part."

I smile and kiss his lips.

"You're quiet today," Travis says to me in the car. We're driving back to the police station after dealing with a stolen-car situation.

"Am I?" I murmur, looking from out the window to him. "I guess I'm just a little distracted."

I've been thinking about how to handle the Elizabeth situation all day. Ranger said he's going to talk to her first and see if he can handle things without it getting messy and having her get angry, so I'll see how it goes, and then I'll speak to her myself. I don't know what he's going to say. Is he going to tell her he's seeing someone or is he going to tell her he's seeing me? Two very different situations.

"Want to talk about it?" he asks, turning down the volume on the radio. "Is everything okay with your cousin? Or is she not settling back in well?"

"She's actually doing pretty great," I tell him. "She's going back to work next week, and plans on helping other women coming out of similar situations. She's trying to turn what happened into a positive."

"Good on her," Travis answers, nodding. "So if it's got nothing to do with her, then what is it?"

I take a deep breath. "It's nothing, really."

. "Don't lie to me."

"It's not something you're going to want to hear about, Trav," I say, shifting on my seat. I look at the side of his face and add, "It's not something we usually discuss, so it's a little uncomfortable for me."

"Is this when we have the sex talk?" he jokes, turning to look at me, blue eyes dancing with delight. "Are you finally getting laid, Jo?"

"Mature, Trav," I grumble, looking straight ahead and wishing I never mentioned anything. "It's not the sex part that's an issue, it's who it's with."

Might as well just tell him everything now, he's going to annoy me until I do.

"Who is it?"

I smack my lips together and just blurt it out. "Ranger, the biker I went and saved Elizabeth with. The same biker who happens to be someone Elizabeth loves and wants to be with, although I didn't know that when I got involved with him. And now I'm in too deep to get out."

He stays silent for a few moments before he explodes. "Really? A fucking biker, Jo? Have you not heard of the Wind Dragons and their reputation? They think they're their own law! Faye is one thing—she's a lawyer, and she's kind of respectable. But the others?"

"Of course I've heard of them," I snap, crossing my arms over my chest. "It's not like I wanted to want him, or wanted him to want me, it just happened. He's a nice guy, and he's good to me. And I can't get enough of him, so yes, I'm screwed. You asked, you pushed, and there's the God's honest truth!"

"Fucking hell, Jo," he grits out, slamming his hands down on the steering wheel. "I have never even seen you with a man before, and now you're dating a biker? How do you get into these situations? Fuck. Only you, I swear!"

"What do you mean *only me*? All the men in that clubhouse have women, it's obviously not only me!" I say, pursing my lips. "I didn't ask for this, Trav, but I wouldn't change it either. I've never met anyone like him."

"A criminal? Pretty sure you've met a lot of those in your time," he mutters under his breath. I narrow my eyes on him. Ranger isn't a criminal. Sure, he's been arrested a few times, but he's never done time. I should know, I checked. "This guy could ruin everything you've worked so hard for, Jo. Your career, your credibility, everything. Are you sure you want to go down this path?"

He's acting like I have a choice, but I don't.

He doesn't understand that. I don't think anyone does.

Ranger is made for me, and I'm made for him.

There's nothing else to it.

"Have you ever been in love, Trav?" I ask him in a small voice.

"No," he says quickly, and I can feel his eyes on me before going back to the road. "Are you saying you've fallen in love with the biker? You haven't even known him long, Jo. You're usually the most levelheaded woman I know, and to hear this shit coming from you . . . Wow. I did not see this coming."

I roll my eyes at his dramatics. He's acting like I've told him I robbed a bank or something. Forbidden love. Is that what I have with Ranger? Do I love him? Do I even know what love is? The questions running through my mind give me a headache. I rub my temples and wish that we never had this conversation. In fact, I'm going to pretend it never took place.

"Can we change the subject now? Please?" I beg, turning the music volume back up and pretending I can't feel the tension radiating from him. He's not happy, and he's clearly not trying to hide it.

We spend the rest of the ride in silence.

TWENTY-NINE

Ranger

"So," I start, wanting to get this conversation over with. I look over at Elizabeth; she's sitting on the couch, eating some ice cream. "Faye has extended an open invitation to the clubhouse any time you feel like you need protection. I think that you don't need me here anymore, Elizabeth. You're doing so well, and you have your sister."

She puts down her spoon and scowls at me. "What do you mean? Don't you like hanging out with me? That's what friends do, you know?"

"Yeah," I say slowly, dragging the word out. "But they don't do it every night on a schedule. It's random. Different times and different places, which we can still do. And if you ever feel like you truly do need me, I'll be here."

"You'd be doing the same thing at the clubhouse, wouldn't you? I don't see the big deal about why you don't want to stay here," she says, blue eyes flashing with sadness and confusion.

Fuck.

I don't want her to be sad, but this truly can't go on, especially when she's secretly hoping something might happen between us. She hasn't made a move on me or done anything inappropriate though, so it's also awkward as fuck for me to bring this up right now. How do I get into these situations?

"So here's the thing. I'm kind of seeing someone right now, so I'd kind of like to be able to spend the night with her. Don't get me wrong, if I thought you truly needed me I'd be here, but you don't, do you?"

"You're seeing someone?" she asks softly, looking down at her bowl. "I had no idea. Why didn't you say anything?"

"Kind of new," I say, trying to brush it off. "And I wanted to make sure you were okay, you know? It's not like I don't like hanging out with you, we can still do stuff, I just can't come here and watch shitty movies with you every night anymore. I have shit to do, and so do you, yeah?"

Her lip twitches when I mention the shitty movies. "I guess I just don't know how you don't see it."

"See what?" I ask, tilting my head to the side and studying her.

"That we'd be perfect for each other," she says, smiling shyly. "Why don't you see it, Cam? I know we were just friends back then . . . but you still—"

"Elizabeth," I say softly, cutting her off. "I think you're amazing, you know this, and trust me, there's someone out there for you. He's going to be a lucky-ass man, but it's not me."

"But it could be."

I shake my head. "No, it can't. The woman I met, she's in deep, Elizabeth. She's under my skin, and there's no digging her out. I don't even want to. I'm sorry. I hate to see you hurt, but trust me, you'll know exactly what I mean when you meet the man who's meant to be yours."

She stays silent for a few moments. "I've never heard you talk like this before. You're a cynic."

"I guess I'm more of an 'I'll believe it when I see it' type, and now I've seen it."

Fuck, I sound like a pussy-whipped little bitch, but I'm being real right now. I'm not going to act like I don't care when I do; I'm not going to fuck around and possibly lose Jo, no fuckin' way. Good women don't come along every day, and one who gives you everything you've ever dreamed of? Yeah, I'm no fool. I want to take care of her, give her everything she needs and wants, and just love her until she knows nothing else. Until she doesn't remember anything before I came into her life, because it wasn't as important.

"I'm not going to lie, I'm disappointed," she admits, puffing out a deep breath. "I guess if it's meant to be, it will be, right? I want you to be happy, Cam. Sure, I wanted it to be with me, but hey, I can't always get what I want, and I know that." She closes her eyes for a moment. "So this is what unrequited love feels like, huh? Never thought I'd be on the other end of that."

I stand up and sit next to her, taking the bowl out of her hands and putting it on the coffee table. I pull her into my arms. "Trust me, you're dodging a bullet. I'm a pain in the ass."

She clings to me like I'm a lifeline, burying her face in my T-shirt. "I know you are, but I thought you'd be *my* pain in the ass one day."

No.

Honestly, I don't even like her holding me like she is right now, but she basically just admitted she loves me, so what else can I do? She may think she loves me, but she doesn't. Only time and experience will let her figure that out. Such hard lessons we all have to go through sometimes.

"We're friends, Elizabeth," I say, hoping she hears what I'm saying. I mean *really* hears it. Even if Jo and I don't work out, we'll never be. Nothing will ever happen, and she needs to understand that and move on. She's a pretty girl, and has a lot going for her; she's not going to remain single for long. Everything will be worth it in the long run, one day she'll thank me.

But that day won't be today.

"Uncle Ranger!" Clover hollers, running into the kitchen with a giant lollipop in her hand.

"Hey, Clover, where did you get that?" I ask, eyeing it. I don't think I'll ever get used to little kids referring to me as uncle, but they're good kids, cute and badass. They treat me like I am their uncle, and the feeling makes me both uncomfortable and grateful.

"Uncle Arrow gave it to me," she says, taking a lick. "It's strawberry. Do you want one? He has more."

I kind of did, but shake my head. No point adding "taking candy from a baby" to my list of shitty deeds for the week. I already have breaking Elizabeth's heart on that list, and that's where I want to leave it.

"No, thanks," I tell her, glancing up as her mother joins us.

"Ranger," she says, beaming. "Just the man I was looking for."

I cringe exaggeratedly. "What now? You want me to give up an organ? Save a kitten from a tree?"

Clover's eyes widen. "There's a kitten stuck in a tree? We have to save it! Uncle Rake has a ladder."

"Like mother like daughter," I say, flashing Faye an amused glance. "Now what's up?"

"Arrow wants you. I don't know why." She cocks her hip against the doorframe, then adds, "Okay, I do know why. He needs a few extra men at Rift tonight and wants you to be one."

"I can't wait until I'm old enough to go to Rift," Clover says, still licking her lollipop. "I'm going to own that dance floor."

Faye and I both stare at her in a *Yeah, we'll see about that* way, then share an amused glance.

"Is that right?" Faye asks, brow rising. "You should have that conversation with your dad."

"Good idea," she says, walking out of the room to go find Sin.

"What happened with Elizabeth last night?" Faye asks, stepping farther into the room and stopping in front of me. "Is the Cinderella scheme still on?"

"I told her I was seeing someone. I don't know, do you think it's a good idea?" I ask, leaning back against the counter. "I haven't even properly spoken to Jo about what happened yet; I'm going to go to her place after she finishes work."

"How are you going to tell Elizabeth her own cousin is the other woman?" Faye asks bluntly, then winces. "Fuck, that sounds bad."

"It is bad," I say, scrubbing my hand down my face. "I don't know, maybe one blow at a time, get her used to the idea, maybe even move on before she finds out that it's Jo?"

"It's going to bite you in the ass."

"I know, but I've got nothing else right now," I admit. "I just don't want Jo to freak out and bail because she feels bad. I feel like how Elizabeth handles this controls Jo's reaction, and I don't like that."

"Because you can't control it yourself?" Faye asks, smirking. "Typical alpha behavior. You still can though, because you can talk Jo off the ledge. You'll just be doing a lot of reassuring for a while. It's hard to deal with guilt, even if it's misplaced."

"I know," I mutter. "You should have your own TV show. Like Dr. Phil."

She playfully slaps my arm. "I need a reality show—how cool would that be? Although we'd probably all get arrested at some point."

"Which would also make for great TV."

"Very true. Now when are you going to bring your cop around for everyone to meet? Isn't it funny? I inadvertently set you up with her. I'm like a part-time cupid."

"Maybe you need a new hobby. And the answer to that is I'll bring her here when everyone stops referring to her as 'the cop.'"

"What? She is one."

Talon walks in and grins when he sees me. "I haven't seen you since I dropped you off at the cop's house, drunk, after you spent the night dancing with strippers to 'Pony.'"

"Great song," Faye adds, but then narrows her eyes and points her finger at me. "You went to Toxic?"

"Talon had to drop in," I say, shrugging. "It's not like I fucked one of the strippers."

I couldn't even get hard watching them, as a matter of fact, not that I'm going to admit that though.

"But we didn't have to stay for two hours," Talon, the shit-stirrer adds.

I turn the tables on him. "Does Tia know you stayed there for so long?"

"Yep," he replies cheerily, jumping up on the counter and sitting. "I told her you were upset and turning to the bottle so I couldn't just leave you there. I was being a good friend."

"Does Jo know you went there?" Faye asks, glancing between the two of us. "You two are hilarious by the way, like an old married couple."

"So, like you and Sin," I fire back, moving out of the way of her swatting hand.

"Sin and I are not old. We're a hot, young married couple."

"Uh-huh," Talon says, grinning. "We're going to Rift and you're coming."

"So I've heard," I say, saying 'bye to Faye and following Talon to the front.

I'll help Arrow with whatever he needs, then go to Jo's house. I miss her.

And I hope my telling Elizabeth makes Jo feel better about being with me.

THIRTY

Johanna

"So how did she take it?" I ask Ranger.

"She was upset, but she'll be fine," he says, squeezing his arms around me when I try to move off his lap. "There is no avoiding upsetting her, Jo. I'm never going to be with her, no matter the circumstances, whether you're in the picture or not. I don't feel that way about her. Yes, I care about her; no, I don't want to be with her. We've been through this. It will all get better in time, we just have to hold on, all right?"

I let his words penetrate, but it still doesn't take away the pain and guilt that I'm contributing to my own cousin's unhappiness right now.

"All right," I reply, burying my face in his chest. "Why does everything have to be so complicated?"

With Travis's words still in my head, and the fact that he's pretty much giving me the silent treatment, everything is really starting to pile on my shoulders. I can feel Travis's disappointment in me every time I'm near him, and although I don't think his judgment is fair, it still hurts to get the cold shoulder from him. Where's the support? Or at least "You're an idiot, but I'll have your back anyway because it's you who has to live with your decisions." Anything other than what I'm getting from him.

"Everyone has their little bumps in the road," Ranger says, then mutters, "At least that's what I've heard. But at least ours has nothing to do with our relationship with each other; it's just outside things that are giving us hell."

"That doesn't make it any easier," I groan, lifting my face up and placing my hands on his stubbled cheeks. "When are we going to tell her that it's me?"

"I don't know, Jo. It's your call. I'll listen to you on this," he says, resting his forehead against mine. "I love you. I don't care what else happens, but I don't want to lose you."

My eyes widen as I hear him say those three words for the first time. It's the first time a man other than my father has said them to me. I swallow hard and look him right in the eye.

"I love you too, Ranger," I say, smiling, bending forward to kiss his lips. I close my eyes, just enjoying the moment, feeling it.

He loves me.

And it feels good to say those words out loud to him; no matter how crazy they may seem, they're the truth.

"You better," he says as he ends the kiss, smiling against my lips.

I pull out his hair from the ponytail and run my fingers through it. "You love me?"

"I do," he says, slamming his lips down on mine, kissing me with a passion that matches his words. He stands with me in his arms and carries me to my room. I love the way he lifts me as if I weigh nothing, how big and strong he is. He makes me feel so feminine, which is a difficult feat in my career. He puts me down, my feet hitting the carpet in my bedroom, then helps me undress until I'm completely naked. I help him do the same, then get down on my knees and take his hard cock into my hands. He looks down at me, eyes dark and heavy-lidded, watching my every move as I stroke him a few times and then take the head of his cock into my mouth. I suck it, then take it out and lick it with my tongue, teasing him a little before sliding as much as I can of him into my mouth and then back out again. I hold the base of him in my left hand, even though my hand doesn't close around him, and suck up and down, hollowing my cheeks.

"Fuck, Jo," he whispers, tangling his hands in my hair and gently tugging on the short strands. "Yes, just like that."

I keep at it, sliding my mouth up and down, until my jaw starts to hurt, so I use my hand for a few pumps, giving my mouth a little break. I lick the underneath of him, from base to tip, then slide him back inside and suck. He makes a sound in the back of his throat that has me sucking him in deeper, until my gag reflex kicks in and I pull him out. I'm about to suck him into my mouth once more when he lifts me up by my arms and pushes me back onto the bed. He spreads my thighs and then his mouth is on me. I'm already wet, I know it, being turned on from giving him head, and when he licks my clit I lift my hips up to him, eager for more. He grips my thighs with his hands and pins me to the mattress, his talented tongue making me moan and make noises I'd never make if I was in control of my own body right now.

"Ranger," I beg, wanting to come so badly. He sucks on my clit, which sends me over the edge, my hands gripping the sheets, my nails digging into them as the orgasm consumes everything in me. I'm still lost in pleasure when he slides into me, bracing himself on top of me, his lips now on mine, his body bringing me more pleasure than I've ever known. I run my hands down his back, feeling his muscles work with each thrust, raising my hips to meet his. In a quick move he pulls out of me and turns me over onto my stomach, sliding into me from behind. I push up on my knees and groan as he reaches his hand over to play with one nipple, then the other, cupping and squeezing my breasts with delicious pressure. His hand then moves to my clit, where he starts to rub in a gentle circular motion that has me biting down on the pillow in front of me.

"You are so fuckin' perfect for me," he grits out, kissing the middle of my spine. "You're mine, Jo."

I'm unable to speak at this point, and I hear his deep chuckle when he realizes as much.

"Tell me when you're going to come," he says, kissing my neck. His lips move to my ear as he whispers, "I want to come with you."

He's kissing down my jawline when I tell him, "Now, I'm going to come now."

"Thank fuck," he groans, placing his hand on my nape and squeezing gently as he finishes. I bite down on the pillow, the pleasure more intense than before. When I come back to myself and Ranger slides out of me, I sink onto the mattress, every last bit of energy wrung out of me. I feel happy, sated, and well loved.

He kisses my spine again.

I smile and close my eyes.

When Elizabeth calls me, sounding on the verge of tears, I feel like the worst person on the face of the earth. I've been so happy today. Ranger slept over, and we spent the whole night talking and making love. It was a perfect night. And if it's possible, I'm crazier about him now than I was yesterday.

"Cam's seeing someone; I had no idea," she says, making a sound of frustration.

"Oh," I say, not knowing what to reply to her. "I'm sorry."

"Me too. I made such a fool of myself. I honestly thought that eventually he'd see that we could be great together, but I guess that's not going to happen. Maybe I've been reading too many romance novels. Things like that don't happen in real life, do they?"

They do. It's happening to me right now, except mine comes with a price, and this is it.

"I don't think you made a fool of yourself. No regrets, right? I'm sure you'll meet someone amazing."

"So I've heard," she grumbles, then says, "I kind of want to have a night out . . . just to distract myself. I haven't been out since everything happened. So you want to come out with me and Helen?"

"Where?" I ask, brow furrowing as I wonder how this is going to go.

"To a bar or a club. We can have a few drinks and a dance, it will be fun," she says, sounding upbeat all of a sudden.

I can't remember the last time I went to a club. It has to have been years ago, maybe three or four. I was never really into the club scene. I don't mind hitting a bar every now and again, but a club? Not really my thing.

"I don't know, Elizabeth—"

"We'll pick you up at seven," she says, hanging up on me. I stare at my phone and wonder what I'm going to do. It feels so fake to spend the night with her, especially when she doesn't know the truth about Ranger and me, but she wants me there and she's trying to get out and about again. I don't even have a valid excuse for not going, because tomorrow is my day off. I send Ranger a quick text saying I'm going to be out late, so we're going to have to change our plans.

What, why?

Elizabeth wants to go out to a club and apparently attendance is compulsory.

I hit SEND and continue cleaning my house. What will I wear tonight? I'm sure I have some dresses in the back of my closet, but it's been a while since I've had to get all dolled up. Or do I have to? Maybe I can pull off a more casual look. I go into my room and start rummaging through all my clothes. I decide on a simple black dress, it's plain but tight-fitting, and a pair of black ankle boots. They have a small heel, enough to be sexy and comfortable at the same time. Nothing worse than having your feet hurt halfway through the night. I lay the dress out and place the boots in front of the bed.

I have a feeling tonight is going to be very interesting.

Cop is going clubbing, hey?

I imagine the amusement in his tone.

Yes, you got a problem with that?

Send me a pic, babe.

I'll think about it.

Do you want me to drop you girls off?

No.

He can't drop us off. Elizabeth is trying to forget him, and it will just be awkward. What if she brings up their conversation? This whole thing is so fucked-up. I'm such a bad person.

Jo.

No.

Why?

You know why, Ranger.

Fine. I'll send one of the men.

Not necessary. We're going to a club, not to war. And I'm a cop, or have you forgotten that already?

Call me if you need me. And call me when you get home.

Why?

So I know you're safe.

I smile at the phone when another text from him comes in.

And so I can come over.

THIRTY-ONE

LOOK in the bar's bathroom mirror, making sure my makeup is still on. The red lip stain is in place and my eyeliner isn't smudged. I actually look pretty decent. I take a quick selfie, probably my first mirror selfie ever, and forward it to Ranger. My hair is slicked back in my version of a dressier hairstyle, but somehow it works on me. In fact, I look pretty glam. The black dress clings to me like a second skin, showing the curves of my toned body. I nod in the mirror, then return to the bar, where Elizabeth and Helen are sitting, already on their fourth drinks. They keep checking out the bartender, a cute blond guy, one who goes by the name of Ryan. He's a charmer, that's for sure, so I can see why they're interested, but the ring on his finger says he's not.

"There are so many hot guys here tonight!" Elizabeth gushes. "None as hot as Cam, but after a few more drinks I'm sure that will change."

I look to see Helen's reaction, but she's just laughing and drinking along with her sister. Do they plan on going home with someone tonight?

"There are three hot guys over there," Helen says, pointing to a group of men in the corner. "We should go and sit with them. I call the one in the blue shirt."

"What?" I ask, voice going up an octave. "I'm going to stay here, thank you."

"Oh, come on, we're three single women, we should go and have some fun. We've never even been out together before," Elizabeth says, rubbing her hands together. "Come on, let's go."

Three single women, right.

Shit.

Elizabeth leads the way as we approach the men. I hide in the back.

"Hello," she beams, turning on her charm. "Is it okay if we join you?"

"Of course," one of the men says. He has dark hair and a dimple in his chin. "We'd love for you to."

I roll my eyes. I bet they would. I awkwardly sit down, between Helen and a lanky bald man. We all introduce ourselves, shaking hands and in the girls' cases, giving flirtatious smiles. There's a man in the corner of the bar who keeps looking over in our direction. I've been keeping an eye on him, and I'm pretty sure I'm not being paranoid—he's not just here for a casual drink. He's got shaggy light blond hair, almost white, and he's tall and good-looking. He's wearing all black, leaning against the wall, and keeps looking over here every now and again. He's been watching us since we walked into Knox's Tavern, and of course I haven't missed it.

"So what do you do for work?" Elizabeth asks the gentleman she's obviously into, Mr. Chin Dimple.

"I'm an accountant," he replies, taking a sip of his wine. "And you?"

I block them out while they exchange pleasantries, wondering what that man is up to. Is he here for Elizabeth? Did we miss someone? What if we did? What if he knows her face, knows that she got away, and wants to take her out? Well, not on my watch. I jump as the bald guy touches my elbow, trying to get my attention.

"How are you doing tonight, beautiful?" he asks me, smiling.

I blink slowly a few times before I reply. "Not bad, how are you?"

"Much better now," he says, eyes dropping to my boobs. I look down where he's looking, then back up at him with a raised brow. From the corner of my eye, I see the man leave the bar, so I excuse myself and follow him outside. His back is to me and he's on his phone, so I pull my gun out of my handbag, wanting to catch him off guard. I walk up behind him and push him face-first into the brick wall.

"Who are you?" I growl, pressing my gun into his back.

"Fucking hell," the man says. "Put the gun down, Jo."

I still. "How do you know my name?"

I hear him mutter, "I told him not to fuck with a cop."

"What did you just say?" I ask, losing my patience and digging the gun deeper into his spine.

"I'm a friend of Ranger's," he says. "My name is Talon. Call Ranger and ask him yourself."

Talon?

Ranger's best friend?

Wow, this is a first impression he isn't going to forget.

"Talon?" I say, taking a step back. I pull out my phone and hit CALL on Ranger's number. He answers on the second ring.

"Babe?"

"Did you ask your friend Talon to keep an eye on me?"

Silence.

Then, "Jo—"

"Answer me before I shoot him."

"Fuck, babe, don't shoot him. He was in the area, so I asked him to drop in on you after you told me where you were going."

"Seriously, Ranger?"

"I should be the angry one; Talon sent me a text saying you're sitting at a table with some fuckin' assholes," he growls.

I lower my gun and hang up on Ranger, awkwardly putting away my gun and phone.

"Hello, Talon," I say, waving awkwardly.

He shakes his head, lip twitching. "Nice to finally meet you, Jo."

"Sorry about the whole almost-shooting-you thing," I add. My phone starts ringing again, Ranger no doubt, but I ignore it, something Talon seems to find amusing, because he glances at my bag and then starts laughing.

"What?" I ask him, clearing my throat.

"Nothing," he says, nodding to the entrance. "Do you want to get a drink?"

"I'd love one."

I hold my stomach, because I can't stop laughing right now. "So he lost at beer pong against the women and he's been practicing for a rematch that no one has even agreed to?"

I've had four drinks with Talon and over those drinks, I've learned so much about Ranger. He has three degrees, which I didn't know but I'm not surprised by, because he's such a smart man. I've heard stories about him and Talon, the two of them getting into trouble and saving each other's asses, and I've also enjoyed getting to know Talon. He's a nice guy. I should have known that he'd be a nice guy, because Ranger likes him. That makes another nice biker whom I would have otherwise judged.

"Yeah, he's a little competitive," Talon says, taking a swig of his beer. "And speak of the devil . . ."

I look to the entrance and watch as Ranger stalks inside, a very unhappy look on his handsome face. The white T-shirt he's wearing is stretched across his broad chest, and drunk me would like nothing more than to jump his bones right now.

"Jo," he growls, taking the glass from my hand and putting it down. "Fun time is over."

"Fun time is just beginning once I get you home and in bed."

When both men look at me, I realize I said that out loud. And this is why I don't drink much.

"Talon, you could have brought her to me instead of drinking with her while she ignores my calls," Ranger says to him.

"Where's the fun in that?" Talon asks him, downing the last of his beer and placing the bottle on the bar.

I have to agree with him.

Ranger throws some money down on the table, probably for the bartender having to deal with us all night, and practically drags me out of there with Talon following behind us. Elizabeth and Helen thought I met Talon and liked him, so they were excited for me, and left with those guys' numbers. I'm glad they didn't go home with them on the first night because it's less worrying for me to do.

"Leave your bike here," Ranger says to Talon. "I'll text one of the men and ask them to come and pick it up."

Talon stares at his bike longingly but then nods and gets in the backseat of the car while Ranger puts me in the passenger seat and closes the door for me. I glance in the back and share a grin with Talon.

"Who will come and get your bike?" I ask him.

"Vinnie and Ronan will probably come in one of the cars and then one of them can ride it back," Talon explains as Ranger gets into the car and starts the engine. The music comes along and I start bopping to the beat.

Drake's "One Dance" comes on the radio. "I like this song," I think it's important to announce as I shimmy in my seat.

"I can see that," Ranger muses in that deep sexy voice of his. He sounds like he doesn't agree with my choice of music, but I couldn't care less.

"Isn't this the song Faye is always playing?" Talon asks, sticking his head between our seats.

"Yep," Ranger replies, shaking his head. "Can't get away from it."

"Who would want to?" I ask, doing a little dance.

"The cop dances." Talon chuckles, finding it hilarious. "And listens to R and B."

"What am I supposed to listen to?" I ask, scowling. "Police sirens?"

Ranger glances at me, blinks, then concentrates on the road. When I realize we're not going in the direction of my house I ask, "Where are we going?"

"To the clubhouse," he says simply.

"What? Why?" I ask, panic starting to set in. "I don't want to go there. I want to go back to my house and have hot sex and live in denial."

"Denial from what? That your man is a biker? You're going to have to deal with that, Jo," Ranger says, reaching over and taking my hand. "We'll be fine. Everyone is going to love you just like this idiot in the back does."

"How do you know he loves me?" I ask, glancing at Talon, who simply smirks.

"Because I know him. If he didn't he wouldn't have spent hours drinking and talking with you, he would have sent me a text telling me that he's sick of the babysitting gig and is going to bail."

"Oh."

"Yes, oh."

I guess I'm going to the Wind Dragons clubhouse. I'm glad I'm drunk.

THIRTY-TWO

Ranger

I WATCH in amusement as she walks into the clubhouse, glancing around like she has no idea what or who to expect. It's 2:00 a.m., so everyone has gone back to their own houses; it gets pretty empty here after dinnertime. Some nights it's just me and Ronan, but other nights some of the members sleep over. Vinnie and Ronan left to get Talon's bike, so now the whole place is empty.

"No one's here, Jo," I tell her, my hand on the small of her back, leading her to my bedroom.

"Good night, you two," Talon says, slapping me on the back. He turns to Jo and says, "Was nice meeting you, cop."

"Right back at you," Jo says, smiling at him. "Thanks for saving the night."

It seems like she had more fun with Talon than her cousins. Sounds like an interesting night, one that I wasn't invited to. When we get to my room, I open the door for her, turning the light on, then nodding my head for her to enter. She walks in and looks around, not that there's much to see. There's a king-size bed, and on it black sheets and a black blanket. A wardrobe and a desk, and the door that leads to the bathroom.

"This is where you live?" she asks, sitting down on the bed and removing her cute little boots.

"Yep. Why? You don't like it?" I ask, curious as to what's going on in her tipsy little mind.

"It has no personal touches at all," she says, staring into my soul. "It looks like no one lives here, or maybe someone who isn't planning on staying here long. You don't even have anything on your desk."

I take off my own shoes and sit down next to her. "Maybe I don't know how long I'm going to be here."

She looks confused, her brow furrowing adorably. "This is who you are, isn't it? Or who you want to be?"

I change the subject, because I don't know how to answer that. Yes, this is who I am, but I feel restless here, like something isn't right. "You hung up on me today."

"You had me followed," she says, lifting her chin stubbornly.

"I just wanted to make sure you were safe," I tell her, raising my hands in surrender when she's about to object. "Yes, I know you can protect yourself, but I'm still your man, and I just wanted to make sure. Is that the worst thing in the world? Bad shit happens every day, and I don't want any of it touching you."

"I was in a public place and not alone. You're being paranoid. Talon didn't need to waste his night just making sure I was okay," she says, licking her lips. "And the girls wanted to talk to those guys, not me, before you decide to bring that up. I don't have eyes for anyone else, Ranger. I'm not a woman you have to worry about whenever I go somewhere. I only want you."

Everything in me softens, except for my dick. That hardens. Fuck. The shit she says. "I know that, Jo. I trust you. You wouldn't be here right now if I didn't."

She places her hand on the center of my chest. "Good, I'm glad. I mean I almost shot Talon today, but I didn't know it was him, so I don't think that really counts."

I grin. "You're going to have to tell me that story from the beginning."

She gives me a quick rundown of the night, and I can't help laughing, picturing Jo with a gun pressed up against Talon's back. "You're something else, babe."

"Are you going to kiss me now?" she asks, her teeth running along her lower lip. "Ever since you walked into that bar, I've just wanted you to be inside of me. Stop making me wait, Ranger."

Fuck.

I lift her onto my lap and start kissing her

She doesn't need to tell me twice.

I wake up with her wrapped in my arms. I love having her here in my bed, and even though it hasn't been mine for very long, it's still good to have her in what I consider my domain. Not wanting to wake her, I slide out of bed and throw on some sweatpants. I head into the kitchen, wanting to make Jo breakfast in bed, since I've never really done anything like that for her. I make some pancakes and fry some bacon and eggs, then pour orange juice and coffee, and take it all back into the room, setting it on the side table closest to her. Then I climb back into bed and start kissing her neck. I wonder if she's going to be hungover today. One thing I do now know is that she's much louder in bed after she's had a few drinks, something I particularly enjoyed.

She's amazing.

" 'Morning, babe," I say, sucking on her neck gently so it doesn't leave a mark. "I made you breakfast. How are you feeling?"

" 'Morning," she whispers, voice thick with sleep. "What did you make?"

"You hungry?"

"Yes," she says, opening her eyes and wincing. "Do you have any aspirin?"

"Yes," I say, kissing her forehead. "I'll get you some with some water. The food is next to you."

She glances to the table next to her, her eyes widening. "Oh wow, Ranger." She sits up and takes the orange juice first. "You made all this?"

"Yes."

She finishes the whole glass. "You're the best ever."

"Dehydrated, are we? Is there anything else you want from the kitchen?" I ask, getting out of bed and waiting for her response.

"No, that's it, thank you."

She takes a piece of bacon in her hand, takes a bite, and groans. "So good."

Nothing like the noises she was making last night, but my dick still twitches. Fuck—it's like he's enslaved to her.

I smile and head to the kitchen, grabbing the pills and water and giving them both to her when I get back to my room.

"Thank you," she says, swallowing two of them with some of

the bottled water. "I can't believe I pointed a gun at Talon last night."

I throw my head back and laugh. "Babe, that and the picture you sent me were the best things of the night. I know I didn't tell you, because I was too busy fuming, but you looked so fuckin' beautiful."

In fact, that's kind of why I sent Talon. I didn't want any assholes hitting on her, and I knew they'd try because look at her. I was being a little possessive, I couldn't help it, but she's mine and any other man can fuck right off. Do I trust her? Fuck yes. Do I trust men? Fuck no. Whenever there's a pretty woman about, men turn stupid, and if anyone tried to touch her inappropriately, like that amazing round ass of hers, I'd want to murder them with my bare hands.

"Thanks," she says, ducking her head. "Aren't you going to eat something?"

"I'll eat after," I say, getting back into bed. I kind of just want to lie here with her for a bit. I'm not hungry yet, but I can't let her go hungry. I want her to come back here. I hear noise in the kitchen and know that the men must be awake.

I hear Talon yell, "Where's my breakfast?" then, "Have you ever seen him make breakfast before?"

I hear Ronan say, "Nope." And make a whipping noise.

Vinnie starts laughing, then calls out, "I'd ask his woman to cook for us, but I don't want to get shot."

More laughter.

I glance up at Jo to see how she's taking this, but she just looks amused.

"I should go out there with my gun just to teach them a lesson," she says, smirking and eating another piece of bacon before starting on the pancakes. "So you don't make breakfast for all your women then?"

If only she knew.

"Only for you. And I've never had another woman in this bed, Jo," I say, lying back and just watching her. "I don't think you understand just how different you are for me."

She stops chewing and lowers her hand. "You're different for me too, Ranger. I'm in a biker clubhouse right now. I don't think I've let that sink in. Before you, the only time I'd be here would be if we were doing a raid." She pauses, then adds, "I don't know where the boundary line is, but it's been crossed. I told my partner about us and he's not happy at all. I hope he'll get over it soon though."

I hate that her partner is giving her shit because of me.

"Do you want me to talk to him?" I offer, flashing my teeth. "Say the word, babe."

"No, I'll handle it," she says, her tone final. "It's between Travis and me. He heard things about your MC, about raids here, and how Arrow was put behind bars. He's not taking all of it very well, having me associated with all of that."

I bite my tongue and let her have that. It's her work, her career, and her relationship with her partner, and I know she's a strong woman who values her independence. It's hard to step back and watch when you care about someone though, sometimes you just want to fix everything for them.

She finishes eating and then we spoon for a little bit, and eventually fall back asleep.

Best fuckin' morning ever.

THIRTY-THREE

Three Weeks Later

USE the key Jo gave me to let myself into her house. She's running late, so I make myself at home, grabbing a drink from the fridge and sitting in front of her TV. When she comes home she closes the door behind her and rushes at me, jumping on my lap and wrapping her arms around me.

"I missed you," she says, kissing me.

"Same," I say, smiling. "How was your day?"

The last few weeks with her have been amazing. We've been spending almost every night together, usually here but sometimes at the clubhouse, and Elizabeth just started dating someone else. It almost seems like everything is going to work out for us just fine, like we pulled this feat off. Everyone said it wouldn't work, and we're proving them wrong.

"It was okay," she says, burying her face into my neck. "Next week I have all night shifts, so we're going to have to work out when we can see each other."

I don't like the thought of her working nights. She's done it several times already, and I find myself staying up and worrying about her. I now know how the women must feel, waiting for the men to return. It fuckin' sucks. Once, I had the urge to follow her, but I didn't, because I know it would be crossing a line. Jo was a cop before she met me, and it's who she is. I need to accept it, and although I worry about her and wish I was there with her so I can protect her, I know that she's a badass in her own right. My woman is my very own superhero. At least when she's not harassing bikers.

"We'll work it out, don't worry," I say, standing with her in my arms and throwing her over my shoulder. "But right now, we're going to bed, and then I'm taking you out for dinner."

I slap her ass through her uniform pants and carry her to her bedroom.

"We're going out for dinner?" she asks as I lay her gently on the bed and start to undress her.

"Yes," I say, kneeling before her to remove her shoes. "I want to take you on a proper dinner date. It's going to be romantic as fuck."

She laughs, and I just watch her, enjoying the moment, the way her eyes light up and the upward tilt of her perfect heart-shaped lips. "Romantic as fuck? Yeah, I can imagine what your version of romance is."

"Hey, I can be romantic," I say, a little on the defensive side. "I'm on my knees right now taking off your shoes, and I'm about to stay on my knees so I can eat your pussy. That right there is modern romance."

Her eyes dance with humor. "I'm not complaining, Ranger. If you didn't treat me properly you wouldn't be sitting here right now. You're always so good to me, in and out of bed. And I try to be just as good back to you."

I kiss her as I undo the buttons on her shirt, slide it off, and then lay her back on the mattress as I work on her pants next. Taking her panties with them, I push them down her legs, leaving her in nothing but her red bra. Gently spreading her thighs, I get straight to business. I love going down on her. Her taste and the sounds she makes drive me insane. I love it when she squirms because the pleasure is too intense, lifting her hips and so restless in her desire that I have to pin her body down so I can continue to please her. She loves it, I know she does, and so do I. It's satisfying to pleasure a woman, but to pleasure *your* woman, that's something else entirely. Jo will never be left wanting, I will always take care of *all* her needs—financial, sexual, and emotional—everything. I'll be everything to her.

"You're perfect to me," I tell her before I lower my mouth to her.

She moans and says fuck under her breath just as my tongue touches her clit.

"You look stunning," I tell her as I sit opposite her. She's in all black, jeans, and something she tells me is called a crop, which is a tight black top that shows off her toned stomach. She looks fuckin' hot, and if anyone saw her they would never guess she's a cop.

"Thank you," she says, color hitting her cheeks. She looks down at the menu. "What are you going to get?"

I haven't even looked at the menu yet, so I pick it up and glance over it. "Probably the steak. How about you?"

"Maybe the chicken," she says, taking a sip from her glass of water. "Creamy chicken with mashed potatoes and asparagus. Sounds perfect."

The waiter comes and takes our order and then we're left to our own company again.

"Faye wants to take you out for lunch sometime," I tell her, smirking. "I told her I'd ask you, but you don't have to if you don't want to. She can be a bit much."

She laughs softly. "I know. But I don't mind. I've already met her, so I know what she's like."

"Next all the women will want to meet you," I tell her, cringing. "I don't think they'll be as nosy as Faye though."

"I can handle them."

"I have no doubt," I say, leaning back in my seat, eyes on her. "I know you can handle anything, babe."

My cock included.

We enjoy our dinner with a glass of wine. I pay—she complains, but I don't care, because there is no way she's paying for anything. We walk back to my bike hand in hand, where I kiss her deeply, my hand on her nape, her ass pressed into my Harley.

And that's when everything goes to shit.

"Cam?"

I hear the voice behind me and I still. I know that voice, and no one else calls me Cam, and basically, right now we're fucked. Jo has frozen in front of me too. My lips are still on hers, so I pull my face away and look down into hers. Her eyes are filled with dread. We've been pretending this situation doesn't really exist, but it looks like we're going to be confronted with everything right now. Jo is scared because she doesn't want to hurt Elizabeth, but the reason I'm scared is for a whole different reason.

It's not Elizabeth I'm afraid of hurting.

It's Jo.

I turn around and face Elizabeth, who is standing with the guy she's seeing. Jo steps out from behind me, and I can tell the second Elizabeth sees her.

"Jo?" she says, confusion laced in her tone. She looks between us, then her eyes widen in realization. "Are you fucking kidding me right now? *She's* who you've been seeing, Cam?"

"Elizabeth wait, we can explain," Jo says, stepping forward, her arm outstretched.

Elizabeth's face is etched with pain. She glances at me and smirks before she sneers, "So my cousin is fucking the guy who took my virginity behind my back. Isn't this just gold? I hope the two of you are very happy together."

She then storms off, dragging her guy with her, leaving behind the wreckage of her words.

"What did she just say?" Jo says after we watch Elizabeth disappear. "You took her virginity? What happened to *just friends*, Ranger?"

This is the thing I never wanted Jo to know, and I was hoping Elizabeth wouldn't say anything, but I should have known better. I've fucked up. I should have told Jo the truth from the start, before we got in too deep—trust me, I know—but I didn't want to lose her. She was already so unsure, and felt so guilty about what was growing between us, how was I meant to tell her that all those years ago, Elizabeth admitted to me that she was a virgin and told me she wanted me to be her first? We got drunk one night, and I ended up saying yes. How the fuck can I explain this? How did I know that years from then, I'd meet the love of my life and she'd be related to Elizabeth? I now know that I was meant to meet Elizabeth, and she was meant to be in my life because she was meant to bring Jo into my life.

If I was a romantic man, I'd say she's my soul mate.

So yeah, I fuckin' omitted some shit because I didn't want to lose that. I was scared. I am scared. And now that the truth is out, I just have to hope that I'm under her skin enough that she'll forgive me.

"We were never anything more than friends," I tell her in a calm voice, glancing around. "Come on, Jo. Let's go home and talk about this."

"Home?" she asks, looking at me like I've lost my mind. "Ranger, you lied to me! What do you expect me to do with this? You should have told me the truth. What else have you lied about?"

"Nothing," I say, trying to touch her arm, but she moves away. "I haven't lied about anything, Jo. Yes, I omitted the fact that once, many years ago, we slept together, but it meant nothing!"

"Maybe to you it meant nothing," she says, eyes flashing with hurt and disbelief. "But it obviously did to her. The fact remains that you lied, Ranger. You knew this would hurt me, and you purposely chose to keep me in the dark about it."

"Jo—"

"Take me home, Ranger," she demands, looking away from me.

I know she's not going to listen to me until she calms down, so I take a deep breath, and I listen to her.

I take her home.

THIRTY-FOUR

Johanna

W HEN I told him to take me home, I meant just me.

Not him.

He can leave me the hell alone right now.

"Ranger, I just want to be alone right now," I tell him, trying to push him out through my front door. "Why don't you give me some space, and we'll talk about it another time. Like when I don't want to shoot you in the nuts."

"What did I say about what happens when we fight? I'm not walking out on you this time," he says, standing there like a rock. He's so big that when I push him, he doesn't even budge. "I don't want to leave when you're angry at me. I don't want you to go to sleep angry."

"Oh, *now* you're thinking about my feelings?" I snap, losing my patience with him. "Ranger, I don't want to do this with you, not now. I just want to crawl into bed and pretend that my cousin doesn't hate me and isn't telling the whole family right now what a whore I am."

"Don't ever say that again," Ranger growls, reaching down to take my chin in his hands. "You didn't do anything wrong, you're not a fuckin' whore, and only you and I know what we have between us. They don't know, Jo. You didn't even fuckin' know about Elizabeth and me!"

He's getting angry now, and I have no idea why. There are no ramifications for him. My cousin will forgive him, but she won't forgive me. It's bullshit, but that's just how it goes. I didn't know about their history, I didn't know Ranger and Cam were the same man, or that Cam took her virginity. And when I found out, yes, I could have ended it and explained it to my cousin, but I was already in love with him.

So, yes, I was selfish.

And right now I need to deal with the consequences.

"I'm going to bed," I state, getting sick of arguing with him. "Do not join me."

I walk into my bedroom and slam the door shut, just so he gets the hint.

I go to bed, but I don't go to sleep.

I can't.

When I walk out of my bedroom in the morning, feeling like shit, I head to the kitchen to make some coffee. I feel like I've been hit by a truck, mainly because I didn't get any sleep and because I have no idea how to fix the situation I've landed myself in.

No idea.

Cup of coffee in hand, I walk into my living room and come to a stop when I see Ranger fast asleep on my couch. He stayed the night here? He looks so boyish and innocent as he sleeps with his cheek pressed against my red pillow, I can almost forget what a lying bastard he is.

Almost.

Ignoring him, I jump in the shower and start getting ready for work. I'm buttoning up my shirt when he barges into my bathroom, shirtless, coffee in his hand. "'Morning."

"Ranger what are you doing here?" I ask him, looking at him in the mirror. "Pretty sure I told you to leave last night."

"I didn't want to leave you."

I puff out a breath. "Why did you lie?"

"Because I didn't want you to look at me the way you are right now, like I'm not the same person I was yesterday," he admits, resting his coffee on my bathroom counter. He places his hands on my shoulders, running them up to the back of my neck. "I'm sorry I didn't tell you."

"Me too," I say, shrugging off his hands. "I have to go to work."

"Can we talk later tonight?" he asks, running his hand through his hair, his biceps flexing with the easy motion. "Don't even think about cutting me out, Jo."

I nod, just to get him out of my space.

He gets on his bike and I get in my car, and we go our separate ways.

"Everything okay?" Travis asks, standing by my desk. "You look like you want to kill someone."

I do.

"I'm fine," I tell him, glancing up at him. "Do we need to go on a call or something?"

"Why?" he asks, pulling out the chair next to me. "You looking for a distraction?"

"Are you my best friend now after weeks of ignoring me?" I ask, pursing my lips. "Thanks, Trav, but I'm fine. Now what's on the agenda today?"

He sighs and rests his hands on the desk. "I'm sorry, all right? I care about you, and I don't know how to deal with the fact that you're with a criminal. I've gone about it all wrong, but I'm still your friend, Jo. And if something is wrong you know you can come to me."

"I don't really want to talk about it," I admit. When his face drops, I say, "Elizabeth found out about Ranger, and now she hates me, okay? I'll have to deal with it, and I'm just a little . . . off today, but it won't affect my work, so it's fine."

"She won't talk to you?"

"I tried to call her this morning but she didn't answer, which is understandable."

"Maybe you should just give her some time to cool down. This is just temporary, Jo. It won't always be like this. Anger doesn't last forever."

"I just want her to forgive me," I admit.

I know it's not that easy, but that's the only thing that's going to make me feel better. Great, I'm making this all about me—I really am selfish. How is she feeling right now? She's probably feeling betrayed by her own blood, but she doesn't know the whole story, and she isn't going to want to hear it. I know she needs time, but it's still hard to give her that, which is probably how Ranger is feeling right now.

"She'll get over it," Travis says, placing his hand on mine.

"Even I could see how happy you've been recently, all right? As much as I hate to admit it, this guy obviously is good to you. I don't think I've seen you smile so much in the last few years as you have the last few weeks."

"Is this you coming around?" I ask, finding it ironic that this is happening on today of all days. I don't even know what I'm going to do about the whole Ranger situation. He lied, and I'm angry. No, I'm hurt. And I don't know how to forgive him.

"Yeah," he murmurs. "I guess it is."

He smiles, and I grudgingly return it.

He's not at my house when I get home, but the coffee table is covered in bouquets of flowers. There's one note in the middle.

Jo,
Forgive me,
I'll be holding my breath until you do.
I love you.

I put down the note with a sigh, taking in the beautiful red roses. I'd told him they're my favorite, and he obviously remembered. Even with the nice gesture, I'm glad that he's not here, because I want some space and he must have realized that. I try to call my cousin again, but she doesn't answer. It hurts to think that she and Helen are probably sitting there discussing me right now, and I'm trying not to think about it too much. The pain from Ranger's lie is also hitting me right in the gut, because the one thing I thought I could count on, I'm now thinking that maybe I can't. The thought of him sleeping with her . . . I know it was a long time ago. He took her fucking virginity though, no wonder she never forgot about him!

You always remember your first.

And he kept that very important fact from me. How did he think that was okay? Did he think it would never come out? He made me look stupid, left me in the dark, and the bottom line is that he lied. On purpose.

How do I trust him now?

THIRTY-FIVE

Ranger

I WAIT and hope that the flowers make her reach out to me, but they don't. I'm trying to give her a little bit of space tonight, but it's not easy. All I want is to go to her house and demand that she forgive me. When Faye walks into the clubhouse with Asher on her hip, she looks at me and grins. "Haven't seen you in a while."

I hold my hand out and she passes me the baby. "I've been busy."

"Doing what? Or should I say who?"

"If I ask you something, will you promise to never bring it up ever again?" I ask, rocking Asher in my arms as Faye rummages through the cupboards, looking for ingredients.

"Of course. What's up?" she says, pausing and giving me her attention.

"If Sin hypothetically fucked up somehow, how could he make it up to you so that you forgive him quickly and without holding a grudge?" I ask, looking at Asher's face instead of hers.

"Wait a minute, has Sin actually done something? Because I will kill him. Or is it you who's fucked up and wants me to help you fix it?"

"The latter," I admit, cringing. "I kind of omitted something to Jo. She found out. She's pissed. How do I fix this so I'm back in her bed by tonight? And I've already tried flowers."

"So you lied," Faye states, slamming a cupboard harder than necessary. "What did you lie about, Ranger?"

"Nothing you need to know. Can you help me fix it or not?" I ask, not wanting to tell her about my taking Elizabeth's virginity. No one else needs to know that.

"So you lied and sent flowers? Lying is a hard thing to overcome. I think you need to prove that you won't lie again and that you can be trusted. Honesty is everything, Ranger. Lying is a hard thing for someone to forgive," she says, scanning my face. "I wouldn't take you for a liar, Ranger."

"I'm not," I growl, narrowing my gaze on her. "I didn't want to hurt her, so I kept something from her. She found out and now I have to deal with the consequences."

"You didn't want to hurt her or you didn't want to hurt your chances with her?" she asks, sitting up on the counter.

"Both," I admit, passing Asher back to her as he starts crying.

"I don't know, Ranger," she says, tilting her head to the side, her long hair touching the table. "I think you need to have a good talk, an honest one, where you tell her why you did it and why you can guarantee you won't do it again, along with a nice apology gesture."

"Yeah, okay," I say, racking my brain.

"There's something I need to admit to you."

I look to her, watching as she rocks Asher from side to side. "What?"

She takes a deep breath, then blurts out, "The reason I took Elizabeth's case was that I already knew Jo was her cousin and I was going to ask her for a favor."

I blink. "You're ice-cold, you know that? And I hope you know you're not asking her for shit."

There's no way I'd allow it. Faye can sort her shit out without bringing my woman into it.

"I know," Faye says, smirking. "Trust me, I know. I just wanted to come clean about it. I wanted her to help me with a case I'm working on. She was the cop on call that night."

"And you wanted her to what . . . lie about what she saw?" I guess, narrowing my eyes on her.

She shrugs but doesn't elaborate.

I put my hands up. "You need to stop."

"I've already stopped," she says, lifting up her chin. "I like the girl, and she's yours. Family first. I'm not going to mess things up for you." She grins and adds, "Looks like you've done that all on your own."

Right, back to the task at hand. I have to get Jo to forgive me. I miss her already, and her not forgiving me isn't an option. She must be so hurt right now, and it fuckin' kills me that I contributed to it.

I need to fix things.

Now.

"What are you doing here?" Elizabeth asks as she opens the door, her expression as sour as can be expected. "You're the last person I want to see right now."

"Well that makes two of us," I say with extreme honesty.

"But we need to talk. So we can do it at the door, or you can invite me in, but either way you'll be listening to what I have to say."

She studies me for a few seconds, giving me a dirty look, but then mutters, "Whatever," and walks away, leaving the door open. I follow her inside, closing the door behind me, then join her on the couch.

"Now, I know you're pissed," I say, turning to face her. "But hear me out. The second Jo and I met, there were sparks flying. While working together to find you, we grew really close. We fell for each other. Jo only knew me as Ranger, not as Cam, so she didn't know who I was. I didn't know you had any kind of feelings for me or even thought about me for the last few years, so I didn't think it would be a big deal if I went for Jo. You and I were friends. Yes, as you kindly pointed out, we slept together once, when we were drunk and you wanted to lose your virginity to someone you trusted, but that's all it was. So please, do tell me why the fuck you're so angry and why you're acting like Jo stole your boyfriend when I was never yours to steal?"

I've decided to go with some tough love. She needs to know the truth, and there's no point babying her anymore.

"Are you serious right now?" she snaps, shaking her head. "I woke up and wanted you. Why didn't the two of you just tell me straight out you were together to save me from looking like an idiot? I'm glad Jo didn't know who you were, that makes the betrayal a little less cutting, but still, no one told me shit, and I feel stupid now. How about some honesty?"

I cringe when her words ring true. "You had just been rescued. After going through everything you did, you expect us to hit you with this too? We were waiting for the right time to tell you, which turned out to be never. And Jo feels like shit, Elizabeth. She's been questioning us the whole time, and I love her. She's the only woman for me."

"You love her?" she asks, eyes narrowing. "Truly?"

"She didn't know that we'd slept together, and now she hates me, but yes, I love her," I say, smiling sadly. "I'm sorry, Elizabeth. You know I care about you and I never want to hurt you and I'm an asshole, but Jo doesn't deserve your anger."

She sighs and buries her face in her hands. "I don't know what you want me to say, Cam. I'm sorry that she's angry at you? I can't believe you came here and spent those nights with me just because what . . . you thought I'd have a nervous breakdown if you rejected me?"

When she puts it that way, it sounds fuckin' ridiculous. "We just didn't think you needed any more pain in your life. For fuck's sake, you'd just been kidnapped and almost sold off as a slave! Can you really blame us?"

"What do you want me to do?" she asks after staying silent for a while, thinking.

"I want you to talk to Jo."

She crosses her arms over her chest, making me think she's about to say no, but then she says, "Fine."

"Really?" I ask with suspicion. "Just like that."

She sighs and says, "It sucks. I think you were both wrong for not telling me, but I don't want to stand in the way. I care about you both and if you make each other happy, then fine. I've met someone now, and he's a nice guy and treats me like a princess. It will take some time for me to get over everything, but yeah, I'll talk to her. She's family, and she saved me. I can't forget that."

"Thank you," I say, pulling her in for a hug. "Now I just have to get her to forgive me."

"Good luck," she says, smirking. "Jo holds a mean grudge."

I leave her alone for one more night before I show up at her house. I walk in and find her on the couch in nothing but a T-shirt and panties. I love her like this. No makeup, no fancy clothes, just her. She's most beautiful like this, in my opinion.

"Hey," I say, sitting down next to her. I pull her into my arms and kiss the top of her head. "I shouldn't have lied. I was wrong, and I will never lie to you again, Jo. I'm so fuckin' sorry, babe. I've tried to give you a little space, but fuck, I'm going crazy without you and I'm not ashamed to admit that."

"How do I know you're never going to lie, conceal, omit— whatever you want to call it, again? And I'm just supposed to forget that you've slept with my cousin?" she asks, sadness and resignation in her tone. "I don't know, Ranger. I was willing to do anything for you. To have people judge me at work and possibly fuck up my career, to go behind my cousin's back, to change all my rules, and you couldn't even give me honesty in return."

Her words hit me right in the chest, which has suddenly become tight, because she's right. I've really fucked up, and getting her to forgive me is going to be a lot harder than some nice gesture and sweet words. I'm going to have to get her to trust me again. I don't care what I have to do though—I'll do it all and more.

Anything to go back to how things were.

THIRTY-SIX

Johanna

WHEN Elizabeth reaches out to me, I'm nothing short of surprised. She comes over and we order a pizza and have a chat.

"Cam came to speak to me the other day," she says, wringing her hands together. "He explained what happened, how you two fell in love when you didn't know who he was to me. I wish you'd told me, Jo. Things could have ended up so differently. Yes, I would have been upset and disappointed but I wouldn't have felt betrayed. Still," she says, smiling sadly, "I shouldn't have said what I said."

"It's me who should be apologizing," I say, looking into her beautiful face. "If I knew Ranger was your Cam, I wouldn't have touched him, Elizabeth. When I found out, it was too late, and I guess I'm selfish because I couldn't give him up."

"Yet now you're still angry with him?"

"He never told me the two of you slept together," I say, awkwardly laughing. "So you weren't the only one surprised that night."

"It was years ago, and it meant nothing to him, as much as it hurts me to say. He loves you, Jo, and him admitting that is something huge. The Cam I know wouldn't let any woman get her claws into him—he never got attached and always kept the upper hand. With you though, even just the way he talks about you, it's something. So he fucked up and kept something from you. Maybe you should give him the chance to redeem himself?"

"Now you want us to be together?" I ask, wondering how she can feel this way. Maybe she's falling for the guy she's seeing, or maybe she's just not as selfish as me.

"I want you both to be happy. Cam's not mine, with or without you in the equation. I'm not going to be the reason the two of you aren't happy. Stop being stubborn and forgive the man, Jo."

"Team Ranger, hey," I grumble, taking the biggest slice of pizza and taking a bite out of it. "I don't know what to do."

"Forgive him."

"That easy, huh?" I ask, chewing and swallowing thoughtfully.

"It is if you let it be."

Those words ring in my head for the rest of the day.

I pull up at the clubhouse and wonder how I'm going to get in. I want to surprise Ranger, but I have no way of getting through their gate. Luckily for me, a woman opens it and drives through, so I quickly walk through it before it closes. She gets out of her car and quickly approaches me.

"And who the hell are you?" she asks, giving me a once-over. She's pretty, with blond hair and green eyes.

"I'm Jo. I'm looking for Ranger," I tell her. "Do you know if he's in there?"

"The cop?" the woman asks, arching a brow. "I'm Anna."

So this here is the woman in charge, then. Funny, because when I met Faye I assumed that she was the boss lady, but Ranger explained that Faye handed over the reins to a woman named Anna.

"Nice to meet you, Anna," I say, lifting my chin. "I kind of wanted to surprise him, but if he's not here or if I'm not welcome, I'll just leave."

I've never been here during the day before, and have met only a handful of the male members and Faye. Ranger has always said that I'm welcome here, but who knows. I am a police officer. It's probably not appropriate that I'm here anyway, in fact, I know that it's not, and if someone in the force wanted to give me hell over it they could.

"No, it's fine," she says, nodding toward the door. "Come on in. Everyone's been dying to get a glimpse of the woman who nabbed Ranger." She puts her hand up. "I guessed you would be a blonde."

I smile and follow behind her.

"He's probably in his room."

"Thanks, Anna," I say, heading straight to his room and opening the door without bothering to knock. I find him lying on his back, watching *Supernatural*. He sits up when he sees me, eyes widening in surprise.

"Jo?"

I lock his door, then practically jump on him.

His arms around me, he brings me against his chest and kisses my head. "Best fuckin' surprise ever."

I lift my head and look him dead in the eye. "Lie to me one more time and you will never see me again."

He swallows hard and nods once. "I'm not going to do anything to fuck this up, all right?"

I manage to get out the word *okay* before he's kissing me, rolling on top of me, and my wrists are pinned above my head. When he pulls back and says, "I didn't even get to do my big gesture," he has me curious.

"So I should have waited before coming over here?" I ask, bringing his lips back to mine. "What did I miss? I still want this so-called big gesture."

"Right now?"

"Is it something that can be given to me in bed? Because I'm all about that," I tease, kissing the stubble on his jawline.

"Oh, I'll be giving you something in bed, all right," he murmurs, kissing me again, then leaning over to his top drawer. What is he getting from there? Can it wait? I kind of want him to make love to me first, and I say as much. He tells me to wait one second and then he will take care of me. When he pulls out a velvet ring box, I still. Wait, that better not be a . . .

He opens it, exposing the most beautiful ring I have ever seen, a pear-shaped diamond on a white gold band, and says, "Jo, I love you and I want to spend the rest of my life with you. Will you marry me?"

This is his gesture? Proposing? Has he lost his ever loving mind?

I shake my head. "Ranger, no."

And that's how the next fight started—before we can even make up for the previous one.

"We don't know each other well enough to get married, Ranger. What's the rush? We're both not going anywhere," I say, disbelief pouring from my voice. "Do I want to marry you one day? Sure, maybe if we're still happy and in love then, but to propose now? And as an apology gesture? Did you come up with this yourself?"

I'm kind of hoping he didn't. I also realize I'm being a bit of a bitch right now, but I'm in shock. Who proposes to a woman after such a short time?

I cup his face in my hand. "I love you, but now isn't the time."

"If you want me, I don't see what the big deal is!" he growls, jaw tight. "I want you, and I know that's never going to change. I fuckin' love you and want you by my side. You're acting like it's the craziest thing in the world when it's not. We don't have to get married this year, it can be next year. I've never even thought about marriage before, you know that? And now I plan this romantic proposal, which I ruin by doing it now instead, and you say no?"

"Ranger," I say in a sweet voice, trying to butter him up a little bit. "I love you, and I love being with you, and I'm yours, and you are mine, but can we talk about the marriage thing a little bit later?"

His expression goes blank. "You rejected my marriage proposal. I don't know how you expect me to react to this."

"I'm not rejecting you, I'm just saying not right now," I say, wincing. Shit, I don't want to hurt him, but getting engaged is not what we need. I don't see what the rush is.

"Jo, I don't see why—"

I kiss him, wanting to shut him up. I don't know what I expected from him but a marriage proposal isn't it, and although it is the biggest of gestures, it's not the one we need. I distract him with my mouth, with my hands, with the seductive gaze that trails all over his skin. I go down on him until he comes in my mouth, and then he does the same to me. We make love, looking into each other's eyes. We tell each other we love each other, and although we still have shit to work out, all of a sudden, everything is right in the world.

THIRTY-SEVEN

Ranger

EYES darting between Jo's naked body and the door, I want to ignore the knocking, but whoever it is probably won't stop until I answer it. I cover Jo's sleeping form with my blanket, then open the door just a little bit.

"Hey," I say when I see Talon standing there.

He grins, flashing his teeth. "You going to stay in your room all day and night or are you going to come out and socialize a little? You gotta feed your woman more than just your d—"

"She's asleep," I say, cutting off his charming comment. "When she wakes up I'll bring her out to eat."

"Okay," he says cheerfully, then walks away. I close and relock the door and climb back into bed. The open ring box still sits on my side table, taunting me. I can't believe she said no. She's so stubborn. Isn't that what most women want, the ultimate commitment? Fuck, I sound like a little bitch. This hellion in my bed right now is definitely giving me a run for my money. Women are so hard to figure out sometimes. I'm glad she came over here though—I thought she was going to stay mad at me forever. I wonder if she spoke to Elizabeth and that's what brought her here. Either way, I'm thankful.

She's in my bed, where she belongs, and even though the ring is on the table and not on her finger, she's still mine. I haven't lost her, and she's forgiven me for lying about fucking her cousin. Yeah, that sentence doesn't exactly paint me in a good light. I wonder if she's one of those women who will keep throwing shit in my face, even after she says she's forgiven me. Like months from now is she going to bring it up every time we fight?

Remember the time you fucked Elizabeth and lied about it?

I really hope she isn't like that, but if she is, then I'm going to have to handle it, and her. If she fucked someone I knew, I don't think I'd take it very well, never mind someone I was related to. When she stirs I sit down on the bed, the mattress going down with my weight.

"Babe, are you hungry? We've been in bed for hours," I say, kissing her forehead. "I need to feed you."

"Hmmm," she hums, opening her eyes. "What are we going to eat?"

"I don't know, but everyone is waiting to see you out there," I warn her. "There's probably food in the kitchen, otherwise I'll take you out to get something."

"Who is here?" she asks, sitting up and rubbing her eyes. "I met Anna, she's the one who let me in the gate. Are all the women here gorgeous?"

"Pretty much," I say, shrugging. "I don't know—I don't see them like that."

"Really?" she asks, eyes flaring. "I don't even swing that way and I've checked out both Anna and Faye."

I lift the sheets off her and pull her out of bed. "Well, you can see who else is here. What do you want to bet Anna called all the women?"

Jo rolls her eyes and stands up. "So, what, it's let's-all-stare-at-the-cop day? Are they going to give me shit? Never mind, don't answer that. Either way, I'll handle it." She goes into my bathroom and washes her face, squares her shoulders, then says, "Okay, let's do this."

I grin and lead her straight to the kitchen, because I'm starving. Like I'd guessed, almost all of the women are in the kitchen, with the exception of Tina, Anna, and Faye.

"Oh, look who's here!" Tia says, smiling widely. "What a lovely surprise."

I glance around the room, expression blank. "Anna called you, didn't she?"

Lana takes off her glasses and smiles at Jo, then at me. "She may have sent a group text."

I sigh. "Everyone, this is Jo. Jo, these are the Wind Dragon women."

I point and tell her the names of each woman. Jo says hi to each one, smiling amiably.

"There's spaghetti," Tia says to me while she pulls out a chair. "Jo, why don't you sit with us while Ranger sorts you out?"

Jo takes a seat and I start serving the two of us.

"You're so pretty," I hear Shayla blurt out. "It's nice to finally meet you, Jo."

"You too," Jo replies, and I can hear the smile in her voice. "It's nice to put faces to the names."

"What's Ranger been saying about us?" Tia asks, making a *tsk-tsk* noise. "I can only imagine what you've heard. We're not that bad, promise."

"Although she probably likes bad," Bailey throws out.

"Yeah, bad at beer pong," Lana adds, laughing.

Fuck, I'm never going to live that down.

"I heard about that," Jo says to Lana. "Talon told me. I think we should have a rematch."

I'm going to have to kill my old Wild Men president, and I'm totally fine with that.

"When, tonight?" Tia asks, sounding interested. "Getting drunk on a weekday, isn't that spontaneous. I wonder if Talon will stay with Rhett so I can get in on this."

I approach the table and set down a bowl and fork in front of Jo. "Do you want anything with it? Parmesan cheese?"

"No, I'm good, thank you," she says, picking up her fork. "I'll save room for all the beer I'll be drinking soon."

"So, we're having a beer pong match on a weeknight, against a cop and a former enemy turned family member?" Lana asks, eyebrows hitting her hairline. "Our lives are definitely interesting. Who's going to play? We only need two."

"Me!" Tia says, waving her pink-tipped fingernails in the air. "I nominate myself." She looks around the table. "Who is joining me? Shayla? What say you?"

Shayla looks to Lana, who shakes her head. "You go ahead, Shay. I think I'm going to enjoy this from the sidelines."

"You scared, Shay?" I taunt, sitting next to Jo and digging in. "I won't lose a second time. Tell Vinnie to expect you home very drunk."

And getting Tia drunk can be my 'payback' to Talon for doing the same to Jo that night at the bar.

"We'll see about that, Ranger," Shayla boasts, lifting her chin. "Eat. You're going to need a full stomach."

These women.

All I know is I better not lose this time.

Everyone comes for the event, like it's a birthday, not a midweek beer pong game. The kids are all here too, but they're playing outside while we're in the game room. The red cups are lined up, and everyone is waiting to begin.

"Have you played before?" I ask Jo, not knowing how much she partied in the past. I probably should have asked her these things. But then, she's the one who started this whole thing, so she probably deserves to get intoxicated tonight.

She nods, giving me an amused glance. "I haven't been living under a rock, you know."

"Ladies first," I tell her, giving her the opening shot.

She throws the white ball but misses all the cups. She throws overarm, which I think looks weird, I prefer the underarm technique.

"Nice try, babe," I tell her, trying to curb my competitive streak and be encouraging.

Tia goes next and also misses. "Dammit!"

I get my shot in, and Shayla drinks the cup, everyone cheering as she finishes it. Shayla misses her shot, and I taunt her for a bit, enjoying annoying the shit out of her.

"Maybe next time, Shay."

"Shut up, Ranger!" she calls, poking her tongue out at me. "You haven't won yet."

This game really brings out the immaturity in everyone.

"I'm not losing." I look to Jo, then smirk at Talon. "I have a better partner this time."

Talon picks up a candle off a table and fuckin' throws it at me, but I duck and it smashes against the wall. See what I mean about the immaturity thing?

"I'm an excellent beer pong buddy! Not our fault Bailey and Anna are fuckin' sharks," he calls out, and I actually agree with him on that one. Bailey is sweet as pie, so no one ever suspects her, but you need to remember who her company is. Any girl who is best friends with Anna can't be sweet.

When Jo plays her next shot, she gets it in, and I've never been so proud. I lift her in the air and cheer as Tia chugs down the cup. Speaking of the devil, Anna arrives and smirks, approaching the table. "Well, isn't this déjà vu."

"Not going to lose this time, Anna."

"That's because I'm not playing," she says, a smug look on her face. "And because Bailey's not here. Convenient how both of us aren't here while this is going on!"

I throw a Ping-Pong ball at her. "Call Bailey. After I win this game, Talon and I will happily take you both on."

I hear Talon groan, but I ignore it. He's in this too, and Anna isn't going to shut up until she's taken down a notch. I only hope she doesn't open her mouth about my kidnapping her in front of Jo, because that will open up a shit storm and I really don't have any way of talking myself out of that one.

Fuck. I really should have thought this through before bringing her here. Damn Anna and her lifelong grudge! What's a little kidnapping among enemies turned friends?

"All right, I'll call her now," she says, sliding her phone from her jean pocket.

In the meantime, the game goes on until we have one cup left, while they have three.

So we need only one shot to win.

And it's Jo's turn.

Everyone is watching, and the pressure is on. If she gets this in, I'm going to go down on her for an hour tonight. Who am I kidding? I'm going to do that anyway.

She throws the ball and it seems to spin through the air in slow motion as it plops gracefully into their last cup.

When she gets it in, I'm so fuckin' happy, I take her into my arms and kiss the shit out of her. Everyone cheers, except Tia and Shay I imagine, while I dip her backward and congratulate her with my lips, a promise of what's to come later tonight when we're alone.

Bailey comes to the clubhouse just for the rematch.

"Bailey, this is Jo," I say, arm around my woman. "Jo, this is Bailey. Don't be fooled by her sweet demeanor."

Bailey rolls her eyes and hugs Jo. "Welcome to the family, Jo. We should get to know each other a little after I kick your man's ass."

"Told you," I mouth to Jo, who starts laughing and takes a seat next to Shay to watch the game.

Talon looks at me, amusement dancing in his green eyes. "Brother, if we don't win this we'll never be able to show our face here again."

Dramatic, but true.

"We're just going to have to win it, then, won't we?"

"Not all of us have been practicing," he says so only I can hear.

"I can carry us," I say, slapping him on the back. "I've got this."

I play the first shot and miss on purpose. Let them think they've got this. We got hustled, and now it's their turn.

Every shot after that, I get in.

And when I take the winning shot, I look Anna right in the eye, and I smile.

Lucky for me, she doesn't use the kidnapping against me in front of Jo, for which I'm grateful. I even give her a kiss on the cheek. "Good game, Anna."

She rolls her eyes, but I don't miss the quirk of her lips.

What a damn good night.

THIRTY-EIGHT

Johanna

Two months later

"REMEMBER that time I proposed to you and you said no?" Ranger says when we walk through the door of my house.

I laugh, my body shaking. "You're not going to let that go, are you? Where have you been?"

"I had to drop by a few of the businesses and do some accounting stuff," he says, stepping behind me as I wash the dishes and kissing the side of my neck. "Then I came straight here. I've missed you today, and I was thinking about something."

"What?" I ask, turning off the tap and spinning around.

"Do you like this house? As in do you want us to live here, or should I buy us a new house?"

My eyes widen. "How is this a casual conversation for you? And since when are we moving in together?"

We practically live together anyway, so I understand his train of thought, but his asking if he can buy us a house is not a normal conversation. It wasn't even "Should we buy a house together," he just asked if *he* can buy us a new house. Am I a kept woman now?

"We sleep together pretty much every night and I have a key to your house. How is that not already living together?" he asks, raising a brow. "I don't have time for your commitment issues, Jo. If you want the milk, buy the cow."

I burst out laughing at that, and glance around my house, considering. "I do love this house, but it's not very big. What do you think, Ranger? I just want to be wherever you are."

"And I just want to make you happy."

"You do," I whisper.

I don't remember ever being this happy before. Everything in my life is going well, and I'm in a place I never thought I'd be. I'm in love. I have a man who will do anything to make me smile, and keeps me satisfied in every way. I have a house, a good job, friends, and family. I'm a lucky woman.

"Maybe we could get a new house and rent this one out," I suggest, then add, "We're going to need room for any possible children we have."

His eyes dash to me, widening. "You think you're having kids without us being fuckin' married? What? You gonna give them hyphenated names and shit? I think not, Jo. Nice try, but my good genes come with a ball and chain."

I smile, step forward, and rest my head on him. "You really want me to marry you that much, Ranger?" I ask him. "It's that important to you?"

"Yeah," he admits. "I don't know why, but it is. And I've never even considered marriage before; I just want it with you. I want you to be mine in every way, even the traditional ones."

I smile and peep up at him. "Okay, Ranger. I'll marry you."

He lifts me into the air, kisses my lips, then takes me to the bedroom and shows me just what I'm signing up for.

And trust me, I'm not complaining.

We're still in our post-lovemaking daze when Ranger gets a call from Arrow.

"What?" he growls, sitting up. "What happened?"

I sit up, alert.

He glances at me as he continues to speak. "She's with me. Okay, I'll be there now."

He hangs up, throws his phone on the side table, and jumps out of bed. I can't help but stare at his naked body as he picks up his pants from the floor.

"What happened?" I ask, lifting the sheets up. "Is everything okay?"

"Cops raided the MC," he says, getting dressed. "They didn't find anything. Thank fuck they didn't find any of the weapons."

What the hell? I have to wonder why I wasn't told about this, or at least had any idea it was taking place. Did Travis not tell me on purpose? Did they have a reason for the raid?

I cringe, ignoring his mention of weapons, and also start to get dressed. "Ranger, I had no idea they were going to do this."

I know I don't have to explain myself, but I don't want him to think I knew and didn't tell him. It's a fine line, and if I did know I don't know what I would do anyway.

"I know, Jo," he says, softening his tone. "It's okay. Arrow just wants me to go in because he's calling a club meeting."

"Do you want me to come?" I ask him, not sure what to do here.

"No, babe," he says, walking over to me and kissing my forehead. "I'll be back as soon as I can."

Right, it's not like I'd be welcome to a club meeting, but I feel a little helpless right now and unsure what to do.

Did Arrow ask where I was to see if I knew about what was going down? Is the club meeting about me? What if they don't want me to be with Ranger anymore?

Should I go to the station and ask what happened? Or will that make me look like I'm siding with the MC? I can't win here. It's a conflict of interest, and I can't choose either side. I'm stuck in the middle. I want Ranger to be able to trust me, and I want to know what's going on in his life, but at the same time I can't know too much, because if I'm asked . . .

Is it possible to be a good cop and a good girlfriend to a biker?

I don't know how, but I need to make it work. I want both, and I need to make it so I can have both. Can't I just be Switzerland? Neutral ground? Even I'm not so naïve as to think so. Shit is going to blow up, it's just a matter of time, and I don't know how I'm going to handle it. Being a cop is who I am, but Ranger . . . Ranger is who I love.

I slide back into bed and wonder what the hell is happening right now.

"Never thought I'd be having lunch with a cop who's dating one of the Wind Dragon men," Faye says, the beauty in her smile almost blinding. "But I like you, Jo. To be honest, I was kind of worried about Ranger before you came into his life."

"What do you mean?" I ask her as I take a bite of my chicken salad.

She tilts her head to the side, then explains. "He was restless becoming a Wind Dragon. It's like he felt like he didn't fit in or something, although I tried everything to make sure he felt like he did. I gave him your cousin's case to distract him. I thought he was going to leave us, and I didn't want him to."

"He loves being a part of that lifestyle though."

"He does," she says, nodding. "But it was a big change. When you're with a club, you become so loyal to them. He was loyal to the Wild Men. So was Talon, but his loyalty changed to Tia, and he already had ties to the Wind Dragons, so it was an easy transition for him. Ranger had only Talon, and he knew Shayla; I think that was it."

"So it was like a whole new life. New people, new environment, and new loyalties?"

"Exactly," she says, nodding. "Also a very different biker lifestyle. More family environment, less drugs and alcohol, less club whores, et cetera. All the men have settled down now. So maybe that made him feel left out, I don't know. He's a good man though, and I'm glad he found someone worthy of him who makes him happy."

"He is a good man," I agree, then broach the topic I want to ask her about. "I didn't know anything about the raid, you know."

"I know," Faye says, studying me. "It's going to be hard to keep your work separate from Ranger, but you can do it. Ranger told us you had nothing to do with it, and we believe him, and you. Nothing happened anyway. They were looking for something but found nothing. I also think that if they did find something they'd have tried to drag you down with us."

I never thought about it that way, but she's probably right. Shit.

"There's something I need to admit to you," Faye says, cringing.

I look at her expectantly, waiting for her to continue.

"There's a reason I took Elizabeth's case," she says, shifting on her chair. "Ranger asked me once why I chose to help with finding her, and I didn't tell him the whole truth then."

"What's the reason?" I ask, brow furrowing.

"I kind of told Ranger I wouldn't bring it up, but I was going to ask you a favor," she says, clearing her throat. "I didn't know that you and Ranger would end up all in love and shit, but I'm glad you did, and I just want to say that I'm sorry. I won't ask anything from you, and I feel a little guilty that I was going to." She smiles and takes a deep breath. "Okay, well, I feel better now, how about you?"

I open my mouth to ask what her original plan was, but then decide against it. I have a feeling that I don't want to know, and if I change my mind I'm sure Ranger can enlighten me. So I ask her something that has been bothering me instead. "I have a question for you."

"Shoot."

"How do you keep everything separate? Being in the MC plus your work with the feds—it must be hard to juggle the two?" I ask, hoping she can give me some advice.

She looks at me and sighs. "Since Sin stepped down as president, it's actually a lot easier for me. I don't have to worry about

what everyone is doing anymore, although I still do. It's hard
to step down from a role that I've played for years, plus it's just
me—I'm a caring and thoughtful person. But now with Anna
handling everything, when I go to work, it's work. No one
throws being a biker in my face, they know I'm good at what
I do. Yes, I'm a lawyer, but I'm so much more. I'm well connected, I can defend myself and others, and I'm smart. I'm an
asset. They treat me as such. My family comes first, always, so if
they call me or need me, I'm there. I think it would be harder in
your position as a police officer than it is for me, a lawyer."

"So, basically, I'm screwed?" I groan, covering my face with
my hands. "I don't know how this is going to turn out."

"Whatever happens, you will handle it," she says with such
confidence that even I believe her.

"Ranger wants us to move in together," I say, changing the
subject, since I still don't know what the right thing to do is.

"Oooh, housewarming party!" Faye beams. "If you need any
help moving or decorating or looking for a house, basically if
you need any help at all, you have my number."

"How do you have so much time on your hands with two
kids, a husband, and working with the feds?" I ask, shaking my
head. "You're Wonder Woman."

"That's only half of it," she says with a wink. "I like to stay
busy, and I like to make sure I can take care of my extended
family, but I also like to help others. I'm blessed; not everyone
is. If I can help in some way, I will."

Asher stirs in his little carrier thing, so Faye picks him up
and taps his back gently as he rests on her chest. "I'm glad you
two sorted out the whole Elizabeth thing. Now, that was some
drama."

My lip twitches. "That's an understatement. She's really liking her boyfriend, so I think that is helping her move on, you know? And she's forgiven me, which I'm grateful for. She could have chosen to be bitter and hold a grudge."

"You didn't do anything that bad," Faye says, sniffing. "Don't be so hard on yourself. Love doesn't come easy—there's always a war, or a battle, but it makes you appreciate it more."

I wonder what her battle was.

"I don't think my cousin shares your thoughts," I utter, then change the subject again. "So you know a lot about houses and interior decorating, then?"

Faye nods. "Yep. What do you have in mind? Oh, you should buy a house near mine! That would be so cool. Are you more of a country or modern woman?"

"Modern," I say, watching Asher as he falls back asleep. "I don't know what Ranger has in mind, but he said he wants to go see some houses next week."

"This is so exciting! A cop and a biker shacking up. A police car parked next to a Harley. The forbidden love story writes itself."

I laugh, but the truth is, our love *is* forbidden.

And our battle isn't over yet.

I walk out of the police station, fuming, and get into my car. When I was called in for a chat with the chief, I had no idea it would be about my personal life. Everything has finally caught up to me; everything Travis warned me about is coming true. Apparently a woman of the law should not be fraternizing with an MC gang, and as such, I need to cease all contact with them if I want to keep my job. Also—an investigation into my activities may be taken. I wanted to tell her it's not a gang, it's a club, but I don't think that would have been appreciated. The chief, who was once my ally, the woman who I've known for years, now tells me that I can lose my job just for falling in love. It was hard to hear it, even harder to hear it from her.

I haven't done anything illegal, and it really sucks that this is happening to me. I'm a good cop—I love my job and I'm good at it, but I guess I can see it from her perspective too. I just don't know what to do now. Sure, I could stay away from the clubhouse, but there's no way I can stay away from Ranger.

Shit.

I head home and give myself a little bit of time to lie in bed and feel sorry for myself. I send Ranger a message that says we need to talk, so I'm not surprised when he shows up not an hour later at my house.

"What's wrong?" he asks as he walks into my bedroom. "Are you okay?"

"I don't know," I answer honestly, glancing up at him. "I don't know how we thought this would be okay, that I could be with a biker and be a cop at the same time. We got away with it up until now, I guess."

"Tell me everything," he demands, sitting down and gently stroking my hair. "Who do I need to kill?"

I throw my hands up in the air. "See! You can't say shit like that. I don't even know if you're joking or not."

I feel like crying, and that's just not me.

I have to choose—my career or Ranger.

THIRTY-NINE

Ranger

'M not joking.

"And unless you're going to kill the whole police station, nothing else can save me."

"Babe, tell me what happened. I can't fix it if I don't know," I say, wondering what has happened. I can guess, but I want to know the whole story. Whoever is giving her shit will pay. She hasn't done anything wrong, has never crossed the line by doing something that goes against her ethics or morals, except love me. And that shouldn't be a crime.

It can't be.

She tells me everything that was said in her meeting, and I listen, already forming a plan in my head. She's right: we were naïve to think there would be no repercussions from our union. Of course they wouldn't want a cop with a biker. I don't want her to lose her career, her identity, and then resent me forever after that, and I don't want Jo to have to change who she is; I would never expect her to.

"I don't know what to do, Ranger," she admits, sitting up

and shuffling back against the headboard. "And don't you dare say I don't need to work, you know how much I love my job."

"I know," I tell her, my hand on her bare knee. "And I want you to keep it because I know that it's a part of you."

She hasn't said that we shouldn't be together yet, which means running isn't on her mind. I hope she's not thinking it though. There has to be an alternative, but I can only think of one option.

The thing is—I'd do anything for this woman, and I'd never regret it. I look at the ring on her finger. This woman is going to be my wife. She's all in, and so am I.

"I'm going to fix this," I tell her, standing up. "And no, not by killing anyone."

"What are you going to do?" she asks in suspicion. "I'll just stay away from the clubhouse is all. They can investigate all they want, I don't have anything to hide. Sure, it will be annoying, but once they figure that out I'm sure they'll leave me alone."

I don't think it's going to be that easy. They have something over her now, and they might even try to use her to take the Wind Dragons down. I won't put her in that position. Not that the Wind Dragons do any illegal shit like the Wild Men did, so really we don't have anything to hide.

"Do you trust me?" I ask her.

"You're quoting *Aladdin*," she says, but then adds, "Of course I trust you, Ranger."

I love being a biker, and being in an MC. The Wild Men were my family, and now the Wind Dragons are my family, and they always will be.

But they don't need me.

Jo is the most important person in the world to me, and I

only see one way out of this. It's not like I haven't been thinking about this for a while anyway, but my plan was to go nomad, not to quit the lifestyle and settle down. I don't think anyone saw that coming, myself included, but here we are.

My first thought: Talon isn't going to take this very well.

"Have you lost your fuckin' mind?" Talon yells, pacing up and down the patio. "No, Ranger. I can't let you do this. We're your family, your brothers, you can't give up on an MC you never gave a real chance to."

"I second that," Faye says, her eyes filled with sadness. "If I knew she was going to take you away from us, I would have taken her out."

"Faye," I growl, but she just stares at me defiantly. "She doesn't even know I plan on doing this, so don't blame her."

"So you're leaving the MC voluntarily? That makes it so much worse," she says, sniffing. "I know I haven't known you long, Ranger, but you've become one of the brothers. I care about you. Stop being selfish. I can fix this. I'll talk to the feds, ask them to handle it or something, I don't know."

"What are they going to do? Put out a new law that cops can fuck bikers without any repercussions?"

"Ranger, you're my brother. I fuckin' love you. Don't make a decision you're going to regret," Talon says, stopping in front of me.

"It's not like I'm not going to see all of you!" I tell them, scrubbing a hand down my face. "You're still my family, and always will be. Sin and Faye stepped down, and they're always still around. It's going to be the same thing. When I joined, I felt like something was missing here, but that something was Jo. Just because I hand in my cut doesn't mean we aren't still a family, okay? It's not like that. I'm not going anywhere. Fuck, Faye, we're looking for a house right near yours! We'll be fuckin' neighbors—get that sad look off your face because I can't deal with it!"

I didn't know how much she'd grown on me until this very moment. She's just always been here for me, every time I needed someone to talk to, and even when I didn't think I wanted anyone to talk to. "And, Talon, you're my brother. My best friend. We've been through hell and back together. If you think I'm going to turn my back on you, then you don't know me as well as I thought you did."

His green eyes fill with pain, and it hurts me to know I'm the cause of it. "You're serious about this."

I nod and repeat, "I'm still going to be here, Talon."

"Fuck," he grits out, looking to Faye, who simply shrugs.

"It sucks but it makes sense, Talon," she says, tapping her fingers on the chair arm. "When are you going to tell Arrow? Make it final?"

"As soon as I see him," I say, rubbing the back of my neck. "I'll hand in my cut tonight."

Talon shakes his head and storms off angrily. We both watch him, then turn to each other. "I don't want to hurt anyone."

"He'll come around," she says, smiling sadly. "Especially when he sees that you'll still be in his life. He's probably just hurt. We'll miss you around here. But maybe one day you'll be back."

I look around, my gaze stopping on the playground. Will my kids ever get to play here?

"You never know," I tell her.

She comes over to me and kisses my cheek. "I'm always here for you if you need me, Ranger."

"Right back at you, Faye."

She heads inside and I'm left with the image of Talon's pain in my head. I know he will come around, and accept my decision, but it's still hard. He was once my president, but he was always my friend. I'm all he has left of the Wild Men, of the legacy his stepfather left for him, and I wonder if that has something to do with it. He's happy here though, I can see that so clearly, and he needs to let me go so I can be happy too.

I've made my decision.

Now I just have to tell Arrow to make it official.

"Are you sure?" Arrow asks, stroking his beard. "We can try something to make it work, Ranger."

"I'm sure," I say, looking him in the eye.

He's silent for a few moments but then nods. "You do what you have to do, but I'll be sad to see you leave. You're a good man."

"It hasn't been an easy decision," I admit to him. "Kind of terrifying really, but I'll still be around, you know. Just not a part of the MC." I place my cut on the table. "I'll have my stuff moved out by tonight."

This is hard. Seeing everyone sad to see me go is very difficult for me. I had no idea they all cared so much, but I should have. It's in the way the women look after me, in the way the men treat me. Sure, I haven't known them as long as some, but they still saw me as a brother. I don't think it was them, it was me.

Something was missing here; I just felt like I couldn't find my place. But what if it was me? What if I didn't try hard enough? I don't like change much, and following Talon to the Wind Dragons was definitely a big change. I don't regret it though. The Wind Dragons are better than the Wild Men could ever be. A family unit. A force to be reckoned with. No one can touch the Wind Dragons without getting burned, without making enemies for life. And yet, they're some of the kindest people I've ever known. Fuck, now I'm starting to feel emotional, but I mask it. No one needs to see that, especially not my president.

I stand up and walk to the door when he calls my name. "Yes?"

He studies me, then says, "You ever want back in, you're in, you got it?"

My eyes widen at the offer, one I never expected on receiving. I nod and leave the room, closing the door behind me.

FORTY

"YOU did what?" Jo yells, her face going pale. "Are you crazy? Those people are your family, that is your life. I'd never ask you to give that up!"

"You didn't have to," I say calmly, watching her pace and rant in a similar way that Talon did. Jeez, there's just no pleasing anyone these days, is there?

"What if you regret this, Ranger?" she asks, looking on the verge of tears. "What if you start hating me because it's my fault you lost all of it? How am I supposed to live with that? You love everyone in the MC. Talon and Faye are going to hate me!"

"I made this choice alone," I tell her, crooking my finger for her to approach. "It's not on you; it's on me. You didn't ask this of me, and I know that you wouldn't. I'd never regret choosing you, Jo, and I'd never blame you for my decisions. I don't want you to have to give up your job and life because of things I've done in my past. The Wind Dragons aren't going anywhere. I'll still see them, they're still my family, I just won't be an official member, nor will I know whatever shit is going on with the club. I still get to see them, I still get to ride my bike, and you get to keep your job. Where's the downside in this?"

"Well, when you put it like that," she mutters, dropping down onto my lap. "Are you sure though, Ranger? If you're doing this just for me, please don't. I wouldn't want you to. It's too much to give up."

"I'm sure," I assure her, burying my face in the crook of her neck. "I've decided: it's done with, all right? Maybe now I can use one of my degrees and get a real job."

"That's your plan?" she asks, cupping my cheek with her palm. "You're not going to be a man of leisure? I know you have enough money to do that if you want to."

"I don't like not working," I say. "I was kept busy with the accounts at the club, but now I'll find something new. I don't usually like change, but I feel like this will be a good change. If my mom was alive, she'd be so happy right now."

She lifts my head and kisses me. "I can't believe you just gave up everything for me."

I look her in the eye and say, "I can't believe that you're surprised."

We decide to go for one last ride together, but before we do, Talon pulls me to the side.

"I'm sorry I was a dick before," he says, shifting on his feet. "I'd do the same for Tia and Rhett." He pauses and slaps me on the back. "Just don't be a stranger, okay?"

"You know I won't," I say, eyeing his cut. "You're the only

friend I have left who's known me for years. You're family, and nothing can change that."

He nods, flashes me a sad smile, and then walks to his bike.

The end of a fuckin' era.

We keep busy for the next week looking at houses, happy when we finally find one that we both like just down the road from Faye and Sin's. It's a two-story, recently built beautiful house with a modern design, a pool, and a large garden. It has four bedrooms, two bathrooms, and an amazing security system, which is important to me. Jo takes Faye to see it, who instantly loves it, and we make an offer the next day. While we wait to hear back from them, we start to pack up Jo's stuff, adding it to the boxes of my possessions from my clubhouse room. My other house is being rented, and I'm going to leave it as an investment. I want a fresh start with her. And I wanted her to help choose our new house. I don't really have much, to be honest. Clothes, boots, and my bike. I'm not a materialistic person, and I don't need much. Jo is packing up her clothes while I'm doing the kitchen for her, just leaving out the basics to get us through until the move.

"Ranger?" I hear her call out.

I go to her bedroom. "Yeah?"

She walks out of her closet, and my eyes practically bulge out of my head. "Holy fuck."

"Look what I found," she says, winking at me and doing a little spin. She's dressed in a black teddy, knee-high stockings with garters, and hot red pumps. "Do you like?"

My dick definitely likes. I narrow my eyes on her as I approach. "And who have you worn this for, Jo?"

"No one," she says, scowling.

"Then why did you buy it?" I ask, circling her. Her ass looks amazing and I can't help but reach out and touch her.

"I didn't have any lingerie, and I wanted to buy something," she says, shrugging. "I never wore it for anyone. It's just been sitting here."

"Well I wouldn't want it to go to waste," I say, licking my suddenly dry lips. I head to the iPod dock next to her bed and turn it on. "Fine by Me" by Chris Brown starts to play as I sit down on the bed. I raise an eyebrow, daring her.

"You want a lap dance?" she asks, laughing. I thought she'd balk at the idea, which is why I never verbalized anything, I just waited. "I think we need something a little sexier," she says changing the song to "Feel It" by Jacquees. The atmosphere in the room instantly changes, the air getting thicker. She mouths the first line in the first verse of the song, then starts to dance, moving her hips in a sensual grind.

Fuck.

She turns in a circle slowly, hips swaying in a way that has my dick so hard it's straining against my track pants. She bends over slightly, giving me a full view of her round ass, and I can't help but cup the globes with my hands. When she turns around and says, "No touching," I think I've died and gone to heaven. She starts to roll her stomach in that sexy move women like to do, then straddles me, grinding her pussy onto my hard cock. She runs her hands down until she's cupping her breasts enticingly, looking me right in the eye as she pulls the cups of her lacy bra down, exposing her nipples. I lick my lips, wanting to suck on them badly but playing the game. I love how she's becoming so comfortable around me. She definitely wouldn't have done something like this when we first met. She continues to dance on my lap, her bare breasts in my face, her body moving in a seductive motion that has me wanting nothing more than to be inside of her. She slides off my lap, making sure she rubs the length of my dick at the same time, then spins and starts to shake her ass. When she bends over and touches her ankles, I have to wonder who this little temptress is. Having enough of being teased, I grab her by the hips and pull her so she's sitting back on my lap but facing away from me. I start to kiss her neck, my hands roaming over her nipples, gently pulling them just the way I know she likes it. Her head falls back on my shoulder, and I take advantage of her exposed neck, biting down gently. My hand moves from her breasts, down her stomach to between her legs, where I slide my fingers inside her panties to find her already soaking wet.

"My baby liked doing that, didn't you?" I murmur into her ear, sliding a finger inside of her slick heat. She groans as I move up to her clit, stroking her. I stand with her and use my other hand to slide my pants down, then rip the center of her panties with one hard tug.

"Ranger," she moans. I think she was trying to sound angry but failed.

I bend her over a little with a hand on the small of her back, then slide into her, watching my cock disappear inside of her inch by inch. When I'm fully inside of her, I start to gently thrust, the perfect view turning me on and making my cock so fuckin' hard that I could break glass with it. With me still inside of her, I lift her and place her on the bed on her knees, then continue to thrust. I reach over to play with her nipples a little, then her clit, loving her little moans and gasps.

"Fuck," I hear her whisper. "I'm going to come, Ranger."

"Come, babe," I command, wanting to feel it on my dick. Fuck, I love it when she comes. I can feel her tighten on me as she comes, which pushes me into my own orgasm, even though I wanted to last longer because it feels so good right now. Once we're both finished, I pull out of her, kiss her nape gently, then lay down next to her.

"I love you," I tell her, pushing her lightly damp hair off her forehead.

"I love you too, Ranger."

FORTY-ONE

Johanna

WE got the house.

Although everything has happened so fast, everything feels so right, and I don't have any regrets. Sometimes you just need to do what feels right, as long as you aren't hurting anyone, instead of letting outside factors control your reactions and views on things. I'm sure anyone would tell me I'm crazy to buy a house with a man so soon, a man who didn't even let me pay for the house but still put my name on it, but I just know that this is where I'm meant to be. I'll never regret my time with Ranger, no matter what happens with us in the future. For now, my job is safe, I spoke to the sheriff and explained that Ranger is no longer a part of the Wind Dragons. And even if that's not enough—well, I will make do. I'll find something else. I'll work with Faye, or maybe I'll consider a fresh start in a new career. I love my job, but I love Ranger more.

"This house is amazing," Elizabeth says as she walks through it, taking in everything she passes. "I love it, Jo."

"It's perfect," Helen agrees, pointing to the pool outside. "I know where I'll be this summer."

I grin and open the door so they can go outside and have a look. "You're welcome here any time."

"Where do you want these boxes, Jo?" Talon asks me as he walks in carrying a giant one.

"In the kitchen is fine," I tell him. Sin comes in with the next box, then Tracker. I can see the girls' eyes go wide as they take in the fine specimens that make up the Wind Dragons Motorcycle Club.

"They're all taken," I tell them, laughing as their faces drop. "I know, right? Bikers . . . who knew?"

"Do you know what I do to women like you?" Faye asks, scowling as she fiddles with the throwing star in her hand. A fucking throwing star! Who is this woman?

"I didn't tell him to quit the MC, Faye," I tell her, crossing my arms over my chest. "Did you come here to help me buy furniture or to kill me?"

"Both," she snaps, scowling. Then she sighs, the anger draining out of her. "I'm just sad, okay! We lost a man."

"I know," I say, touching her shoulder. "But he's still going to be around. We're moving in down the street!"

"And I'm on my period," she adds, then points to a black leather couch. "Oh, look at this one! What color theme did you decide on?"

Boy, this woman jumps from one topic to another. "I haven't decided yet, black and gray maybe? And can you put that throwing star away? This is my partner's cousin's store, and he's going to wonder about the crazy woman I'm with!"

"Tell him my name. I bet my reputation precedes me," she says, grinning. She puts her star away and wraps her arm around me. "Lighten up, Jo. We're shopping, and it's always a good time."

Ranger arrives straight from his first job interview, and I'm grateful for his presence.

"How did it go?" I ask him, reaching up on my toes to kiss his cheek. He's so tall he still has to lower his head for me. Our relationship has been amazing, and I know without a doubt I've made the right choice by fighting to be with him. I have never been this happy before.

"Went well," he says, saying hello to Faye. "They said they'll let me know this week."

"Ranger with a nine-to-five," Faye says, shaking her head with amusement. "I'm going to be interested to see how that one goes."

"Why are you here again, Faye?" Ranger asks her, but I can see the affection in his tone. He cares for Faye, and I can see why. She just kind of grows on you.

"Because of my impeccable taste," she says, pushing between us and entwining her arm with us on each side of her. "I have an hour before I have to pick up Asher from day care and Clover from school, so let's make this time count."

Denver, Travis's cousin, walks out.

"Well, hello," I hear Faye mutter as he approaches us. I know exactly what she means. Where Travis is light, Denver is dark, with a headful of thick dark hair and eyes the color of whiskey and Coke, dark with a hint of amber.

"Hey, Jo," he says, eyeing the three of us, Faye's arms looped through ours like we're in high school. I detangle myself from her and go and give him a hug.

"Nice to see you again, Denver. This is my fiancé, Ranger, and my friend Faye," I say, introducing everyone.

"Ranger?" he asks, eyebrows rising. I wince and correct myself, "His name is Cam. Ranger is kind of a nickname."

"Nice to meet you," Denver says, shaking Ranger's hand. He turns to Faye and kisses her hand seductively.

"She's married with kids."

"Oh," he says, letting her hand go and returning his attention to me. "I haven't seen you since Trav's last birthday, and all of a sudden you're getting married and buying furniture for a new house. Sounds like quite the story."

Travis is such a gossip.

We order all the stuff we need, and on the way out I hear Faye mutter to Ranger, "We should have brought him to Cinderella's ball. Trust me, it would've worked."

I don't even ask what she means. I've learned that with Faye, sometimes it's better not to know.

A week later, and we're finally unpacked. I walk around the house, just taking it all in, pinching myself that this is my life now. I'd be happy living wherever Ranger is, no matter what it looks like, but that doesn't mean I can't appreciate the beauty that's in the home he bought us.

"Jo, what are you doing?" he asks me, giving me a weird look as I touch one of the tables with my finger as I walk past it.

"Admiring our house," I say, sighing happily. "I still can't believe we live here. Together. It's all ours."

He smiles and takes my hand, leading me to our new bedroom. "I got the job."

"Did you?" I ask, jumping on him. He instantly lifts me and I wrap my legs around him. "Congratulations, Mr. Accountant."

"Thanks, babe," he says, kissing me. "I grew up in a trailer park, and now I'm a fuckin' accountant, living in this fancy house with the woman of my dreams. Took me a while, but I got here."

"Will you let me know if you're ever unhappy?" I ask him, pressing my forehead against him. "Your whole life has changed, and like you've done it for me, I'd do it for you, Ranger. So you need to tell me if you ever change your mind about all this."

"I won't change my mind," he says, kissing me briefly. "But I promise to tell you if I'm ever unhappy."

"Okay," I say against his lips. "Now are we going to break in our new bed?"

"You bet we are." He grins, slamming his mouth down on mine.

EPILOGUE

Ranger

Five Years Later

"JO!" I yell through the house, wondering what the hell is going on here. "Why are all the women here? And why the hell are they all dressed as vampires? If I'd have known, I'd have dressed up as Sam from *Supernatural* and kicked everyone out."

I hear her sweet laughter as she walks down the stairs. "Ranger, it's Halloween. I told you we were having the party here about ten times. It's a vampire theme."

I narrow my eyes. She's a vampire too, with fake blood around her lips. First time in my life I've never wanted to kiss the crap out of my wife. "Where are all the men?"

"They said they'll come later," she says, shrugging. "Apparently they all had something important to do."

I'll bet they did.

And thanks to the assholes for not choosing to save me too, instead putting me in the same house as all the women and children, the only man here.

Clover walks past and the tiny vampire hisses at me, exposing little plastic fangs.

Jesus Christ.

Next to walk past is Vinnie and Shayla's daughter, Alexa, who flashes me a sweet smile. She's holding hands with Serena, Anna and Arrow's daughter, who is a spitting image of her mother.

"Where is Isla?" I ask, referring to our three-year-old daughter. Jo calls out her name, and I see my little princess, a cute dark-haired beauty with chubby cheeks and her mother's blue eyes toddle over with her aunty Faye holding her hand. Every time I see Isla, my heart just melts. I can't tell you how much having a daughter has softened me. I thought Jo had done that, but Isla . . . I'm like putty in her hands. I see the whole world in a different light now, my daughter has turned my life around and changed my entire world view. She's also dressed as a mini vampire, wearing a cloak and the same little fangs Clover had.

"Hi, Daddy," she says, her smile exposing them to me.

"My daughter is dressed as a vampire," I say, sighing and picking her up in my arms. "Did Aunty Faye do this to you?"

"No," she answers, giggling. "Mama did."

Faye smirks at me, her fangs sticking out. She says, "Don't blame crap on me. I'll suck your blood," then walks off. I don't think Faye will ever grow up, and I like that about her. At the same time, I'm also thankful there is only one of her. Asher comes and stands next to me, the only kid not dressed up.

"Where's your costume, dude?" I ask him.

He points to the wooden cross on his chest, attached by a black cord around his neck. "I'm a vampire hunter."

I throw my head back and laugh. What a fuckin' great kid. "Whose idea was that?"

"Mine," he says, grinning.

"I had the same idea," I admit to him.

We share a high five.

"Can you protect Isla though?" I say to him, and he nods quickly, a smile on his face.

Yeah, everyone loves my Isla.

I put Isla down, and she and Jo head to the kitchen for some "blood," which is apparently red Jell-O.

Yeah, I need to bail.

I call Sin, and he tells me they're at his house, so I drive straight there.

I could have walked, but I wanted out of there fast. The sight I come across is hilarious. All of the men from the Wind Dragons are sitting in front of the TV, beers in their hands, watching a basketball game.

"Thanks for saving me, guys," I say, scowling and taking the only spare seat left.

They all laugh, and I know that they did it on purpose. "Whose idea was the vampire theme?"

"Faye and Jo came up with it," Sin says, shrugging unapologetically. "Did you see Asher though? What a little legend."

"I did," I say, lip twitching. "He's hilarious."

Over the last few years it's been such a change, but we've all stuck together, even without my being in the MC anymore. I don't go to the clubhouse, but I still see all of them every week. They're still my family. Our kids are friends. And Jo is thriving, working her way up in her career, loving her life. I don't have any regrets with the decisions I made.

I now have what I never thought would be possible. A respectable job, a family, and a home. My daughter has a completely different life to what I had, and I'll make sure she always does. I made this little life for me, and I love it. I fall in love with

Jo all over again every single day, and Isla makes the sun shine that much brighter for me. Not everyone is this lucky in life, and I know it, and I'm thankful every damn day.

I'm also thankful for the men in this room, the ones who took me in when they didn't have to, the ones who still love me even after I left them. The ones who were at my wedding, my daughter's birth, and who celebrate with us all of life's achievements. The Wind Dragons are one of the best things that have ever happened to me, after Jo and Isla, and I wouldn't even have my girls if it weren't for them.

Arrow glances around the room. "Want to go for a ride before we hit the vamp party?"

We all stand up at the same time.

Some things never change.